The Raging Quiet

The Raging Quiet

SHERRYL JORDAN

Aladdin Paperbacks
New York London Toronto Sydney Singapore

First Aladdin Paperbacks edition November 2000
Copyright © 1999 by Sherryl Jordan
Aladdin Paperbacks
An imprint of Simon & Schuster
Children's Publishing Division
1230 Avenue of the Americas
New York, NY 10020
Also available in a Simon & Schuster Books
for Young Readers hardcover edition
Designed by Paul Zakris
The text for this book was set in 11-point Meridien Roman.
Printed and bound in the United States of America
10 9 8 7 6 5 4 3 2 1

The Library of Congress has cataloged the hardcover edition as follows:
Jordan, Sherryl.
The raging quiet / by Sherryl Jordan.—1st ed.
p.   cm.
Summary: Suspicious of sixteen-year-old Marnie, a newcomer to their
village, the residents accuse her of witchcraft when she discovers that the
village madman is not crazy but deaf, and she begins to communicate
with him through hand gestures.
ISBN 0-689-82140-9 (hc.)
[1. Prejudices—Fiction. 2. Deaf—Fiction. 3. Physically
handicapped—Fiction. 4. Sign language—Fiction.] I. Title.
PZ7.J7684Rag 1999
[Fic]—dc21
98-23283   CIP   AC
ISBN 0-689-82877-2 (Aladdin pbk.)

For Lee, whose love, patience, and
support make this, and all my stories,
possible; and for Kym, who, like Marnie,
is a woman of courage.

With my love

Chapter 1

HE AFTERNOON MARNIE came to Torcurra, the villagers were whipping the devils out of a mad boy. She knew he was mad by the way he cried, his voice high and unnatural, with no words but only strange, wild sounds. She had seen a mad boy whipped before, long ago when she was a child. He, too, had made those outlandish cries, and old women said later that when he had made them, devils with pointed tails flew out of his mouth. There were no devils flying around this day, however. There were only the Torcurra fisherfolk gathered in the stony field beside their cottages, howling encouragement to the man with the whip, and the screaming mad boy stretched against the whipping post with his hands tied to an iron ring.

Rubbing her dusty fingers across her face, Marnie looked the opposite way, toward the placid sea. The wagon jolted over the rough track between the thatched cottages, and she shifted her position to ease the aching in her back. Even over the rumbling of the wheels she could hear the mad boy's cries. Struggling to shut them out, she studied the man sitting beside her. He was more than twice her age, with graying hair curling on his shoulders, and a swarthy beard. Dark-eyed he was, with a careless self-assurance and a charming, easy smile. Sensing her eyes on him, he turned and smiled sidelong down on her. His hat sat on a rakish angle on his head, and under the shading brim his eyes were invisible, yet she felt them roving on her skin.

"What things be on your mind, Marnie?" he asked. His voice was deep, rich and warm like the sun on new-cut hay.

"I'll be glad when we're in our new home, sir," she replied, not looking at him anymore, but at the sweat-damp mane of the horse that drew the wagon.

"It is through this place, in a little cove on the other side," he said. "But I'm stopping first, at the alehouse. I have a mighty thirst after well nigh all day on the road."

Marnie bit her lower lip. Hesitantly she asked, "Could we not get settled at home first, sir?"

His smile widened, and he laughed a little. "'Tis sweet to see your eagerness, lass, but I have a need for an ale. And I think that considering your new situation in life, you might call me by my name. Call me Isake."

She said nothing, but the color rose in her cheeks. Leaning down, she busied herself rubbing at a dusty patch on her long blue skirt. Isake chuckled, amused at her obvious disquiet. Though her black hair hid her face, he knew well what her expression would be like, with its bewitching mix of boldness and modesty. And she, with head bent and face aflame, knew how the laughter would be dancing in his eyes, though she dared not look at them right now. Always, she had liked his eyes. And his voice.

The first time she really noticed him, he was laughing. It was harvesttime last autumn, and she and all the villagers had been working on his father's land to bring in the wheat. The work was done, and a sheep was roasting over a fire in the stubbled field for the workers to feast upon. Everyone was laughing, relaxed with ale and the sun, and tired from the long day's labor. Marnie had looked up, and there was the manor lord's son watching her. Many times that harvest eve she had felt his eyes on her. And later, when the stars shone silver blue beyond the flames, and the fiddlers were playing and the old folk were standing about clapping, he had asked her to dance with him. So overwhelmed was she with the honor of it, that she could hardly bring herself to look upon his face, but when she did, she glimpsed those dark eyes laughing in the firelight, and that roguish smile. She had been fifteen summers old.

"Let me hear you say my name," he said, bringing her back from the warm harvest memory. Lifting her head, Marnie looked at him straight. His eyes remained hidden in the shadow of his hat, but his lips were curved, and almost mocking.

"Your name seems strange to me, sir," she said very low. "But I will call you Isake, if that's your wish."

"My wish!" he exclaimed. "I've been wishing for it a year long, my lovely."

"It wouldn't have been right to call you by your name, you being a lord," she said. "Besides, we never spoke enough for me to use your name."

"True," he replied, laughing. "Not before your troubles began, anyway. Before then, you were always bent over the butter churn or else busy milking cows, or head down, tail up in the straw, looking for hens' eggs. Mind you, they all were pretty sights, though not conducive to lengthy conversation. Still, we shall make up for that."

Her face burned again as she thought of future summer evenings sitting with him in a strange house, knowing his eyes were watching her. Whatever would they talk about? Milking cows? Plowing? Sowing grain? But that life was forever gone, and she did not know, now, one thing they held in common. She pulled her cloak closer about her, and tried to calm the quivering in her limbs. Isake chuckled again, then flicked the reins at the horse, making the wagon bound over the stones. Marnie clung to the seat and tried not to bump against the man as they lurched down a sloping track to the beach. Once she looked behind her to see what was happening with the villagers and the mad boy, and glimpsed a priest running toward them. He was red-faced, furious, his fists raised; and the people were moving back, leaving the boy slumped by the post. The priest began to untie his hands, and Marnie looked away again, inexplicably relieved that the whipping was finished.

For a short distance the road was a stony track along the beach. Between it and the cottages scattered along the shore was a sturdy wall, the only protection the buildings had against the high and stormy tides. A few boats were pulled up against the wall, tied to metal rings set into the stones. At the end of the beach track, just before the wall petered out and the road swung inland to grassy slopes, stood a weather-beaten stone alehouse, ancient haunt of smugglers and pirates. The sign hanging above the door proclaimed the name: THE SAGE AND FOOL.

"Well, that's a fitting title," Isake remarked, handing Marnie the reins and climbing down from the wagon. "We've seen a lot of sages beating the devils out of a fool."

"Maybe we've seen a lot of fools beating a sage," she murmured.

Isake was yawning and did not hear. "I'll have an ale, and be back," he said. "Stay with the horse. A village that has a madman is bound to have a thief or two as well, and all we have to live on, at the moment, is on that wagon."

The wall was interrupted by steps leading directly to the alehouse door, and Isake's boots crunched on coarse sand and stones as he strode up them. He was a big man, stalwart and tall, and strong from laboring on his father's land. Unlike his two brothers, he had not been too proud to work, and the common people had loved him for it. He disappeared through the low door into the alehouse, and Marnie got down off the wagon and stretched. Never had she traveled so far on a

wagon before—never been more than half a day's walk from home—
and she was weary.

More used to labor than to sitting still, her small body was shapely
and strong. Her face was striking, with astonishing blue eyes and a
forthright look that got her into trouble on the farm. Various youths,
reading her boldness as brazenness, had at different times tried to grab
her in the hay barn or behind the stables, and been soundly walloped
for their trouble. Humiliated, they each crowed of success, and gave
her a name she did not deserve. They were one part of her old life she
did not grieve to leave behind.

Going for a short walk along the road, Marnie inspected the tiny
fishing hamlet she had come to. The cottages were small and tumble-
down. Built of whitewashed stone and with low thatched roofs, they
seemed dormant and withdrawn, as if centuries of battling against the
sea had worn them out. Above their windswept roofs the sky glow-
ered, heavy with impending rain.

Reaching the end of the beach track, Marnie peered past the bend
to where a few more cottages crouched, unwelcoming and sullen, in
the spiky grass. Between them, the road led to bleak hills, then
beyond to farming villages where Torcurra fish was sold on market
days. Marnie remembered her mother buying Torcurra fish at a market in her own pastoral village of Fernleigh.

Fernleigh. Marnie's heart ached with longing as she thought of it.
It would be warm now, in her home, the air thick with smoke and the
scent of rabbit stew. Her eleven younger brothers and sisters would be
making noisy fun of their afternoon chores, and her mother . . . her
mother . . .

Marnie pressed her fists against her eyes, and swallowed hard.
When she felt calm again, she walked back to the wagon. Isake was
still in the alehouse. Realizing she was hungry, Marnie reached under
the heavy oiled cloth covering their belongings and took out a small
parcel wrapped in white linen. It contained goat's cheese, fresh-baked
bread, and apples. She sat on a rock with her back against the wall,

unfolded the cloth, and selected an apple. As she ate she looked at the sea. Before this day she had not seen the ocean, except once from a great distance. The vastness of it frightened her, and she marveled that the water did not all pour away over the remote edge. Did it endlessly claw its way up onto the sand and stones, she wondered, to keep itself from flowing out the other way? Did it never rest? And what happened to boats that went too close to the far edge? She sighed, too tired now to contemplate such wonders. Enough that there was pleasure in the salty tang of the wind, in the wild cries of the seabirds as they fought over fish, and in the way the sky colors lay in a long ribbon along the wet shore.

Finishing the apple, she put the remaining food in the wagon, and climbed back up to her seat. To pass the time she tried to imagine her new home. Isake had told her little about it; only that it had belonged to his grandmother and not been lived in since, and that it was worth more than all his father's lands put together. It must be grand, she thought.

The skies darkened, and rain began to fall. There was nowhere to shelter, and she refused to crawl under the wagon cover like a dog. So she sat there, pretending she did not notice the rain. People came running to their homes, and a few children stopped to stare at the stranger sitting on the wagon in the downpour. Their mothers hurried them inside, banging the doors shut against the weather and the newcomer. The rain fell more heavily. Marnie dragged her cloak over her head, and looked hopefully toward the alehouse door. Surely he would come out soon to take her home. But he did not, and she waited another hour, while the rain pelted down in torrents. It stopped at last, leaving her cold, angry, and soaked to the skin. Wringing out a corner of her cloak, she dried her face. When she looked up she saw that she had company.

The mad boy was standing between the wagon and the sea, watching her. Fear swept over her, but there were no demons crawling out his ears, and he looked too calm to be menacing. Curious, Marnie observed him.

He was not a boy, she realized; he was a young man, perhaps a little older than herself. His eyes were age-old, sad, and an unusual violet gray. Long hair, dark as coal, shone wet against his pallid skin, and a shadow of a beard darkened his jaw and chin. His cheeks were bruised, there were welts on his wrists from the binding, and his knuckles were raw. He had been cut badly on the head, and blood, faint-colored from the rain, ran down his shoulder and chest. He was wearing a ragged brown knee-length tunic, but no leggings or shoes.

"Good day," Marnie said, and immediately thought it was a heartless thing to say to one who had just been whipped. But if her words seemed callous, the youth gave no sign of offense. He just stared at her, his eyes wise and knowing, the color in them melting with the sky, with the rain that still fell on the distant sea.

"What's your name?" Marnie asked, smiling.

The youth did not reply, but seeing a rare friendliness, he stepped closer, limping on the sharp-edged shells and stones. Marnie could smell the wetness in his tunic, and the blood and sweat on him. He looked hungry, hungry in his body and his soul.

"Would you like something to eat?" she asked.

He said nothing, so she reached behind her, lifted the waterproof covering, and took out the packet of food. As she raised the covering, water poured off it onto the mad youth, and he leaped back, making unearthly grunts. Fearfully Marnie glanced at his mouth, expecting to see it contorted by escaping demons, but he was only laughing. His face was transformed, appealing, and something in it, in the look of him, tugged at her heart. She unwrapped the cloth and held it out. He took it in both hands, wonder in his gray eyes.

"Take it all," Marnie said. "We don't need it. My man will be so full of ale, he won't have room for food."

Carefully the youth wrapped the cloth about the food again, flashed her a stunning smile, then turned and hobbled away. The back of his tunic was stained with stripes of blood.

"I'd like the cloth back!" she called, but he ignored her.

She watched him run awkwardly up the rough road toward the dismal hills, then sighed, stretched her cold and cramped body, and looked again at the alehouse. But no one came out. Other men went in, and sometimes she heard loud laughter and a shout or two.

Day darkened to night, and the early summer air grew chill. In the patches of deep blue between the clouds, stars glimmered.

The alehouse door opened, and Isake staggered down the steps.

Chapter 2

LURCHING, THE MAN stumbled to the wagon and hauled himself up, swearing at his clumsiness. He belched loudly, grinned at the drenched young woman, then clicked his tongue and shook the reins. The wagon jerked on, turning inland to the hills. As they passed the little church and the last few cottages, Marnie glimpsed candle glow in the windows, and heard laughter and the merry music of a fiddle. Shivering, she thought again of the warmth of home, and longing went through her like a pain. Her shoulder was touching the man's, and he felt her shaking, and glanced sideways at her.

"Not a word of reproach, my lovely?" he asked with a crooked, entrancing smile. "My first wife—God rest her tetchy soul—would have belted me over the head by now!"

She looked away from him and said nothing. She did not care about his wife, four years in the grave. Everyone said she was a shrew, even his sons and daughters, who all were married now.

"You may hit me if you like," he said, slurring his words, "but not so hard that you knock me teeth down me throat. She did that once, and I had the devil's own job to cough 'em up again, and plant 'em back in their sockets."

Leaning close, he peered through the darkness at Marnie's face, searching for a smile. Against her will, the corners of her mouth twitched. Isake chuckled and leaned back, and they sat in a silence that was amiable enough, while the wagon lurched and slithered on the miry track. Soon the village was behind them, and there were only barren fields broken by craggy rocks and low stone walls. The earth was ghostly, drained of color under the light of the brittle moon.

Suddenly Isake halted the horse, passed Marnie the reins, and got down from the wagon. He vomited noisily, then wiped his mouth on a handful of grass. Fumbling with the front of his leggings, he unlaced them to relieve himself. Marnie looked away, but even the sound of it embarrassed her. When he climbed back up to his seat, she handed him the reins without looking at him, and they drove on.

Leaving the road they turned sharply left, climbing a steep grassy slope. The horse struggled, its flanks quivering with fatigue, its breath misting the cold night air. They came to the crest of a hill, and Isake halted the wagon. Before them lay a small cove, its water silver in the night, the land around it black and rugged against the sky. At the bottom of the hill, almost on the beach and barely visible in the dark, was a tiny cottage.

"That's it, my lovely," said Isake, and drove the horse down the slope.

Marnie's breath caught in her throat. The dwelling faced the cove, and she could see only the end wall of it, windowless, and rising to the chimney. At the back stood a small grove of trees. They stopped beside it, and Marnie got down off the wagon.

"It's little," she said, staring at the front of the cottage, at the two tiny window holes overshadowed by the low thatched eaves, and the thick wooden door. There was a broken step leading to the door, and weeds grew tall along the stone walls.

"What did you expect—a king's manor house?" growled Isake,

belching as he heaved himself off the wagon, the ale playing havoc with his usual alacrity.

"You said it was worth more than all your father's land," she said.

"Aye, so it is," he replied.

Gingerly, she climbed the step. "Should we speak a blessing, since this is the first time we enter in?" she asked.

He gave a short, humorless laugh, and pulled the wet covering off the wagon. "It will need to be a powerful blessing," he said, "if it's to cancel out the thing *she* put on it."

Marnie stood very still, while a coldness crawled across her skin. "What thing?" she asked.

Isake did not reply, but busied himself lifting some of the belongings off the wagon. "Open the door!" he said. "'Tis not all night we've got. I'm bone weary."

Facing the house, Marnie said as solemnly as if she were in church:

Jesus enter, demons go,
Keep us safe in weal and woe.
Guard us in our humble place,
Don't let the devil show his face.

She pushed the door and it creaked back on its ancient hinges. The stench of wet straw and musty air swept over her. With growing apprehension she walked in, and was engulfed by utter dark. Water dripped all around, and she almost slipped on the wet floor stones. Years of wind and neglect had destroyed half the thatch, and she glimpsed stars between the rafters.

Behind her, Isake grunted and groaned under the weight of his large box of carpenter's tools. Staggering through the blackness, he collided with a wall, and swore as he put down the box. "I'll fetch us a candle," he muttered.

He went out again, and Marnie waited in the doorway. In the moon-light she saw him search among his belongings, then heard him strike a flint, and saw a tiny glow. Sheltering the flame with his hand, he came back to the cottage. The wavering light revealed dank moss-stained walls, a wet stone floor, and a squalid fireplace gleaming with black water. Rough beams spanned the single room, and over one of them hung a sack, rotten and dripping. It was over the fireplace end of the house that the roof was gone. Marnie noticed, in a corner at the opposite end, a pile of straw. She realized it was the bed. There was nothing else.

Isake swore under his breath. "Well," he said grimly, setting the candle on the mantelpiece, "'tis not exactly the manor hall at Fernleigh, but I dare say we shall knock it into shape. It's as well you're a strong wench, and not afraid to get your hands dirty." He started to go back outside but stopped beside her. "Don't look so gloomy, lass," he said more gently. "I said we'll fix it up. Now get a fire going and cook us supper."

While Isake continued unloading the wagon, Marnie went to look for firewood. On the far side of the cottage she discovered a small brook, and she cupped her hands in the swift waters, and drank. For a few moments she stood looking at the beach, listening to the waves tumbling on the dark sand. Desolate and mysterious, the sea seemed alien after the homely farmlands. Gathering an armful of broken branches, she went back to the cottage, and found inside a sturdy but graceful lit-tle table with two hand-hewn chairs. They were things he had made. On the table were piled kitchen utensils, a cast-iron pot to hang over the fire, and a long-handled frying pan. There was a jar of honey mead too—a gift from her parents. Isake was bringing in something else, and she heard him cry out as he fell over, and the crash of pottery breaking. After a lot of panting and muttering, he came in and dropped a basket on the table. It rattled with broken bowls and cups, and Isake grinned and scratched his beard with one finger, while he looked sheepishly at the angry young woman standing with her arms full of wet wood.

"Damned me if the ground out there didn't leap up and knock the basket from me arms!" he said, his speech still slurred. Ruddy-faced in the candlelight, he gave her one of his irresistible grins, but she looked away and dropped the wood on the hearth.

Isake stomped outside again to tend to the horse.

Searching among her jumbled belongings, Marnie found a broom and tried to sweep the slimy puddle from the fireplace. With mounting despair, she piled wet sticks in the pitch-black space and attempted to light them from the candle, but the sticks hissed and spat, and would not catch the flame. Isake came in with the waterproof covering from the wagon. "You'll need witchcraft to get that wood burning," he remarked.

"Then there won't be a fire tonight," she replied, "since I know nothing of such things."

"I think you do, since you bewitched me." He smiled. Leaning down, he took the candle from her, and she felt his fingers warm and damp on hers.

"Come, my lovely," he said quietly. "Don't hold a little drink or five against me. I was celebrating. And this place—we'll make it right. Tomorrow I'll go into the village and get some straw to mend the thatch. It'll be homely soon enough. In a few days I'll go back to the manor and fetch us a proper bed, and mats for the floor. We might as well be comfortable for the time we're here."

"We're not staying here always?" she asked, astounded.

He looked at her shocked face, and laughed. "In this hovel? There's something I need to do here, then we'll be gone. In the meantime, even a bewitched man needs feeding. Since we're not to have hot food, we'll have the rest of that bread and cheese we started at noon."

He placed the candle on the table, then went over to the bed, spreading the waterproof covering over the wet straw, with the dry side of the covering uppermost. Then he spread out the bedding he had brought, his movements clumsy because of the ale, his shadow huge and black on the candlelit wall. Marnie watched him bending over the sleeping place, her emotions in turmoil.

Isake finished preparing the bed, and came back to the table. "Well, where's the food?" he asked.

"I gave it away, sir," she replied.

He waited for an explanation, and she hung her head. "There was a—a beggar boy," she faltered. "He was starving. I gave it to him."

Isake cursed, and wiped a hand through his long hair. "That's the last of anything of mine you'll give away, woman," he said.

"I was thinking it was my food as well," she said very low, "and not only yours."

"Well, it belongs to neither of us now," he said, "and your beggar boy eats while we go hungry. At least we have the comfort of a little drink." He found a cup that remained intact, poured some of the honey mead, and offered it to Marnie. The mead was rich and sweet, and she took several mouthfuls before giving it back to him. He drained the cup, then went over to the bed and removed his fur-lined cloak, dropping it over the toolbox to keep it off the muddy floor. He removed his belt with its attached velvet purse and costly knife, and began to undo the gilt buttons on his tunic.

Embarrassed, Marnie turned her back on him. She could hear every move the man made; could hear him take off his wet boots and drop them on the floor, and heard him grunt as he peeled off his leggings and linen shirt. Then the straw rustled under the blankets as he lay down.

He said softly, in that voice like silk, "Come to bed, my lovely."

Shyly she glanced at him, hoping he would face the wall, giving her a little privacy to get undressed. But he was leaning up on one elbow, his dark eyes shining in the candlelight, watching her.

Quivering, her limbs like water, she bent to blow out the candle.

"Leave it," he said. "I want to see what all the fuss has been about."

Slowly Marnie straightened. Red-faced, she asked, "What do you mean, sir?"

"You know well enough what I mean, lass. Now come to bed, afore I fall asleep. I'm hellish tired, and the drink is playing havoc with my head."

Sherryl Jordan
14

"I *don't* know what you mean," she said, confused. "I don't know what you mean, by 'all the fuss.'"

"For Christ's sake, woman, don't harp on about it! Your moral weaknesses I can overlook, but henpecking I'll not tolerate."

"My moral weaknesses?" she repeated faintly. "What—"

"I said, enough! Are you trying deliberately to provoke me? Now hold your silence; and come to bed!"

She stared at him as if he were a stranger, seeing him altered by the ale, hot-tempered, belittling her with words she did not understand; and for the first time she was afraid of him.

"Come to bed," he said again, impatiently.

She replied, stalling, "I'll come to bed soon, sir. But I want to say my prayers first."

"Then be quick about them," he muttered, lying down. "This isn't the Sabbath, it's your joyful wedding night."

Not daring to look at him, Marnie sat in one of the chairs, her hands clasped tightly on her lap. Bending her head, desperate to find inner strength, she whispered, "Our Father in heaven, blessed be your Name. Your kingdom come. Your will . . . your will be . . . done."

"Nobody's will's going to be done tonight, if you don't come to bed," growled the man. "I'm getting mighty tempted to forgo this uncertain pleasure, for some sleep."

"In a moment, sir," she said, and finished the prayer. But still her nerves were jittery, and she could not go to him. "Lighten our darkness, we beseech you, O Lord," she went on, "and mercifully defend us from all perils and dangers of this night . . ."

Isake sighed heavily. After a while, as Marnie prayed, a sound disturbed her, and she opened her eyes and risked a glance at the man. He was sprawled on his back, snoring.

With mixed feelings, she went over to the bed and stood looking at him as he slept. He was naked, the blankets drawn up almost to his waist. His head was on a pillow he had brought from the manor house, white as snow and edged with lace; it seemed foreign in this place. Dark hair covered his throat and chest, and his body was well muscled and rugged like her father's. He smelled of sweat and ale.

Slowly she unlaced the front of her dress and removed her outer garments, placing them across the box of tools, and thinking how odd they looked together, her rustic clothes and his fine ones. Though it was very damp, she left on her long homespun shift, and crept under the blankets. Immediately she was aware of his body's heat, the strange and potent strength of him; and she moved as far away as she could, apprehensions rushing over her.

Sleepless, she lay staring up at the stars through the broken thatch, listening to his irregular snoring, the wind moaning in the trees behind the cottage, and the sea sighing over the pebbles. The candle sputtered and went out, and somewhere in the dripping dark a rat squeaked. At last she dozed, dreaming of wild beasts howling, and of herself pressed against a broken door to keep them out. But the door turned to smoke, and she felt the beasts swarming over her, suffocating her. Waking suddenly, she felt the man moving. He turned toward her, his breath hot on her face, and stinking of ale and stale vomit. He leaned up on one elbow and looked at her, saying nothing, his breathing hoarse and uneven. She could not see his face, except for the glimmer of his teeth as he smiled. Still clumsy from the ale, he fumbled with the front of her shift, undoing the ribbons that tied the two sides of the bodice together. She tried to push him away, but he moved onto her, his hands pulling at her clothes, ripping them. Crying, she begged him not to—to wait, that she was not ready—but he kept her quiet with his mouth over hers, his breath making her retch, his body crushing, overpowering.

Afterward he rolled off, away toward the wall, and began to snore.

Curling onto her side, Marnie lay with her back against his, her hands pressed hard across her mouth, so he would not hear her sobs of despair and disappointment and pain.

Chapter 3

THE GRAY-EYED youth stood on the hill above the cove, watching the young woman down on the beach. She had lit a fire on the sand, and was carrying out straw from the house, and burning it. Beyond her, on the rocks, clothes and wood were spread to dry in the sun. The man was nowhere in sight, gone, along with the horse and wagon.

The youth began to run down the hill toward her, but halted several times, hesitant and afraid. Still bent over the fire, Marnie looked up and saw him. She stood up straight, and pushed back her hair.

"Good morning!" she called, smiling.

The youth grinned and approached with surer strides. A little way from her he stopped, his face uncertain again, and tense. Marnie noticed that he carried a small basket. The acrid smoke from the fire drifted across him, and he coughed.

"Would you like a cup of mead?" Marnie asked. "I've nothing for us to eat, I'm afraid, but you're welcome to a drink."

The youth simply gazed at her, his expression intense and compelling. Then, to Marnie's horror, he began opening and shutting his mouth, making ungodly noises deep in his throat, the muscles in his face and neck working as if he were choked by something terrible. Marnie fled into the cottage and slammed the door. But there was no way to bolt it, and she could hear him coming up the grass, still making the awful sounds.

"Jesus defend me!" she whispered, frantically making the sign of the cross against him, and leaning with all her weight against the wood.

But nothing happened, except that after a while there was a scuffle on the step, and the sound of something placed there. Then she heard him running away. Long minutes passed before she had the courage to open the door to see what he had left. It was the basket, with six brown eggs inside. And on top of them, washed and folded carefully, was the white cloth from the food she had given him yesterday.

Mystified, she picked up the cloth. Who had washed it for him? And where did he get the basket of eggs? Not stolen them, surely? For her? She felt something small and hard inside the cloth, and unfolded it. A tiny bronze cross lay in the whiteness. Suddenly she smiled, then laughed, collapsing against the door, her fears vanished. "Sweet Jesus!" she said. "I thought he was going to spit devils on me, and he gave me instead a gift from the priest!"

Savoring every morsel, Marnie sat at the scrubbed table and ate two boiled eggs. Afternoon sun spilled through the broken roof, radiant on the tiny cross in front of her, and on the foxgloves she had found growing beside the stream. The cottage shone, the cauldron steamed in readiness for the fish and vegetables Isake had promised to bring back from the village, and the bed was remade on a pile of fresh grass. Beside Isake's toolbox stood a carved chest containing his clothes and other belongings. Before he went he had locked the chest, putting the key in a little bag he wore around his neck. Marnie's things were in a smaller chest, beside her old spare shoes and winter boots. She owned only a few clothes, most made by her own hands, a basket of sewing equipment, and a painted plate her parents had given her for a wedding gift.

The clothes she had worn yesterday were drying on the beach, and after her meal she went down to collect them. The blue dress she folded and placed with the shoes. Then she picked up the shift she had worn to bed last night. For a long time she stood there on the sand, staring at the torn garment. A tiny rust-colored stain lay by the neck of it, where she had pricked her finger while sewing. Despairing, she thought of all the winter evenings she had spent by the fire with her mother and sisters, carefully making her clothes. She had been sewing the shift that fateful night when all this calamity began.

Stricken with sudden, overwhelming grief, she sat on the stony shore, her ruined clothes crumpled in her hands, remembering.

That night her father had been working late on Sir William Isherwood's property, helping to search for a horse that had broken loose and run away. Her father's name was Micheal, and he held a high position on the lord's estate, ensuring that all the work due to the lord was done correctly and on time, and that nothing was stolen or wasted or lost. Responsible for all the farm equipment, for the allocation of fodder for the beasts, the maintenance of buildings, and for the animals themselves, Micheal answered for any losses or thefts. That was why he was late that night, searching for the missing horse.

All the children were in bed, and only Marnie stayed by the fire to wait with her mother, Dedra. While they waited, they sewed. It was a blustery night in early winter, and a draft whistled under the old door and through the gaps in the window shutters. The flames of the candles leaped in the gusty air, and the writhing shadows made needlework difficult. In the dim edges of the room stood shelves and chests for belongings, all handmade by Micheal. Along one wall were stairs leading to the two bedrooms above.

Marnie thought she heard a sound outside and raised her head, thinking it was her father home at last. But it was only the grunting of unsettled animals in their walled enclosure behind the house. There were not many animals left, now. Food was scarce in winter, and only the strongest animals were kept alive for breeding next spring. Two of the pigs, killed for winter meat, hung on chimney hooks above the fire, being preserved in the smoke. The smell of bacon mingled with the smoke that billowed into the room.

"Go to bed, child," Dedra said, near midnight. "I'll wait for Micheal, and keep some soup hot for him. You need your sleep."

"So do you." Marnie smiled. "Besides, tomorrow I'll be working for us, so I can sleep later in the morning, if I want to. If it's not raining tomorrow, I'll take a sack of wheat to the miller. We need more flour."

Like all those old enough to work, Marnie labored for three days a week on the lord's property. In return for the labor done for him, Sir William gave each family a house on a small portion of his wider estate, so they could keep animals and grow food for their own use. It was not easy tending two lots of land. At the busiest times of the year, the villagers were bound to give all their time to their lord, until his land was plowed, his grain sown, or his harvest brought in. And only then could they tend to their own small holdings, and make the best of it somehow if rain had spoiled their own harvests, or the weather ruined their farming schedules. At sixteen, Marnie was the only child of Micheal's old enough to render weekly service to Sir William. Because her father had been elected as overseer on the lord's estate, she could have been given lighter duties, but she took no privileges, and worked harder than most. That worried her mother.

"I heard that your father had you mending thatch on the manor barn," remarked Dedra now, contemplating her daughter's roughened hands. "He should give you lighter work."

"I asked if I could help with the thatching," Marnie replied. "It was not so dull as milking cows. And it was a wonderful view from the roof. I could see over the manor house, past the village and the church, over the windmill and the hills. I saw the sea, Mama. I saw the sea!"

"'Tis the only view of it you'll be likely to get," said her mother, trying not to smile. "And you're lucky it wasn't your last. Your father should know better. Maids aren't meant to climb up ladders. It's dangerous."

"He let me because I asked. He often lets me help with his tasks. I helped him mend the plow the other day. I like to know how to do these things. It keeps my mind sharp."

"Your mind, child?" cried Dedra, laughing. "What do you need a mind for? You have a perfectly fine body. And from what I heard, it'll get you all you need."

"What do you mean?"

A shrewd smile played about Dedra's lips, and she said softly, "I heard mention of the lord's middle son, the other day. I heard he was seen talking to you."

Marnie blushed, and in her confusion pricked her finger with the needle. A tiny spot of blood stained the milk-white undergarment. "It was nothing," she said, her head bent low over her sewing. "He wished me a good day, that's all, while I was winnowing grain in his barn. And he said he liked the way I acted my part in the village play. It was politeness, that's all; it was nothing."

"If it was nothing, then why so red about the cheeks?" said Dedra softly. "It's nothing to be ashamed of, Marnie. If Sir William's middle son has a liking for you, that's a fine thing."

"He's old, Mama! He's seen as many summers as Papa has! His children all are married!"

"That's no matter. He's a handsome man, and good-tempered, and he's the only one of those three sons who'll roll up his sleeves and do any work. And since his wife died, he's given no cause for gossip. They say he likes his drink, but that can be overlooked. You'd never do better. And it's not as if you've got a lad you have a liking for."

"But he's a lord! He'd never consider the likes of me!"

"True, he's a lord, but his family's lost most of their land, one way or another, and he's not so grand anymore that he wouldn't favor a common lass. Besides, you're not as common as most; you're the overseer's daughter, and our house is one of the best in the village—excepting the manor itself, of course."

"But he doesn't even know me, Mama! We've hardly spoke! We danced, that's all, on harvest eve."

"And he fetched you a cup of ale, and gave you a basket of apples, and twice he told your father how your work pleases him."

"He often praises his workers. He's a fair master."

"Aye, and he'd make a fair husband, too. If he ever asks you, Marnie, you'll be a fool to turn him down."

Remembering that conversation now, Marnie thought how strange it was that they had talked of Isake Isherwood. It was almost as if, in speaking the words, they had set loose a force on earth and had invited fate. And fate it was, surely, that struck their home that night; because, soon after that talk, the door had burst open and three men carried Micheal in, unconscious, foaming at the mouth, and with his eyes rolled back in his head.

They said he had been found facedown in a field, palsied but alive. No one knew for certain what had happened, but as it was the midnight hour, it was presumed that he had most likely been chased by ghostly hounds, or attacked by the devil himself. And when, two days later, Micheal regained consciousness but was unable to move or speak coherently, it was evident that he had encountered something too dreadful to describe.

They put him to bed, and the children were made to creep around so they would not disturb him. Dedra spent every hour at his side, trickling broth into his gaping mouth, changing his bed and clothes when he fouled himself, and talking to him in a vain effort to bring back his wandering mind. The priest came and exorcised the stricken man, but it made no difference. In secret a powerful old woman was brought in to stroke Micheal's body while she spoke magic incantations, but that accomplished nothing either, except that Dedra lived in fear after, in case the priest should find out.

On most days Marnie worked about their own house, tending to the animals, mending clothes, cooking, and trying to keep the youngest children quiet. The older children helped her, and relatives took the two babies, to free Dedra to nurse her husband. They were terrible days, for everyone knew that unless Micheal could take up his work again, they would lose their house and farm, which Sir William had allotted them, and face poverty and starvation. As Marnie snatched brief moments at the windows, looking out at the bleak earth and the flurries of snow across their own small piece of land, fear settled over her; and all the time she grieved for the strong, vibrant father who now lay babbling and incontinent.

Theirs was not the only tragedy. Two days after Micheal's misfortune, they heard there was a fire at the manor house, and elderly Sir William had been burned to death. The priest was very busy then, exorcising fields and houses and even animals. The bad luck stopped after that. And then Gerard, the eldest of the dead lord's three sons, came to the house of Micheal.

Solemn-faced, in quiet tones, he told them that since there was no improvement in Micheal's condition, a new overseer had been elected. This house, and the farm that went with it and all the animals, would go to the new man.

"But where will *we* go, my lord?" asked Dedra, her face deathly white. "I cannot move out with twelve children and a palsied husband, and go nowhere! Not with winter coming on. How shall we live?"

The new lord was compassionate but firm. "I'm sorry, woman, but that is not my concern. My father has just died, my home partly burned and in need of repair, and the villagers are disorganized without an overseer. There is a smaller cottage for the new man, if he will accept it. But even if he does, and you stay here, you will have to pay rent, since your husband is unable to work for us, and your sons are not old enough yet to work."

"We can't pay," wept Dedra. "How can we earn money?"

"I can work, sir," said Marnie, coming forward. "I'll work five days instead of three on your land, in exchange for this house and its farm."

Frowning thoughtfully, Gerard regarded her. He had noticed her working alongside her father, doing tasks other women would have refused. "I have no doubt that you can work well," he said, "but it is still not a man's work, and not enough to merit this house and land."

"I'll work as much as any lad, who is my age," said Marnie. "And we'll continue to pay our other dues. We'll still pay an egg out of every six, and two of each kind of animal every year. And my sisters will still weave a garment each season for your household, and—"

"What of your own farm?" asked Gerard. "Is it to be neglected?"

"My oldest son, Nathy, is twelve," said Dedra. "He can work it, with help from the younger ones. We'll not cause you trouble, my lord, nor neglect what you give us."

For a long time Gerard looked into the fire, his face thoughtful and grave. At last he said, "I'll talk it over with my brothers, and with the new overseer. If all are in agreement, so be it."

But it was an agreement not easily reached. The new overseer was bitter at not being offered the house traditionally owned by the man in his position. However, wishing to avoid conflict with the manor lord, which might have jeopardized his own new standing in the village, he moved his wife and two children into the lesser house, and kept his grievances to himself.

Christmas came, and Marnie insisted that Dedra take the children to the great feast in the manor house, while Marnie stayed behind to look after her father. She and Micheal were the only villagers not at the festivities. It was a cold and sorrowful day, though Marnie cherished the time alone with her father, telling him stories and acting out

Christmas plays for him. He did not show any awareness, except that he cried. It was afternoon, and she had already lit the candles, when there was pandemonium outside and the children burst in, powdered with snow, smelling of cider and gingerbread, and with their faces greasy with roasted meat. Shrieking and laughing, they rushed up to Marnie and thrust into her hands a basket covered with a bright green cloth.

"It's from him!" they shrieked, jumping around like frenzied pups, and begging her to open it. "From him, the lord's middle son!"

Marnie set the basket on her father's knee to open it, and found gifts of ham and Christmas puddings, nuts, and candied fruits. And there were scarlet ribbons for her hair.

"It's for you!" the children chorused, grinning.

Marnie bent her head, her cheeks hot. "It's for Papa, mostly," she mumbled.

Plowing time arrived, and the new overseer began supervising the first work of the year on the lord's lands; and people, realizing too late they had voted badly, grew to fear him, and missed Micheal, who had been honest and just and unchanged by the power given to him.

Then Marnie came to the new overseer's notice, and he began to see a way to get the house he so badly coveted . . .

Chapter 4

GROANING WITH THE EFFORT, Marnie hoisted the full sack onto her back. It was evening, and already the stony field glimmered with frost. The field had lain fallow for a long time, but the new overseer had ordered it plowed, and gave Marnie the task of removing the stones and clods the plow had thrown up. As she struggled toward the edge of the plowed land, she noticed a cloaked man watching her, and knew it was the overseer.

Breathing hard, bent almost double under her load, she staggered along the dark furrow to where he stood, and dumped the stones and frozen clods onto the pile beside him. The pile was as high as Marnie's waist, for she had been clearing the field all day.

"These are in the wrong place," said the overseer, just as she finished emptying the sack.

Slowly, painfully, she straightened. She dropped the sack on the ground, and looked at the man's face. It was shadowed by the falling night, but she could see his breath white in the frosty air. He smelled of garlic.

"They're in the wrong place," he said again.

"They're where I was told to put them this morning, sir."

"Then the man who told you must have misunderstood my orders. These are to fill that ditch behind the stables."

"Can't I fetch a horse and wagon to do that, sir?"

"They can't be spared. It's your task. It was supposed to be done today."

"I'll get up early in the morning, sir, and do it."

"You'll do it now. I told the lord it would be done today. He'll not tolerate slack workers, girl. 'Twould be a crying shame to have to tell him that you can't complete your work in a proper manner. You'd be dismissed, and your family would lose that grand house."

"I'll get up before dawn, sir, I promise. All this will be moved by noon tomorrow. I swear."

"Your swearing isn't good enough. If this pile isn't in that ditch by morning, I'll be duty bound to put in a complaint about your idleness."

Then he strolled off, whistling to himself.

"May I go home for a meal, sir?" she called after him.

He ignored her. Shivering, her sweat suddenly cold on her skin, Marnie bent and began to fill the sack again.

All that night she worked. At dawn she trudged home through the fields, passing the other workers on their way to the manor farm, their faces shining in the morning sun, their spades and tools in their hands. Some took their oxen and plows to do their share of plowing for their lord. Several of the men called out to her, wondering why she was on her way home instead of to the fields, and asking how her father was, but she only shook her head, too weary to call back a reply.

At home her mother's face was grim as she put a bowl of porridge on the table in front of her daughter. The other children had eaten, and were out tending the animals on the land behind their house. "'Tis not right, how the new overseer harasses you," Dedra said, sitting down with Marnie while she ate. "He'll break you, girl. He'll drive you into the ground, so he can have this house. I've heard it said that he took the other house against his will, rather than cause trouble at the start. But he'll have his way in the end."

THE RAGING QUIET

"No, he won't," said Marnie, her head low over her bowl. Though she had scrubbed her hands, they were still stained from the soil, and her nails were torn. "He'll not break me, Mama. And you and Papa and the little ones won't be put out to starve, not while I live."

She finished her meal and went back to the field. At noon she stopped to eat. Her mother had given her some bread, hard-boiled eggs, and dried figs wrapped in a cloth, which she ate while sitting against a tree. She was alone, the other workers being in different fields, sowing the barley. The sun was pleasurable, the spring day almost warm. Marnie closed her eyes.

Four hours later the new overseer woke her, kicking her soundly with his boot.

That night, while she was eating supper at home with her family, there was another visit from a son of the manor house. This time it was the man called Isake.

Marnie answered the door when he knocked, and she was shocked to see him standing there, his hat in his hand as if he were visiting people equal to himself. For once the roguish smile was gone and the dancing dark eyes were grave. "I've had a complaint from the new overseer," he said very softly. "Do you mind if I come in to discuss it?"

The color drained from Marnie's cheeks, and she nodded, unable to speak. He came in, bending his head as he passed under the lintel, for he was taller than most men.

Seeing who was visiting, Dedra leaped up from the table, wiping her mouth on her apron, her face white and red by turns. Marnie's sisters giggled among themselves, and their mother told them to take their bowls of food to their room upstairs, and finish their meal there. The younger children looked at the lordly visitor, their spoons halfway to their mouths, potato soup dripping down their chins.

"Sit down, please, sir," said Dedra, moving Micheal's chair toward him.

Marnie remained standing, her back to the fire, her body straight and tense. Isake Isherwood sat and faced her, his hat clenched in his strong hands, his fur-trimmed tunic and handsome face ruddy in the firelight. To Marnie's astonishment, he smiled. "Don't look so alarmed, lass," he said. "I want to hear your side of it."

"Her side of what, sir?" asked Dedra, sitting down suddenly at the table again, and absentmindedly pushing her plate away. "What has she done?"

"I fell asleep today, Mama, when I stopped at noon," Marnie explained. Confronting the man, she said, "I'd worked all night, sir, and I fell asleep. I'm sorry. It won't happen again."

"No, it won't," he said heavily. "No one on this estate is expected to work day and night. Who told you to?"

"I'd rather not say, sir."

"The new overseer tells me that you're idle, that you're defiant and uncooperative."

Silent, she would not look at him. He noticed that there were dark shadows under her eyes, and she had got thinner.

"I haven't seen you lately, sowing barley with the other maids," he remarked.

"No, sir."

"Be straight with me. Is he unfair to you?"

"It's not for me to criticize him, sir."

"He has stated a complaint. It concerns the work you do in exchange for your family keeping this house. You realize the consequences if his complaint is taken to the court, and his accusation proved?"

"Yes, sir."

"We are holding another court in the manor house three days from now. You will be fairly listened to, if you answer him. Would you like to do that?"

"No, sir."

"Then you admit your fault?"

"I do not, sir."

Isake sighed, and stood up. "I'll tell him that I reprimanded you," he said, "and that I have given you a second chance." He added, in tender tones that made her cheeks burn, "If you have difficulties, lass, come and see me. Will you do that much, to help yourself?"

"Yes, sir." She lifted her head then and looked at him, and saw his red lips curved, his eyes dark and smoldering. Without another word, Isake put on his hat and went out into the night.

Marnie did have difficulties, but she never went to him. She endured in silence, and not even her own family knew the heavy work that was required of her, or the words of abuse and scorn heaped on her by the overseer. Then, one evening at the beginning of summer, events changed.

Micheal had been carried downstairs to sit in his old chair by the fire. He was still paralyzed, and Marnie fed him his supper, all the while talking to him about the work being done on the lord's farm, and how the other villagers were. When she talked he watched her face, as if he listened, and sometimes he tried to answer, though his sounds were unintelligible. Marnie was sure he could understand everything, but could say or do nothing, and her heart ached as she imagined his intolerable frustration and suffering. She had just finished feeding him when there was a knock on the door, and one of the children brought in Isake Isherwood.

Isake greeted Micheal and sat in a chair opposite him, but apart from shaking violently for a moment or two, the sick man made no reaction. Marnie stood beside her father, her hand on his shoulder, and faced the visitor. Dedra sat at the table, the younger children gathered about her knees. The older ones saw the grave look in the visitor's face, and guessed their sister was in trouble again. Meek and solemn, they listened to what he said.

"I've had another complaint from the overseer," Isake told them. "But I would rather discuss it just with the lass accused, and with her parents."

Alarmed, Marnie's mother ushered the little ones upstairs, and sent the older girls to look after them. They sat on the top stair, hushed, straining to hear what was said in the room below. But

Isake's voice was very quiet, and they could hardly hear. Watching Marnie carefully, he asked, "Have you any idea what this latest complaint is about, Marnie?"

"No, sir," she replied, white-lipped. "I've done nothing wrong, that I know of. I broke two eggs the other day when the goose attacked me. 'Tis a fearful bird, sir, when it's riled. I'll give you two of our eggs for the manor house, if that's what the bother is."

"It's not the eggs. It's about the plowman's boy, Jonty."

Marnie frowned, confused. "Jonty? But I haven't talked to him since last Michaelmas, when we walked together to take our tithing gifts to the manor, sir. And that was only because we happened on the same path. I don't—I don't like talking to him much."

"Why is that, Marnie?"

Color flooded her cheeks, and she looked away. "He tried to court me once, sir. Well, not courting exactly . . . In the brewhouse, when no one else was around, he tried . . . Anyway, I boxed his ears, sir, and made his nose bleed. He's not liked me much, since."

Isake rubbed his beard, and tried to hide a smile behind his hand. "You look after yourself well, then," he said.

"Aye, sir, I have to."

"And you've not seen Jonty since? You're quite sure of that?"

"I've seen him plowing, sir, and a few days ago I saw him with the sowers in the field by the wild wood. He was shooting stones at the crows to keep them off the new-sown barley. He's cunning with the slingshot, sir."

"Jonty says you saw him yesterday."

"I did not, sir. Early in the morning I drove the sheep to the high pasture to graze on the new grass there, and was all day with them. I saw no one."

In unhurried tones, without reproach or accusation, and all the time studying her face, Isake said, "The new overseer is very clear about what he saw. He says he saw you yesterday, in the hay barn. You and Jonty, together. You were in the hay with him."

"That's a wicked lie! I don't care who said it, Jonty or the overseer or the lord himself—begging your pardon, sir—but it's a lie. All yesterday I was out with the sheep while they grazed."

"Who saw you there?"

"No one. I was alone, shepherding them."

"I believe you. But this scandal, if it spreads, will force you and your family out of this place."

"But it's a lie, sir!"

"That I know. I consider it but a small matter, myself, but the new overseer says he wants no such goings-on while he's in charge. Besides, Jonty is betrothed to his niece, and the overseer wants you gone before you cause any more trouble and put a slur on his family."

"I've done nothing, sir! And what of *my* family? What about the slur on *us*? I'll not let this happen. I'll answer him in court, if I have to!"

"You have the right to do that. But unless you have someone who saw you all day yesterday with the sheep, who will swear in court that you were there, you have no chance. There are two witnesses against you, and the overseer will win his case."

"I don't understand, sir! Why should Jonty lie? I never did him any harm."

"You boxed his ears. You hurt his manly honor. And the overseer may have paid him well, to support this plot—though that could never be proved."

"What of *my* honor?" cried Marnie. "He hurts mine, and gets away with it! It's unfair."

"I know, lass."

"What can I do?"

"Nothing, I'm afraid. But since the overseer has made an official complaint, and it is the second against you, we can't overlook it. Right or wrong, it's a blemish on your character, which folks won't forget. You have to be removed from service on our land."

There was utter silence in the house, and Marnie looked down at the dying fire in the hearth, her eyes full of pain and rage.

໙
Sherryl Jordan
32

"I cannot answer him in court, sir," she said at last. "No one saw me with the sheep. And since it was the overseer himself who told me to take them there, alone, I can't ask him to be my witness. But even if this thing were true—and I swear it's not—it should not cause such a stir. The workers, they're always . . . Well, you know what it's like, sir. But none of *them* are named to you, and what *they* do isn't made a public disgrace. And Jonty—I'll warrant you won't send *him* away, though he's supposed to be as guilty as me. It's only me that's being punished, me that's sent away, because the overseer wants this house. It's all wrong, sir, and it's a lie."

"I know. But there is one way out of it," said Isake softly. He hesitated, looking at Micheal's impassive face. The sick man appeared to be dozing, though his eyes were not quite closed. His head lolled on the cushions, and his hands were limp on the quilt covering his lap. Isake turned to Dedra. "I wish I could say these things to your husband," he said, "but since he cannot speak, I must say them to you. I hope you will hear me out and give me your honest answer.

"When my father died he left the manor to my two brothers and their wives and families. To me he left another house. It's a good day's journey away, near the village of Torcurra, by the sea, and is worth more than all my father's lands put together. I'm going there. Since my brothers and I have valued all that your husband did for us, before this evil struck him down, we do not want to turn you out from your house, or take away the land that you have worked. However, something must be given in exchange. It seems your daughter cannot work any longer on our land, but there is another duty she can do. If you will permit her to marry me and look after me in my new home, we will accept that as a fair and right payment for this house and land, which you may keep for as long as your daughter lives. This would save you from being turned out on the street, and it would get your daughter out of an intolerable situation."

For a long time Dedra was speechless. Slowly, as if in a dream, she got up, curtsied low to Isake, and said, "Sir, I would count it an honor for you to have my daughter. And so would Micheal, if he could but say. And I thank you, sir, with all my heart, for taking our Marnie out of disgrace, and doing her such a great favor. God bless you, sir."

Isake stood up and faced Marnie, and his dark eyes sparkled at the stunned look on her face. "Well, lass?" he said, with one black eyebrow raised, and laughter in his smile. "What is your word on the matter? Is it yes, or no?"

Suddenly there was a movement in Micheal's chair and he lifted his left hand, fluttering it wildly in Isake's direction. Red-faced and agitated, he babbled incoherently, spit dribbling from his sagging mouth. Never had he reacted so much since his affliction, and his family stared at him, astounded. His babble rose to a wail, and he rolled his eyes sideways, trying to see Marnie.

"It's all right, Papa," she said softly, kneeling in front of him and taking his hands in hers. Immediately he became still. She bent her head until her forehead rested on their clasped hands, and for a long time she did not speak, but her breathing was troubled and uneven, and she sighed often. When she lifted her face it was calm, though her cheeks were wet with tears. "This is the only way, Papa," she whispered. "If I do it, it is for love of you, all of you. At least let me see that you will be happy, staying here in your home, and watching your vegetables grow, and seeing your lambs born in the spring. God shall look after me."

Micheal shook violently, but he did not wail again. Marnie stood and kissed him, and whispered something else in his ear that made tears roll down his cheeks. Then she turned to the man Isake.

"Well, lass?" Isake asked. "Will you agree to marry me?"

She replied, so quietly he hardly heard, "Yes."

"'Tis settled, then." He smiled, and he lifted her hand and kissed her fingers.

They were married two days later, in the little church on the edge of the manor land.

Chapter 5

IT WAS SUNSET when Marnie heard the rumble of wagon wheels. She was still down on the beach, her torn shift in her hands. Quickly she gathered up the other garments and her shoes, and hurried back to the house. She put the things away, combed her tangled hair with her fingers, and stood in the doorway to watch the wagon approach. It was piled high with straw, and a ladder was tied across the top of it. As the wagon came nearer she heard Isake singing, his voice loud and unrestrained, and her heart sank. He stopped alongside her and raised his hat, a wicked gleam in his laughing dark eyes. "A beauteous maid, if ever I saw one!" he said cheerfully. "May I enter your lovely castle there, and partake of partridge eggs and roasted lamb, with you?"

In spite of herself, she smiled. "You may," she said, "only it will be fish instead, if that is what you've brought."

Isake's merriment dissolved into a puzzled frown, and he scratched his beard. "I think I might have forgot something," he muttered.

Marnie shook her head and went back inside. The water was boiling in the pot, and smelled of the onions and cabbage they had brought. She placed the frying pan across the flames and selected a few eggs to fry. Though it was not her fault they had no supplies, she felt mortified at the offering, knowing that at the manor house his meals were banquets.

Later they sat opposite one another to eat at the little table. Isake sat next to the fire. Though a candle burned on the table between him and Marnie, he seemed dark against the flame light, powerful and oppressive. She thought of the first time they had danced together, that golden harvest eve, and how she had liked his cavalier manner and merry eyes, and been enchanted by his voice. He had seemed lordly, enigmatic and alluring, unlike the uncouth boys who pursued her on the farm. Where had it gone, the laughter and the charm?

"You're quiet, my lovely," said Isake, belching. He had bought a small wooden barrel of ale in the village, and he poured himself a pewter tankard full, and drank thirstily. In the silence Marnie could hear him swallowing, and the smack of his tongue as he licked the ale froth from his lips. Even his breathing seemed loud in that alien quiet. Marnie would have given half her life to hear her brothers and sisters again, arguing about who broke the sparrow eggs the littlest brother had found, or whose turn it was to collect firewood. But there was only the crackling of the flames on the dry driftwood, the sounds of the man eating, and the awful lack of words.

"I suppose I can forgive your uncanny quiet," Isake said, pushing his empty plate away, "since clever conversation wasn't in the bargain that we made. Still, I was looking forward to some friendly talk, after a day in Torcurra. I've never met such a tight-lipped lot. By the way, where did you get the eggs?"

"The eggs are from the priest," she said, still not looking at him. "He sent them."

"Did he, now? I thought you must have stole them from the gulls. How did he send them—by carrier pigeon, or did Saint Patrick drop them in? It wasn't any of those paragons of Christian charity from the village, I'll bet."

"A boy brought them," she replied.

"I passed no one going back to Torcurra, on my way home."

"It was earlier today." She put down her spoon, though her plate was still half full.

"I'll have that if you don't want it," said Isake, and she nodded. He pulled her plate over to him, and began eating. He had stretched out his legs under the table, and she could feel his feet pressed against hers, though she drew back to avoid them. Presently Isake asked, "What sort of boy? A child?"

"No. Old as me, perhaps."

"Oh, that's fearful old," joked Isake. Seeing that she did not respond, he asked, "Do you intend always to sit with your head bent like that, to rob me of the pleasure of seeing your face?"

"No, sir," she replied, bending it lower still.

To her surprise, Isake chuckled. "Well, while you're in that lowly state," he said, "you may as well start your prayers. That way we'll get them over early, and I won't fall asleep afore you finish them and come to bed."

Though her head was low, Isake could see the flush rising from her neck. Amused, he chewed the last mouthful of her meal, then poured himself another tankard full of ale.

After a few moments Marnie got up and began collecting their plates and spoons to take them outside to wash in the stream. But as she reached for Isake's spoon, he gripped her wrist, pulled her over to him, and drew her down onto his knee.

"Drink this, my lovely," he said, giving her the tankard. "It will loosen you up a little. Lord knows, you need it."

Taking the drink in both hands, she sipped its bitterness.

"That's better." He smiled, his left arm about her waist, his right hand making slow and sensuous circles on her thigh. Marnie placed the tankard back on the table, and tried to stand. Isake held her, shifting his hand from her thigh, moving it up her body to her throat. She turned her face away, but his hand stayed on her, caressing her neck, his thumb moving across her jaw, and over her chin and lips.

"You're different from my first wife," he said hoarsely. "So small, so smooth. And lovely to behold. How old do you be, Marnie?"

"Sixteen summers, sir."

He gave a quiet laugh, his hand still fondling her face. "Younger than my last daughter," he said.

Very slightly she shivered, her body rigid. Isake held her tight, pressing his mouth into the curve of her neck, his right hand roving, urgent and hurting. "Say your prayers quickly, while you sit here," he said softly. "And pardon me if I start my loving before you've said Amen."

"Please don't, sir," she whispered.

His hand became still, and he half laughed, then swore. "By Christ, you mean it!" he said. "You've changed your tune, from what you sang before! Where's your fetching smile? You used to be a tempting wench."

"I was not, sir!"

"Ah, yes you were! Drove me half mad, you did, with your bewitching ways and teasing eyes. Right from that harvest eve when we danced, and you led me on with your blushing smiles and your taunting lips. And why call me 'sir?' Jesus' wounds! You're my wife! This is no time to be playing the chaste maid! Half the men on the farm had you! Why so unwilling with me?"

"They did not!" She jumped up, red with rage, and confronted him. "That's a lie! No one had me!"

"Not even Jonty, the plowman's son?"

"No! No one, ever! Not until you, last night."

"You must hold that memory sweet, then, in your pretty head."

"No."

"What—not pretty?"

"No—not sweet, sir."

He went crimson, and his eyes turned hard and angry in the fire's light. "That is a hellish insult to throw in your husband's face, woman," he said.

"I'm sorry."

"Aye, so am I. Your mother made a grave mistake, giving you to me. She should have put you in a nunnery."

"It wasn't her mistake, sir. You asked for me."

"And you agreed. We made a bargain, my lovely. And you have to keep it, else I shall be obliged to break my side as well, and take away that fine house from your poor family. Think on that, while I go for a walk. And when I come back, I want your prayers done and you waiting in that bed, and willing, like a true woman and a wife. Then we'll see what we can do to sweeten those sour memories of yours."

He strode out, banging the door behind him. She listened until the sound of his boots died away, then, very slowly, she picked up the plates and spoons and stacked them for washing in the stream in the morning. She piled more wood on the fire, and tidied the room. Then, with shaking hands and tears streaming down her face, she went over to the bed and began to undress.

The sun shimmered on the brink of the sea, warming the face of the young woman sitting hunched on the shore with a blanket around her. For hours she had sat there, staring at the ocean, seeing nothing. At last she stirred, and noticed that a new day had begun. Bending her head on her knees, she tried to pray, but the age-old precepts of her faith were scattered, lost in the chaos of her ruined world, and she could not call them back. She wept, grief stricken, bereft.

Beside her, the sands shifted under approaching feet, and she froze. The footsteps stopped nearby, and she held her breath. But no one touched her or spoke, and after a time she ventured a glance. The mad youth was crouching there.

He was so close she could have reached out and touched him. Yet he seemed unaware of her; he was facing the sea, his hands clasped loosely between his knees, his face serene and beautiful. And his violet-gray eyes, vivid in that incredible dawn, were full of rapture and light. It was as if he had flown, spirit-powerful, to his own world, far from this one and unutterably finer.

"What is your name?" she asked.

The youth ignored her, lowering his eyelids against the sun. She repeated her question. Again he ignored her, so she touched his arm, and he turned his head and looked at her, suddenly back from his own world, his eyes wary, half afraid. But he saw no anger in her; only the stains of tears, and an awful despair. His face changed, and a look of profound sorrow and compassion came over him. Very slowly he lifted his hand and wiped the tears from her cheeks. No other man could have touched her that morning; but the mad youth, with his extraordinary tenderness, gave such a depth of consolation that she found herself leaning her cheek against his hand, and sobbing. He wept with her, and there wove between them an understanding, a unity deep and poignant and powerful. Then, suddenly, he got up and ran away. He went up the grassy slope to the right of the cottage, his footsteps long and loping between the wagon tracks. Marnie watched him until he vanished over the brink of the hill, turning right toward the village.

Strengthened, she bent her head and prayed. "Merciful Lord, who understands all things," she said, "please forgive my sin, because of that man in the house. I vowed to love and cherish him, I vowed it in a holy rite, and I can't do it. Please forgive me. And if it's at all possible, let me get sick or ugly or fall ill of the plague, so he can't—won't— want me any more. Please do something to stop him wanting me . . ."

Behind her the cottage door banged, and she glanced around and saw Isake coming out. He was partly dressed, with a loose-sleeved shirt, brown leggings, and old buckskin shoes. He went down to the stream and washed, and Marnie heard him singing a bawdy ballad he must have learned in an alehouse somewhere. The sands crunched behind her as he came down to the beach, and she pulled the blanket more tightly about her body. Out of the corner of her eye she saw him crouch down in the same place where the mad boy had been. She resented Isake's being there.

"Fancy a swim in the sea, my lovely?" he asked.

"No." She had been in the sea last night, washing herself. Washing and washing and washing, and never feeling clean.

"A pity. I had a hankering to see a mermaid," he said, chuckling. "But no matter. We have work to get on with. I have to buy some peat from the farms, since there's little firewood about. But first I'll thatch the roof. The priest loaned me the ladder for it. He's the only one in the village who talked to me yesterday, apart from the innkeeper's daughter and an old drunk in the tavern. Seems we'll be shunned until the friendly folk get used to us. Still, we have each other for company, eh, my lovely?"

She said nothing, and Isake laughed and stood up. He put his hand on her shoulder, patting it the way her father used to, to comfort her when a toy she loved was broken. "I know you're a trifle upset right now," Isake said, "but you'll get to like it, you know. Women do, in the end. When you've finished sulking, come home and get dressed. There's a market day at the village today, they told me. You can go and buy what we need while I'm fixing the thatch. The walk will do you good. You need exercise. That's half your trouble; you think too much."

He went back up to the cottage. Soon afterward she heard him whistling cheerfully while he worked.

A while later she returned to the house. Isake was up the ladder, thatching, binding the loose straw into tight sheaves, which he lay side by side across the wooden rafters and battens, compressing them close with a special clamp while he prepared the next bundle. The thatch was thick and dense, and would last for thirty years or more, when it was done. Laying it was skilled work, and Marnie saw that he did it well, though she wished he would not lean so carelessly from the ladder.

"I can help you with that, if you like," she called up. "My father taught me to bind the wheat, for thatching the manor barn."

He grinned down at her, his face florid in the sun. "What I'd like," he said, "is for you to tidy up that mess in our house, and then go to the village and get us some fish, and make us a decent meal. I have a mighty hunger."

Guilty at having to be reminded of her duties, Marnie went into the cottage. The door had been left wide open, and already the damp floor steamed in the sun's heat. Isake's toolbox was open, and she saw that inside everything was neat and tidy, each tool fixed in its place by a leather strap. Last night's plates and spoons remained on the table, and nearby was the barrel of ale and the half-emptied tankard. Flies buzzed over them. Moving to the end of the cottage where the thatch was whole, and Isake could not see her, Marnie scrambled hurriedly into her clothes. Then she collected the plates and spoons and took them down to the stream to wash.

The water gurgled peacefully over the sunny stones, and dragon-flies hovered over the surface. Marnie recalled washing dishes in her other home, in a bowl of warm water on the table, and with the younger ones arguing about who would dry them and put them away. She used to resent their shrill voices and constant bickering; now she yearned to hear them again. Finishing the washing, she went back to the cottage and put the plates and spoons in the little alcove in the wall beside the fireplace. While there she noticed strange circles and signs scratched into the chimney stones; magical charms to prevent witches flying in through the chimney. Marnie ran her fingertips over them, wondering whose hand had etched them there.

She tidied the rest of the room, and swept the hearth with the straw broom her favorite brother, Nathy, had made her for a wedding gift. As he had given it to her, he had joked, his eyes sparkling, "You can use it, sis, to sweep that grand husband of yours into bed!"

"Hush your mouth!" she had cried, red-faced and laughing. "You ought not to know of such things!" She thought of her brother's play-ful teasing as she straightened the crumpled bed now, and wept.

Finishing her work, she wiped her face on her hands, and went outside. Shading her eyes from the sun, she called up to the man on the roof, "I'll go now, if you give me some money."

He came down the ladder and went into the house. Going over to his locked chest, he removed a velvet purse, took out a few coins, locked the purse away again, and put the key in the little bag around his neck. "Buy yourself a gift too, if you want," he said, carefree and generous, as he placed the money in her palm. "A red ribbon, perhaps, for your black hair. That would please me. I gave you some once, but never saw you wear them."

"I gave them to the children," she said. "I thought they were for them."

Tilting her chin with his forefinger, he looked closely at her face. "Have you been crying again?" he asked.

She pulled away from him, and he swore. "You're going to have to make a bigger effort to be happy, Marnie," he said, "else you'll cause us both misery, and drive me to drink. Lord knows, I'm doing my best, but my patience has its limitations. Now, before you go, I have a thing to ask. Yesterday when you were cleaning the house, did you find anything?"

"Only a lot of dirt, and a little spoon. It was broken and rotting."

"I meant something of value, woman!"

"I found nothing else, sir. Did you lose something? If you tell me what it is, sir, I can look for it."

"For Christ's sake, stop calling me sir! Call me Isake!"

"Yes, sir."

Isake sighed, and ran a hand through his hair. "If you ever find anything, you must give it to me. Don't ever try to deceive me. I won't tolerate lies, or disobedience, or being crossed."

"I wouldn't do those things, sir. I'm your wife."

"Aye, so you are. I thought you forgot that blissful circumstance, last night. Now go and buy those things for us, and don't be all day about it. I'm starving. You're supposed to be looking after me. *That* part of our bargain you ought to be willing to keep."

Marnie put on her old shoes, and placed the coins in the felt purse tied to her girdle. The day was warm, and she put on her white linen hood before picking up the basket that had contained the broken pottery. As she left, Isake was pouring himself his fourth ale of the day. He drank it in a few thirsty mouthfuls, then climbed up the ladder to continue the thatching on the steep and broken roof.

Chapter 6

ROUGH TRESTLE TABLES had been set up on the stretch of flat land beside the church, and the people of Torcurra had put out their simple wares. Other craft folk had come from nearby villages as well, and there was a festive air about the place, with a great deal of joking and laughter. Visiting youths were busy eyeing up the Torcurra girls, and a few kisses had been stolen behind the church, among the high stone crosses in the graveyard, until the priest came out to work in his garden nearby. A group of Gypsies had arrived, and their colorful caravans with rows of trinkets and bright toys were attracting the children with a copper coin to spend.

Marnie stood in front of the potter's stall, and selected two small glazed bowls and a cup for herself. The potter's wife, a busty woman with rosy cheeks and several chins, was sitting behind the stall, busily sewing when not taking money. Over the flashing needle she inspected the young stranger. Never one to miss a point to gossip about, the woman noted the newcomer's swollen eyelids, and the bruises on her wrists as she turned the pottery over.

"You'll be the wife of the stranger who came yesterday," the potter's wife said, never interrupting her stitching, her shrewd eyes flicking over Marnie's work-callused hands and faded clothes. "The handsome man, with the fine tunic and deerskin boots."

Marnie nodded and indicated the pieces of pottery in front of her. "I'll have these, please," she said, opening her purse.

"They say he's from the manor house at Fernleigh village," the potter's wife remarked, taking the coin and delving in her money bag for change. But she did not give the money to Marnie straight away.

Marnie placed the pottery into her basket, and held out her hand for the change.

"They say he's a lord," repeated the potter's wife, stubbornly.

"Do they?" said Marnie.

"Aye, though they say his family's lands aren't near as great as once they were. Still, a lord's a lord, whether he be in charge of a great castle, or a smaller estate, but you don't have the look of a lady, if you'll pardon my saying so. Those are working hands, you have. And he's old enough to be your father. 'Tis curious that you've come here to live, so far from your own kin." Her eyes wandered suspiciously down to Marnie's waist, searching for telltale signs. Disappointed, but still sure of her assessment of the situation, she went on. "Still, 'tis quiet here, and there'll be no talk. And old Biddy can help you when your time arrives. She's cunning when the babes are hard to come, when the father's a big man like your lord, and the wife's so small."

"I won't need your old Biddy," said Marnie angrily, "and there's no cause for your tongue to wag."

The woman's plump cheeks went scarlet, but her voice was cool as she said, "At least he's doing right by you, is your handsome lord, even if he has got an eye for the innkeeper's daughter." Triumphantly, she dropped the coins into Marnie's outstretched palm, then sat down and picked up her sewing again.

Shivering in spite of the heat, Marnie went on to the fish booth. It was crowded and noisy, but the voices dropped as she approached.

She felt curious stares, and heard whispered comments. It took all her will not to run. Calmly, she selected a fish for that night, plus several smoked fillets for the next few days. As she held out a coin to the man behind the booth, a youth leaned on the trestles next to her, grinning into her face. "I didn't think they bred them this pretty in Torcurra," he said, winking at her. "What's your name, sweetheart?"

Marnie ignored him, but the fish seller said, "Watch your tongue, lad! You be talking to the wife of a noble lord, in their first days of wedded bliss! Now get away, afore her husband comes and kicks you all the way back to your own village!"

People around them laughed, and the youth retreated in search of a more likely prize.

Close behind Marnie, an old woman said, her quavering voice barely above a whisper, "I hear they're living in the old cottage in the cove."

"Aye," muttered someone else. "They must be sore in need of a solitary life, to occupy *that* house."

There were other mutterings, but Marnie did not stop to hear them. Quickly, she bought vegetables and bread, and escaped. She was almost running as she passed the village well and the church, and did not hear when someone called out to her. He shouted again, and she stopped. It was the priest, hoeing the weeds in the garden outside his house. The garden had a low wall around it to keep out the coarse grass and tough little yellow flowers that grew along the coast. Seaweed was spread on the wall to dry, for use as fertilizer later on.

The priest waved to her, then wiped his forehead on his sleeve. The long habit was coarse wool, and he looked unbearably hot. But he smiled as Marnie approached, and propped his hoe against the wall of his house.

"Welcome to Torcurra," he said. "Though, from the haste you're in, I think perhaps the welcome wasn't very warm."

"It wasn't, father. Thank you for the eggs you sent yesterday. I forgot to bring the basket back, with the little cross you gave."

"The basket I can wait for, and the cross I'll not be needing. I have

☙
THE RAGING QUIET
47

enough crosses to last me all my life—and beyond it." He smiled, waving his hand toward the graveyard. Then he noticed the pallor of her skin, and the dark shadows under her eyes. "Would you like to come in for a cup of cider?" he asked. "I'm needing one. It's hot work, this gardening. I swear that every year the weeds get stronger and more determined to stay where the Almighty put them."

Marnie smiled a little. "I'd be grateful for a drink," she said. "But I'll wait here, father."

The priest gave her a searching look, then stepped over the little stone wall that edged his garden, and strode down the dirt path to his doorway. Bending his head under the low lintel, he disappeared into the dimness inside.

Marnie put her basket on the grass beside the wall, and removed her hood, using the wide ties to wipe the sweat from her forehead and neck. It was cool in the shade, and quiet after the noise of the market. She could not see the stalls from here, and was blessedly free from prying eyes. Beyond the priest's house stood the little stone church. Square and plain, it was saved from austerity by a quaint timbered porch with rustic hand-hewn rafters and tiny leaded windows. A low gate closed it off from the graveyard, where tombstones and carved crosses leaned crookedly in the long grass, shaded by the only trees in the village. Some of the graves were very old, their stone pitted by the salt sea air, and stained with moss. To her surprise she noticed the mad youth lying on the grass among them, his arm across his face. He seemed to be sleeping.

The priest came out again, two cups of cider in his hands, and he gave one to her. "Did you find all you wanted at the market?" he asked, sitting on the low wall.

"Almost," she replied, thinking how like her father he was, in his gentle manner and easy way of talking. Short and solidly built, he was more muscular than stout, though he looked as if he enjoyed his food—and good wine, occasionally. He was forty summers old, yet appeared younger. His hair was rich reddish brown, receding from his temples, and peppered with gray above his ears. He was clean-shaven, with an honest, candid face, and his lively eyes were vivid blue.

"What couldn't you find?" he asked. "Maybe I can get it for you."

"Ah . . . Nothing important, thank you, father."

"Are you sure?"

"Yes. It was just a ribbon."

"The Gypsies always have those."

"It's no matter."

For a while the priest regarded her, his gaze wise and compassionate, and she had the uncanny feeling that her soul was being read. Blushing, she bent her head and sipped the cider.

"They're a strange lot, the people here," the priest remarked, presently. "They're close-knit, and not exactly overflowing with the milk of human kindness. Most of them have lived in this place for generations, and they know one another's fathers and their fathers before them. They feel threatened by newcomers, especially people they know nothing about. They were even suspicious of me, when I first came here twenty summers ago." He gave a boyish grin, adding, "The old ones still call me the new priest."

Marnie smiled at him over her cup.

"They'll get used to you," he went on. "But it may take them a while."

"How long a while?" she asked, finishing her drink. "If it were twenty summers for you, it will be fifty for me."

"Oh, not so long as that!" he said, laughing. "Forty-five, at most."

Marnie laughed too, then, and gave him back the cup. "Thank you, father. I was needing that."

"How is your husband?"

"He's well. He's mending the thatch."

Watching her, the priest noticed how the laughter died in her eyes, and something like despair came over her.

"How long have you been married, child?" he asked.

"Two days," she replied.

For a while silence hung heavy in the sunlit garden, then the priest said, very gently, "All great changes in our lives are hard to abide. Sometimes at first they seem almost unbearable, overwhelming, and we think we shall never find contentment in them. But all things work together for our good, and God always has our happiness in mind."

Marnie looked away, biting her lip, and tears ran down her cheeks. The priest wiped his sleeve across his face again, and waited for her to compose herself. They were interrupted by the mad youth. He came from the graveyard, leaping over the far wall into the garden, not noticing that he crushed young cabbages.

Seeing his work ruined, the priest jumped up and waved his arms at him. "Mind your feet, Raver!" he shouted, pointing at the little plants. Startled, the youth looked down, noticed the trampled plants, and trod more carefully. He stepped over the wall and touched Marnie's arm, making strange noises in his throat. Suddenly he crouched down, forming a beak in front of his face with his hands, then flapping his elbows like wings, bobbing his head up and down, and wagging his backside. It was a fair imitation of a chicken laying an egg, and Marnie giggled through her sobs, wiping her eyes with her hands.

The priest chuckled too, and said, "I know who she is, Raver. And she says she got the eggs. You did well, and I'm pleased."

"Is that your name?" Marnie asked the youth. "Raver?"

"He doesn't talk," said the priest. "He just makes sounds, and sometimes, if he's angry or upset, he raves. That's why they call him Raver."

"Where does he live?"

"Nowhere, and everywhere. He's an outcast, survives as best he can. He has no home, no family. As a babe he was left on the doorstep of one of the houses, brought here, no doubt, by some poor mother from another village, unwed and unable to look after him. One of the women took him in, but couldn't keep him long. He was devilish wicked when he was little. Still is, sometimes, and impossible to live with. Without warning, a kind of rage gets into him, and he goes like a wild beast. Pray you never see it, for it's a fearful thing. Mostly he's passable, though he hasn't got a mind such as you and I have."

"Who looks after him now?" she asked.

"I do my best to show him charity. I feed him when he's around, and try to encourage the villagers to do the same. But they'd sooner whip him—though they don't dare, if I'm about. That's why he's always out in the fields, away from people."

"Does he really have devils, father?"

"It seems that way, when he's gripped in his madness. Other times, I think it's the spirit of Christ himself shines out of him."

"Where does he sleep?"

"I don't know. The village folk say he sleeps in a tomb. I've tried to get him to stay in my house, but he won't. He's wild, unknowing, like an animal."

Heedless of the discussion, the youth picked up the cups from the place on the wall where the priest had placed them. Throwing back his head, he tipped the last drops of cider into his open mouth. His throat was long and lithe, and his dark hair curled in its damp hollows.

"I'll get you a drink in a moment, Raver," said the priest.

The youth ignored him, licking the rim of a cup with his tongue. All the time he grinned at Marnie, his amazing gray eyes sparkling in the sun.

She smiled, two points of color in her cheeks, and busied herself putting on her hood.

"I have some tools your husband can borrow if he needs to repair the house," the priest offered.

"Thank you, but he has tools. He is skilled at the carpenter's craft. He's using your ladder, though, that you loaned him." Picking up her basket, she turned to go, but hesitated. "Father," she said, looking at him straight, "what is wrong with the house in the cove?"

"Folks have been talking, have they?" he said angrily. "I'll bang their stupid skulls together!"

"What's wrong with it?"

"Nothing, child."

"Something is. Is there a curse on it?"

"I don't think it's a curse so much as the woman who last lived in it."

"My husband's grandmother?"

"Is that his connection with it?"

"He inherited the cottage when his father died. He said his grandmother owned it, but it hasn't been lived in since. And when I spoke a blessing before we went in, he laughed and said it would need more than a blessing to undo the thing that she put on it."

"So you put a blessing on it, did you? That was wise. The woman who lived there, she was a . . . a king's mistress, they say. The king visited her there, in that cottage, so the story goes. And after, the village folk used to hear her singing at night when the moon was full, calling her paramour back to her. And if he didn't come, then she went to him, flying on her broom. So they said."

"She was a witch?"

"That was what they called her. Whether she was or not, is for Christ to judge."

"Did they burn her?"

"I'm afraid so. No one has been near that house, since. Not in the twenty years I've lived in the village, anyway. Don't look so upset, child. I'm sure since you've put a blessing on it, it's fine. There's a power for good and a power for evil, and I know the good is greater."

"Are you sure, father?"

"I've staked my life on it. Now go home to your husband, and don't think on it anymore. By the way, what is your husband's name? I asked him yesterday as he was going, but missed it when he called it out."

For a moment she hesitated. "Isake, father. Isake Isherwood."

"And yours?"

"Marnie."

"I'm Father Brannan."

"Good-bye, Father Brannan."

"God go with you, Marnie."

She went on down the dusty track beside the church, turning around once. Father Brannan was bent over with his hoe again, and Raver had vanished. Beyond them, people swarmed about the market stalls, and the Gypsies were dancing while a man played a fiddle. The sea wind carried the music to her, and Marnie stepped in time to it across the sunny grass, her basket swinging in her hand.

It was half an hour's walk back to the cottage in the cove, and Marnie enjoyed it. The day was shining, and tiny insects rose, glittering, out of the grasses as she walked by. As she reached the top of the hill she saw the cove, curving and blue as cornflowers under the sun. Her cottage was milk white in the shadows under the trees, and its strip of new thatch was golden beside the old roof's darker gray. It was not yet finished. She could not see Isake and thought he must be inside getting a drink, since the day was hot—another ale, no doubt. But her footsteps dragged as she neared the house, and a kind of dread fell over her. It was quiet, too quiet.

The door was half closed, the cottage dim inside. As she approached, she called out, "Sir? Isake? Is all well?"

There was no reply. She pushed open the door. Creaking, it swung back against the wall, making such a crash against the stones that she jumped and cried out. She cautiously went in. And saw Isake, lying on his back on the thatch-strewn floor, his head against the hearth, his eyes open and staring, and the stones beneath him running black with blood. High above him, a broken rafter slanted downward, sharp and jagged, from the roof.

Marnie dropped her basket and sank to her knees beside him. "Isake?" she whispered. A blowfly walked across his pallid lips, and she reached out to brush it away. His lips were stiff, yellow as wax, and cold. No breath came from them. And his eyes were dull and blind, with a strange pale blueness overlying the black. Getting up, she backed slowly away, then staggered outside and vomited into the grass. Then, sobbing and screaming, she ran back to the village.

Chapter 7

ATHER BRANNAN WAS saying his noon prayers in the church, when he heard the crying outside. It was so wild, so desperate, he thought at first it was Raver having one of his attacks. Then he clearly heard his own name, and got up.

Before he was halfway down the nave, the door burst open from the little porch, and Marnie came in. Rushing up to him, she threw herself on the floor at his feet. She tried to speak, but her words were jumbled, incoherent, half lost in sobs and screams.

Kneeling beside her, Father Brannan took her by the shoulders. She was panting, her body hot from running. "Listen to me, child," he said firmly, shaking her a little. "Marnie! You're safe now, nothing's going to hurt you. Stop crying, take deep breaths. That's right. Just get yourself calm, and then you can talk."

For a while she sat regaining her breath, her eyes desperate and fixed at the front of the church, at the plain stone altar with its simple cross.

"Oh, father! He's dead, and it's my fault!"

There was a scuffle in the doorway behind them, and the priest looked around. Three old women stood in the church porch, peering through the open door, their faces avid and curious, and wide-eyed with shock. Father Brannan got up and stormed down the stone floor toward them.

"Get out!" he shouted, waving his arms. "This is a house of prayer, not a puppet show! You'll not stand there gawking! Out! Out!"

They fled, and he shut the heavy wooden door, bolted it, and went back to the young woman. She was kneeling in front of the altar, crying, her hands over her face.

Father Brannan knelt beside her, fingering the wooden cross that hung from his rope belt. "Tell me what happened, child," he said. "Slowly, one thing at a time. In the order that it all happened."

"I got home after seeing you, and he was dead. He had fallen from the roof. There was thatch all over the place, where he had tried to stop himself, and a broken rafter above. His head had struck the hearth, and there was blood running from his skull, all over the stones."

"Are you sure he was dead, Marnie?"

"Yes. His eyes . . . they were blind. And there was no breath. It's my fault, father. It's my fault!"

"But you found him in that state? He was already like it, when you arrived?"

"Yes."

"Then how can it be your fault? It happened while you were away."

"But it *is* my fault! This morning I prayed—I prayed—Oh, father! I can't bring myself to say it!"

"I think you'd better, child. There's nothing you can say that will scandalize me. I've heard more sins confessed than you've had suet puddings."

"I prayed that something would happen to make him stop—to stop wanting me. I couldn't stand it, father. I like him well enough, but not in bed. But I didn't mean for him to die. I wanted to be turned ugly, or to be struck down with the plague. I thought that would let me out of it. I didn't mean for God to kill him. I didn't mean for that, father!" She started to sob again, and the priest sighed heavily and took her hand, smoothing it between his own, to calm her.

"Oh, child!" he said. "God didn't kill him. Neither did you. He was killed because he fell. There's no blame to be laid anywhere. Most surely, none on you."

"I'm forgiven, then?"

"There's nothing to forgive, Marnie. If anyone needs forgiving, it's the man. And now he needs to be attended to. He must be buried."

They got to their feet, and Marnie dried her face on her apron. For a while she stood looking up at the stained window above. Colored light poured in, softening the stone of the altar below, and giving it an aura of holiness. On the wall behind the altar, and all around the church, were paintings of scenes from the Scriptures. They were the Bible of the villagers, who had no books and could not read. Overhead arched the beautiful timber rafters of the roof, dark with age. There were no chairs in the church; the congregation stood for services, and the stone floor was worn smooth, shining from the feet of all those who, for centuries, had stood in this place and worshiped. It seemed that their prayers, their adoration, remained; the silence here shone, and the little church was full of peace.

Slowly, though she was still deadly pale, Marnie's face became calm and resigned. She took a deep breath and said, "I can bury him, father. But I don't know how deep to make a grave."

Father Brannan gave her a small smile. "I honor your self-sufficiency, Marnie," he said, "but I was intending to do the burying for you. I'll get some men to come and help me bring him back here to the graveyard."

"I think he should be buried by the cottage, father."

"Are you sure?"

"It is his land."

"Then that's where he shall be. And when it's done, I'll say some prayers for him. And you could pray for his soul too, if you could find it in your heart to."

"I don't hate him, father."

"No. I didn't think you did. You have a good soul, Marnie Isherwood. Now give me a few moments, and I'll get my prayer book and Bible, and a spade. And I'll find Raver. He can help. I'll take another man as well, who can verify the death, and then come back and send a messenger to your husband's family."

"They might not be there, father. Often the lord's sons weren't there, only Isake, because he was the only one who would work. Should we wait for them to come?"

The priest hesitated, then said, "I'll decide when I've seen your husband, child. Now don't you worry about a thing; I'll see to it all."

Then he went off to get the necessary things. At one of the cottages he knocked on the door. An elderly man answered. He had a strong, honest face, well seamed by the weather.

"I need your help, Finian," said the priest. "There's been an accidental death, and I'd like you to help me for an hour or so."

"I'm not much use at burying, father, with my back."

"It's another matter I need you for. You're the only one in the village, apart from myself, with any understanding in matters of the law. I need you to see the scene of his death, in case there's talk after. Also, I need someone I can depend on to send a message to his family."

"'Tis not one of our folks, then?" asked Finian, pulling on his cloak and following the priest along the road. Then he saw Marnie waiting by the church with Raver, and stopped.

"It's her husband," said the priest.

"I'll not go near that cottage, father."

"You don't have to come in it. Just check the body with me, that's all."

Finian grunted. "I'll do it, father, but I'll not be staying a moment longer than I need to, near that evil house."

Outside the church, the villagers stood in silence and watched as old Finian tramped away with Father Brannan. Ahead of them went the village madman, and the newcomer. The priest was carrying his spade and holy books, and they went up the track toward the cove and the accursed cottage.

As they went, three ancient women hobbled to the front of the watching villagers. One of them lifted a hand and pointed her gnarled finger in the direction of the beautiful young outsider.

"It was her!" shrieked the old woman, her voice high and quavering. "It was her, in the church! Her, we saw! Her we heard confess to murder!"

Chapter 8

MARNIE WAITED OUT in the sun with Raver, while Father Brannan went over to the cottage. Finian shuffled close behind the priest, his wrinkled hands clasped in fervent prayer. They stopped just outside the door. Father Brannan bent his head and prayed, and Marnie wondered if he were exorcising demons out of the house. Then he talked to Finian, but their voices were too low for her to hear. She turned and walked down onto the beach, and Raver went with her.

"I want you to see how he lies," said Father Brannan to Finian. "I want you to tell me how you think he died. Think carefully about it; you may have to remember this, and every detail you see now."

For a long time they stood looking at the corpse, seeing how it lay, and how the broken rafter directly above had been weakened by worms and rot. The thatching remained unfinished.

"'Tis obvious he fell," said old Finian. "There's the rotten timbers above, and the straw everywhere, like he'd clutched at it to try to stop himself. And his head is broke on the stones there on the hearth, and blood running everywhere. He died awful sudden, with his eyes open, and no struggle to get help, or moving after. It was an accident, father—a mortal accident. 'Tis this house; it put a curse on him. And he's already rotting in this heat; you can smell him. Him— or the devil in this place."

"I'll have to bury him now," said Father Brannan. "Listen careful, man. His name is Isake Isherwood, of the manor house at Fernleigh. Will you arrange for someone to go and tell them of his death, and how he died? And ask if there's a will, and if so, when it's to be read, so his widow can be there. I haven't time to write a letter, and I'm depending on you to get things right. Will you do it?"

Old Finian nodded gravely. "I'll send young Conor. He's a good head on him, and he can ride a horse. Shall I go now, father?"

"Aye, and thank you," said Father Brannan, and the old man fled, his cloak flapping about him as he stumbled up the hill.

Making the sign of the cross, Father Brannan went into the cottage. He bent over the dead man, closed his eyes, and said a prayer over him. Before he went outside again he stood for a few moments in the sunlight in the cottage doorway, looking at the charming little table with its jar of foxgloves and the little bronze cross he had sent with the eggs. Next to them was an opened pitcher, a tankard part full, and a pool of spilled ale shining on the wood. On the floor by the table was the basket Marnie had carried that morning, its contents scattered on the floor. Father Brannan picked everything up, setting it on the table, then he went out and called to Raver.

The youth was down on the beach with Marnie, not close to her, but just watching over her as she stood gazing at the sea. He ignored the priest's shouts, but Marnie turned, then Raver looked around as well. Father Brannan went over to them. "I need you to help me bring out the body, Raver," he said. "You stay here, Marnie. Don't come over until he's buried. If you want something to do, perhaps you could go for a walk and pick some flowers for his grave. And do you mind if I take a blanket from your bed, to wrap him in?"

"Take whatever you need," she said.

Father Brannan touched Raver's arm and led him over to the house, explaining again about the corpse inside. Even so, from where she stayed on the beach, Marnie heard the young man cry out in shock, and saw him rush out, as she had, and lean over the long grass. She walked along the shore, trying not to look when they dragged the body out the door and across the grass to a spot under the trees, not far from where the horse was tethered.

The sun was low in the sky when Marnie picked some foxgloves and went to the finished grave. Raver had formed a cross out of driftwood, binding the two pieces with strips of flax that grew along the bank of the stream. "We'll leave the headstone for his family to arrange," said Father Brannan. "But for now the simple cross will do."

Marnie placed the flowers at the foot of the cross, and stood back with Raver while Father Brannan opened his prayer book. But Marnie did not hear the prayers, or anything he said. She was remembering Isake alive, the way he had been that harvest eve, laughing and dancing. She thought of the way he was that fateful evening at her home in Fernleigh, solemn and honorable, offering a way to deliver them out of their predicament. And most clearly of all, she remembered him last night, his face close and overpowering, and the way she had prayed, even while he took her, that everything would end.

"Your prayer, Marnie?" Father Brannan was asking.

"I think I've done enough praying, father," she said.

Father Brannan nodded, his face compassionate, then bent and picked up his spade. The three of them crossed the grass, stopping in front of the cottage.

"I'd like you to come back to Torcurra, Marnie," the priest said. "You can stay with one of the women for the night."

"I don't want to go back there. I want to stay here."

"What—with the roof broken, and blood on the hearth?"

"The weather's good so the roof doesn't matter, and the blood can be washed away."

"It's not just the blood," he said gently. "It's . . . well, there are bits of bone too, and the flies . . . Oh, child, it's not a thing for you to see. If you want to stay here the night, at least let me clean the place for you."

"I can do it, father, thank you."

The priest sighed. "As you wish," he said. "But if you change your mind, you know where I'll be. Would you at least let me fetch his thatching tools down from the roof, for you? They should be put away, safe."

"Thank you, but I can climb a ladder."

"Tomorrow what will you do, Marnie? Will you go back to your own family?"

"No."

She offered no more than that, and the priest did not ask. For a while they stood looking at the sky, ablaze with the setting sun. The light was intense, almost unearthly, covering the land with a fiery glow, and the cottage with gold.

"Father," Marnie said, "who owns this house now?"

"If there's no will, and yours was a lawful marriage," he replied, "it is yours."

"No one will argue that? Not his brothers?"

"Why should they? The Isherwoods are a wealthy family. Why should they want a broken little cottage in the cove by Torcurra?"

"He told me something, father. He said this little cottage was worth more than all his father's lands put together. Do you think he lied?"

"I don't think he was the kind of man to lie. Perhaps he placed a high value on solitude. Sometimes, if one's life is unruly or excessive, peace is worth more than riches."

"I don't think it was the solitude, father. He said we wouldn't stay here for long. Are you sure this house is lawfully mine?"

"I'm certain—unless there is a will stating otherwise. I've been judging disputes in these parts for many a year; I know the laws. If his family wants the house they'll have to buy it from you, or at least you'll have to agree to their taking it."

"Then if you say this house is mine, I shall keep it and live here. I've worked on the land; I know how to live."

"If you really want to stay in Torcurra, there's a better cottage than this in the village. It's been empty for a year or so, since Widow Orley died. I wanted Raver to live in it, but he wouldn't. He doesn't like being in the village. It's a nice cottage, old Orley's. It has two rooms, and a good strong roof and a stone floor. I'm sure for a small rent you could have it."

"Thank you, but I want this place."

"I see there's to be no changing your mind. But if you stay, you'll need help to repair the house. That rotten rafter must be replaced, and the thatching finished. I'll send a carpenter in the morning to do it, and a thatcher the day after that."

"I can do the thatching. My father showed me how. He said a woman ought to know how to do these things."

"He's a rare man, and a wise one. Is there anything else you would like me to do?"

"I'd like some chickens, father, and a goat for milk. Also some seeds, so I can plant some vegetables. I can pay for everything. My husband has some money. I suppose it's mine now."

"All those can be easily provided. I have a boat too, if you want one," said Father Brannan. "The man who owned it drowned a while ago, and no one else will have it. I've used it a few times, but usually I go out fishing with the men from the village. It's a small craft, but strong, and has good oars. You can use it to go fishing in your little cove here, then you'll be well supplied with meat."

"Thank you, father. But I've never been in a boat, and I'd be scared of going on the sea and falling off the edge."

The priest scratched his cheek, trying to hide a smile, his blue eyes twinkling. "Well then, you'll have to take Raver with you," he said. "He's cunning on the oars, and tolerably clever at catching fish. Aren't you, lad?"

But Raver was staring at the burning skies, lost again in his own world.

"Is that how he lives?" asked Marnie. "By catching fish?"

"To be honest, I'm not sure how he lives," replied Father Brannan. "About every third day he comes to my door, and I feed him. But for the rest of the time . . ." He looked up at the sky, and the dark birds wheeling in the light. "Do you know the Scripture, child, that says how the ravens in the fields neither sow nor reap, but the Good Lord feeds them? Well, I think he looks after Raver too."

"Then his name ought not to be Raver," said Marnie, "but Raven. Raven of the fields."

Astonished, the priest stared at her, then slowly he smiled. "So it should," he said.

"That's his name, then," said Marnie. "Do you like it, Raven? Your new name?"

Raven was still looking up, his lucid eyes reflecting the brilliance in the sky. He was rapt, overwhelmed, as if the beauty in the heavens rang with a music only he could hear. While Marnie and Father Brannan watched, the mad youth lifted his arms to the skies and spun slowly in graceful circles, his head thrown back, his eyes closed, his movements natural and unselfconscious. It was like an ancient rite, a dance of innocence and worship and ecstasy.

"I wish I could love the skies, like that," said Marnie. "Is it the way God wants us to, do you think, father?"

Father Brannan chuckled. "There are some would say the devil prompted him," he said. "It could be looked upon as pagan worship of the sun. Though, like you, I tend to think it is his own way of singing psalms. But it's time I got going, to make sure young Conor got away all right to the Isherwood estate, with the news of Isake. I'll come in the morning and see how you are."

Sherryl Jordan
64

"Thank you, father. You've been very kind. I
bless you well for it. You and Raven."

"We're already blessed, Marnie. God be with y

"And with you, father. Good-bye, Raven."

Raven ignored her, still lost in his dance, unti
his arm, and gave him the prayer book and Bible t
walking together up the hill. On the crest they
back at the young woman. She was facing the cottage, her back
straight and determined, her hands clasped as if she prayed.

"We'll have to watch over her, Raven," murmured Father
Brannan. "She's got a difficult road ahead of her."

Raven made meaningless noises, and the priest put his arm about
the young man's shoulder. "Your roads are alike, yours and Marnie's.
They're both solitary, different. I fear for her, Raven. You and her,
both."

Raven grinned, and they walked on. Halfway back to the village
Raven ran off, not toward Torcurra but in the opposite direction. He
still had the priest's books under his arm, and Father Brannan roared
at him to bring them back. Raven ignored him. The priest muttered
an unpriestly word and walked on, his spade over a broad shoulder.
Shortly afterward he looked back and saw Raven on the rim of the
hill overlooking the cove, his figure black against the twilight sky.
Father Brannan sighed, threw down his spade, and began to run back
to the cove. Suddenly he stopped.

"Oh, Lord," he said aloud, panting heavily, "I can't be watching
him every hour. Keep him safe from the madness. Keep them both
safe. And don't let him lose my Scriptures and my prayer book, else
you and I shall have some difficulty communicating."

He made the sign of the cross in the sky over the place where
Marnie's cottage was, and plodded homeward.

Chapter 9

THE FIRE CRACKLED and spat in the
fireplace, and its glow danced across the
smooth stones set in the dirt floor, and shone in
the eyes of the young woman lying awake.
Never before had Marnie slept in a house
alone—never alone in a bed. When she was
small there had been at least one little sister fid-
geting and scratching beside her, and in the past
two years she had shared a bed with Sheilah,
fourteen years old, the sister next in age to herself. Sometimes she and Sheilah had whispered
all night, exchanging daydreams about the kind
of men they'd like to wed, and what marriage
would be like. So innocent, those fantasies, so
far from the reality of her nights with Isake . . .

Marnie shook her head, trying to banish
the memory, the feel and smell of him. Even
now his presence seemed to fill the bed and
the tiny house. She dared not sleep, though
she had done all she could to ward off spirit
powers: There was a bowl of cooked potatoes
outside the door for his ghost to eat, should it
come walking; there was milk on her hearth
for fairy folk, and salt on her threshold and

windowsills to keep out evil. But still she was not safe. Weird shapes wavered in the shadows on the firelit walls, and the wind moaned in through the roof and under the door, blowing like a cold breath across her face. Fragments of straw floated down from the rustling thatch, and she was afraid he was still up there, watching, waiting.

Outside an owl hooted, and the sea washed quietly on the shore. There was a furtive shuffling, a scraping on the wall. Then a noise like something huge sliding along the side of her house, tearing at the thatch, and scratching hard across the stone; then a mighty thud on the ground.

For a few moments she did not move, while there went across her mind half-shaped images of goblins and ghosts. Slowly she got out of bed, padded across the room, and picked up a piece of firewood. Outside the noises continued, much quieter. Something moved along her wall, and there was a grunt, animal-like and gruff. She stared fearfully at the metal latch, and cursed not having a bolt to drive across. To her horror, the scuffling began again, this time on her step. She heard breathing, and a brushing against her door.

In utter silence, her heart thudding, she crept over to one of the tiny windows and leaned out. Raven was there, hunched up on the step as though to go to sleep, his arms across his chest for warmth. Lying on the grass beyond him, where it had fallen, was the priest's ladder.

"Raven, you flaming fool!" she yelled, throwing down the firewood and going over to the door. She flung it open, and Raven fell inside, knocking his head hard on the stones. He had been hugging Father Brannan's books, and they tumbled on the floor. Confused, mumbling incoherently, Raven gathered them up, smoothing the precious pages flat before closing them. He staggered to his feet and put the books on the table, then fingered his bleeding forehead. His expression was one of bewilderment and hurt.

"Fool!" Marnie cried again, slamming the door shut behind him. "I thought you were the devil himself, out there!"

He stared at her, blood trickling down his brow, his eyes like two pale pools in the moonlight. His mouth moved as if he were trying to speak. He pointed to the door, to the level of the step, and shut his eyes tight.

"You were trying to sleep there, is that what you're saying?" she asked more calmly. "I'm sorry, Raven. I was so afraid. Here, sit down, and I'll get a cloth and mend your stupid head."

He remained standing, and she pulled out a chair for him. "Go on," she said more softly, smiling, because he looked so apprehensive. "I'll not bite. Sit down." Then she went over to the chest containing her clothes, and tore two pieces of cloth from the ruined shift. Wetting the smaller cloth, she wiped Raven's forehead for him, tilting his face gently toward the fire with her hand, and inspecting the cut. It was not deep, and she pressed the cloth against it, staunching the blood. She noticed that his skin was flawless, lightly tanned already from the early summer sun. Tiny lines of tension were about his mouth, and his cheeks were hollow and shadowed. His black eyebrows were straight, his eyes translucent and beautiful. A light beard shadowed his jaw, and his chin was well shaped. He was all well shaped, she thought, his body lean and hard from living in the fields. There was something ageless and unworldly about Raven, something akin to innocence. It was as if he were empty, pure, unspoiled by the world's guile and complexity, and she could not fear him, in spite of all she had heard.

"What do you eat when you're in the fields, Raven?" she asked.

He did not reply, and she wiped the cut that still bled on his forehead, and began winding the longer strip about his head, tying it firmly in a knot behind his smooth black curls. With eyes closed, he sat very still, his lips slightly parted and curved, as if he were pleasantly surprised. She realized he was probably rarely touched, except in anger.

"You mustn't creep up on people's houses, Raven," she said. "No wonder they think you're evil. You frighten them." He remained perfectly still, except that his eyes opened a slit, and he looked at her from under the dark-lashed lids. His skin was clean, and she could smell lavender soap on him, though he still wore the ragged clothes stained from the whipping. "Did Father Brannan make you have a wash, after the grave digging?" she asked.

He moved his mouth, straining the muscles of his throat, making awful noises. He seemed so solemn, so earnest, that Marnie turned away, unable to bear the look in his eyes. They were the eyes of a caged animal, full of intelligence and pleading and pain. It was the same look her father had, since his affliction.

"Would you like a bowl of soup, Raven?" she asked, going to the fire and stirring the half-full cauldron that hung on the bar above it. "There's some bread too that I bought today."

Raven gave no answer, and she noticed that he was staring at the box of tools by the bed, his expression intense and concentrated.

"Would you like some fish soup?" she asked again.

He did not react, and she realized he had fled to his other world, the strange world of madness and unknowing. How quickly he moved between this place and that! Unnerved, she took a bowl from the alcove by the chimney stones and filled it with soup. She glanced back at Raven; he was standing by the door as if about to go.

"Don't you want to eat?" she asked.

He smiled and made incoherent noises, back in her world again.

She held out the bowl toward him. "Sit and eat this," she said, "but be very careful, it's hot." Quickly, he crossed the bit of floor between them, took the bowl, and drank. It burned his mouth, and he cried out and dropped the bowl on the floor. Without a word Marnie gave him some cold water in a cup, to ease his pain. He looked at her with hurt in his eyes, and she had the feeling that he blamed her for his burned mouth, though she had warned him.

Marnie cleaned up the mess, replaced the cracked bowl with a new one, and filled it with more soup. She pointed to the bread wrapped in a cloth on the table. "Open that, and break some for yourself," she said. "If you dip it in the soup, it won't be so hot. And sit down, eat properly."

He did not sit, but unwrapped the cloth, discovered the bread, and smiled in surprise.

"You don't understand anything, do you?" said Marnie softly, pushing his bowl of soup toward him. "Sit down and eat, Raven."

Ignoring her, he broke a large chunk off the bread, and began eating hungrily.

"How long is it since you last ate?" asked Marnie.

Raven grinned, his mouth full of food, and turned to go. As he was about to open the door, Marnie said, "You can sleep by the fire, if you like. It must be near midnight. Don't go outside again."

Still chewing the bread, he stared at her, a bewildered expression on his face. "You can sleep here," she said. He remained confused, so she closed her eyes and rested her hand on her right cheek.

Realization dawned on Raven's face. Grunting, half laughing, he pointed to Marnie's bed on the floor, and fear crawled over her. Fighting to keep her voice steady, she said, "That's *my* bed, Raven. You sleep by the fire."

He just looked at her, his gray eyes deep and inquiring. She turned away, picked up her quilt, and pushed it into his arms. "You sleep by the fire," she repeated.

His lower jaw worked, and he made hideous noises again.

"Don't do that!" she cried. "You sound like you're possessed."

Afraid at her anger, sensing her fear, he stepped back toward the door, his right hand already on the latch.

"I said you can sleep inside," she said. "But by the fire. Over there." She pointed to the hearth, and Raven suddenly beamed, his madness gone. Marnie watched as he crouched down, spread the quilt carefully in the fire's glow, and lay on it. Then he drew the sides up over himself, fingering its fine weave, sniffing it. As he sniffed he made strange soft sounds like a contented animal, and Marnie smiled to herself. Then she went over to her own bed, slipped in, and pulled the blankets up to her chin. For a long time she watched Raven, wondering if she too were mad, letting him sleep in the cottage with her; but he lay very still, facing the fire, the strip of bandage pale against his black and shining hair.

"Good night, Raven," she said.

He did not reply, and she relaxed, looking up at the stars through the roof.

"Gentle Jesus, thank you that I'm not alone this night," she whispered. "Bless Father Brannan for helping me today, and bless Raven. And help me to be strong, since I'm to live here by myself. And bless the soul of Isake."

Then she closed her eyes and fell instantly asleep.

Something woke her suddenly in the dead of night, and she sat bolt upright. The fire had gone out, and the room was in pitch darkness. Something banged, loud and echoing, and cold wind blew across her. The door! she thought, terrified. Someone's opened the door! Almost fainting with fear, she thought of Isake, of his grave burst open and his body standing—

"Raven?" she screamed, her voice strangled in her throat. "Raven? Where are you?"

No reply. Just utter dark, and that awful banging again. Then she realized it was the wind banging the door against the wall. Raven must have gone, leaving the door ajar. Praying, summoning all her courage, she got up and groped her way around the table, knocking over a chair in her haste. She slammed the door, and shut the latch. Then, fumbling, she picked up the flints from the table, and lit the candle. The soft glow revealed swirling smoke and ash, and she realized that the wind, blowing down the chimney, had scattered the remaining fire. Marnie glanced at the floor by the hearth, searching for sparks or hot ash; and saw Raven, still curled in his quilt, unaware of everything.

"Does the madness grip you, even in your sleep?" she whispered, thinking of all the noise, and how deep he must be in his other world to have missed it all. Then an astounding thought struck her, and she went and knelt by his head. "Can you hear me, Raven?" she asked. She shouted his name. No response. He snored very softly, the bandage glowing white above his dark brow. A smudge of scarlet stained the white, where the cut still bled.

Marnie got up and stepped over him. Fumbling in the dark, she felt along the cold hearthstones until her hand touched the long handle of the frying pan. Lifting it, aiming carefully, she swung the pan hard against the iron cauldron hanging in the fireplace. The clang resounded around the cottage, reverberating in the stone walls like the boom of a great church bell. Marnie's hands stung from the impact, her whole body felt jangled and jarred, and the explosion of sound hummed long in the air.

But the youth at her feet remained oblivious, as if in all the world there were only his own unutterable dreams, and absolute and unbreakable silence.

Marnie put the frying pan back on the hearth, then sat at the table. She did not notice the coldness in those gray, predawn hours; did not notice when the candle hissed and went out, or when the sun sneaked over the wide stone sills of the tiny windows. She sat motionless, just looking at Raven, and thinking.

Chapter 10

FATHER **B**RANNAN STRODE down the hill to the lone cottage in the cove, and banged on the door. "Marnie, are you here?" he shouted.

"Aye, father," she said, opening the door. "Come in."

He did, sweeping in with a gust of wind and a burst of fresh salt air. "We've slipped back to winter!" he remarked, making the sign of the cross, then striding over to the hearth and warming his hands near the fire. A rush of wind down the chimney covered him with smoke, and he bent over, coughing and spluttering. Marnie gave him a cup of water, and pulled a chair over to him.

"I've brought news," he said, when most of the smoke had whirled upward through the broken roof, and he got his breath. "I'll give you the good news first. There was no will that Isake Isherwood wrote, so his house and all his belongings are yours. And the bad news . . . His family has been told of his death, but they weren't wanting to come here, and they didn't offer you any support, I'm sorry. And I've got other news too that's bad."

"I found out something about Raven," Marnie said, sitting opposite him on the little stool her father had made her. She was tense, elated. "He doesn't have devils at all."

"Of course he does, child! At least, sometimes he does." Suddenly his eyes narrowed, and he searched her face. "He's been here this morning?"

"He came last night. He had your books with him." She pointed to the two books on the table. "I found out what's wrong with him, father."

The priest looked shocked. "He came last night, and you let him in?"

"He fell in, more like! He was asleep on my step, and I opened the door and he rolled in. He banged his head on the floor stones. I bandaged it for him."

"And sent him on his way, I hope."

She reddened, and said defensively, "Where to? To sleep in the fields, where everybody else sends him? He slept by the fire, and left this morning as soon as he woke. He didn't even stop for a bite to eat."

The priest bent his head, rubbing his fingers across his brow. "I don't know that it was wise, Marnie, to have him in your house," he said.

"I think it was very wise. I've found out what's wrong with him, father. He doesn't hear."

"Ah, that's for sure! Lost in his own world half the time, and tormented by devils the other half. Sometimes he's so far gone with them, he doesn't even recognize his own name."

"Of course he can't recognize his name," she said, leaning forward, "he's never heard it! He can't hear anything, father. It's got nothing to do with devils! He can't *hear*!"

"You don't understand, Marnie. You haven't seen him wild, raving. You've only seen him in his better times, when the madness isn't on him. Maybe it isn't devils, but it's something awful powerful that grips him. I know. I've seen it enough times, right from when he was a child. He's not always mad, but when he is, it's something terrible to see. You don't know him. He's dangerous, freakish. There's no accounting for his ways. One moment he's almost like us, the next— gone! Possessed by madness, his soul flown somewhere too terrible to think about. But I'm not here to discuss Raven. I've come to tell you that I've asked at the village for people to help with the rafter and the thatch. I'm sorry, lass, no one will come. And I'm afraid it's not only the cottage that puts them off. There's something else too that's worrying them."

"I can do the thatch, father. Haven't you ever noticed, the times he ignores you, when he's unmindful and distant, are the times he's not looking at you. He doesn't know you're trying to say things to him. That's why he's in his own world. He's not dragged there by devils, or gone mad for a few moments. He just can't hear. That's why he ignores you. And when he does see you talking to him, he tries to talk back. That's why he opens and shuts his mouth all the time, and makes noises. He sees other people doing it, and knows it gets them what they—"

"Marnie, child, I can't believe this! The noises are the madness in him. He doesn't have a mind like ours. I know. I've known him all his life. You know nothing about him. You've barely met him!"

"Maybe that's *why* I've noticed. I've seen him afresh, I've not been swayed by other people's notions about him. He's not mad, father. He can't hear, that's all. He has a mind like yours and mine."

"God forbid! You don't know what you say! Now stop this folly, and tell me what you have to put over the roof, until we can mend it properly. The clouds are building up in the west, and it will be raining soon."

Marnie's mouth folded in a hard line, and she sat looking into the fire. "I'll prove it to you," she said. "I'm going to find a way to talk with him."

The priest shook his head, half amused, half despairing. "And just how are you going to manage that? Is it a miracle you'll be doing?"

"I don't know—not exactly—how I'll do it. But he's never had a chance to learn, father. Not like ordinary people learn, as little children hearing words and then repeating them. There has to be another way. Maybe showing him with gestures. I used to play a game with my little brothers and sisters, to keep them quiet when my father was very ill. In the game we weren't allowed to speak, and the first person to forget that, and to make a sound, had to hold a sage leaf between their teeth, to keep them quiet. Then the next person to forget had to hold a leaf between their teeth as well, and so on. The last person left without a sage leaf was the winner. They always got a little cake, or something special, for remembering so well to keep silent. Sometimes the game lasted for hours. We learned to tell a lot without actually talking. Maybe that's the way it has to be with Raven—showing, not telling."

Father Brannan bent his head in his hands, and was silent for so long that Marnie thought he must be praying. At last he looked up, anguish in his soft blue eyes. "Marnie, child," he said, "I came here with sad news, and I'm afearing it's going to get worse. The people in Torcurra think . . . Well, to put it bluntly, they think you caused your husband's death. Three old women overheard what you said in the church, about it being your fault your husband was dead. I got old Finian to tell them what he saw here, and that he was convinced your husband's death was an accident. That's why I brought Finian with us, so there'd be a witness apart from ourselves. But the village folk . . . Well, they don't let go an idea easily, once it's rattled around a few times in their skulls. I managed to make them see it wasn't murder, but now they think you put a spell on Isake, and by that caused his death."

"Then they're stupid, aren't they?"

"Aye, but they are your neighbors."

"I don't need them."

"I was thinking that you did, if only to help you fix your house. But seeing as they won't, I will. I'll mend the rafter for you when I can, and help you with the thatching. But you will make life hellish difficult for yourself if you befriend the mad boy. It will only make folks even more suspicious of you."

"I don't care what people think. It's like my own world, here. I like this place, father. It's mine. No one can take it away from me, or force me to leave it. And if I choose to share what little I have with someone who has nothing, then you ought to bless me for it, not curse me."

"I'm not cursing you for it, Marnie! I'm just saying life will be difficult."

"It was never anything else, father."

He sighed and wiped his hands over his face, as if brushing away thoughts that troubled him. "Then I can only pray for you," he said, "and ask you to remember that even our Blessed Lord would not invite a madman into his home, without first casting out his devils and making him safe."

"I didn't think our Lord had a home, father," she said. "I remember the priest at Fernleigh telling us that Scripture says the foxes had holes and the birds had nests, but Jesus had nowhere to lay his head. I've always remembered it, and felt sorry for him."

Father Brannan looked surprised, then he grinned. "I'll remember not to discuss holy matters with you, Marnie, in the future. Now, before you start on a sermon, will you fetch me something I can put over that hole in your roof?"

"I have the cover from the wagon. Will that do?"

"I should think so. We'll use stones to weight it down, and it should stay well enough, so long as the wind dies a bit. At least it will keep you dry if it rains. And when the weather's clear again, we'll do the thatching."

"Thank you, father. You're very good to help, considering no one else will, and this house is bedeviled."

Father Brannan's eyes twinkled, brighter than the summer sky. "Oh, bedeviled, is it?" he said. "I thought it was just bedraggled, seeing as it hasn't had a loving touch for a while."

"But you still make the sign of the cross when you come in."

"Just to be safe. I also do it when I enter the church and when I go to bed at night and when I eat my food."

"You think it's safe here, then?"

"I wouldn't be here if I didn't. But you, Marnie—what do you think? You're the one that's living here."

She gazed around the room, at the little table with its flowers and candlestick; the chests of clothes, Isake's covered now with a shawl, and with some wildflowers on it; the tidy bed with its yellow quilt, bright even through the smoky atmosphere; the clay dishes and bowls in the alcoves beside the fireplace, with the little painted plate her mother had given her; and the tidy hearth, with its cheerful fire, and wood neatly stacked, and the gleaming pans hanging on the beam beside the chimney stones. She ignored the moss-stained walls and broken roof.

"I like it well enough," she replied. "It will be better, when it's whitewashed and mended."

"You're not afraid to be here alone?"

"I was afraid last night, but then Raven came."

Father Brannan chuckled, shaking his head. "You were afraid until a madman came, and then you felt safe? Oh, you're a strange one, to be sure, Widow Isherwood. Now make me a cup of peppermint tea, then I shall put that wagon cover on your roof, and go home, and then the weather may do what it likes."

Chapter 11

As MARNIE SAT down to supper, there was a scuffle at her door. It crashed open, and Raven stood on the step, grinning, saturated by the heavy rain. He held up two fish.

"Oh, Raven! You haven't been fishing in this weather, have you?" She laughed, taking the fish and laying them on the table. Raven opened and shut his mouth, making senseless noises. Behind him, rain flowed from the eaves, and the little stream roared as it rushed, swollen and boisterous, down to the beach.

"Did you catch them?" Marnie asked, bringing him inside, and lightly tapping his wet chest with her forefinger. Indicating the fish, she made a motion with her hand as if hauling them from the water, then touched Raven's chest again.

He stared at her, mystified, then noticed her bowl of soup on the table. Picking it up, he began slurping. Marnie touched his arm and he glanced at her, startled, soup dribbling down his chin, mingling with the water that trickled from his black hair. "You," Marnie said, tapping his chest again then pointing to one of the chairs, "sit down."

He did as he was told, and Marnie got more soup for herself and sat opposite him. "Where did you get the fish?" she asked, touching the silvery scales, her expression questioning.

Raven finished the soup, smiled, and got up to help himself to more. Seeing what he was after, Marnie jumped up and took his arm, leading him firmly back to the table. "Not until I know where the fish is from," she said. "Sit." She pushed him onto the chair, and he made pleading noises, pointing to the pot of soup over the fire.

"After," Marnie said. "I want to know where the fish came from. We have to finish what we start, Raven, else we'll never learn anything."

He mimicked her mouth, his sounds earnest and confused, but he remained seated while she pulled her chair around and sat facing him. He was shivering, and Marnie thought of Isake's chest with his clothes locked inside, and wished she had the key.

"The fish," she said, touching them. "Where are they from?" Shrugging, she spread her hands, palms upward, made a gesture as if giving a gift, tapped his chest, and pointed to the fish. She began to repeat the actions, making them deliberate and slow, but halfway through Raven lost interest and stood up, his eyes longingly on the soup. Marnie gripped his shirt and made him sit again. "We're going to work this out," she said, "if it takes till Christmastide."

Making sure she had Raven's attention, she mimed her question again.

At first Raven's face was blank, but suddenly he nodded, grunting with excitement. He pointed in the direction of Torcurra, then signed a cross on his chest.

"Father Brannan!" Marnie cried. Rapidly she traced the shape of a hood over her head, and placed her hands in front of her as though she prayed. Then she made a cross on her chest. "Father Brannan?" she asked. "Did he give me the fish?"

Nodding eagerly, making wild noises, Raven signed the cross again, then touched the fish.

"Thank you, Raven." Marnie smiled, picking up his bowl. "You can have some more soup, now. Sit there by the fire, so your clothes will dry."

Three bowls of soup later, Raven got up from the stool near the hearth, his clothes faintly steaming, and put the empty bowl on the table. Wiping his wrist across his chin, he began exploring the cottage.

Marnie's belongings intrigued him, and he fingered the shawl she had put over Isake's chest, and touched the things in the alcoves and window ledges. Seeing an opportunity to invent names for everyday objects, Marnie followed. As he picked up a bowl, she touched his arm to get his attention, then cupped her hands together as if holding grain. "Bowl," she said, then pointed to the pottery, and made the motion again with her hands.

Raven's gaze went from the bowl to the unfamiliar sign she made. Suddenly he realized that her hands formed a hollow like a bowl. He put the vessel down and copied her gesture, his eyes on her face, inquiringly. She smiled and nodded, and Raven smiled back and made the gesture again. Then he picked up a spoon. Thinking quickly, Marnie made a swift, natural motion as if lifting a spoonful of food to her mouth. Laughing quietly to himself, Raven imitated the move. He picked up a cup, and Marnie made a simple action as if drinking from one. Again he copied her. All around the cottage he went, pointing out household objects, and each time Marnie gestured names for them.

Remembering her silent games with the children, she mimed a simple request, asking Raven to bring her a cup. To her joy and astonishment, Raven understood. As she took the cup from his hands, she almost wept. "We'll talk yet, you and I," she said, and he made unintelligible sounds, his eyes fervent.

Realizing that the room was growing dark, Marnie went to the table and lit the candle there. Raven pointed to the candle, then touched her hands.

"I don't have a hand-word for candle," she said, shaking her head. "I'm sorry, Raven."

Perplexed, he banged the candlestick on the wood. Feeling confused herself, and wishing she had been better prepared, Marnie turned away and went to light another candle on the mantelpiece. Raven thumped the table with his fists, then jiggled the candlestick again, awful sounds gurgling from his throat.

"I told you, I don't know any more hand-words," Marnie said, facing him. "I'm sorry."

He tried desperately to imitate her speech, almost choking with the effort. All the time he pointed to the candle then to her hands, pleading for a defining sign, a meaning, a name. At last he was still, and Marnie gazed at him, helpless, while the chasm of silence stretched wider between them, isolating and profound.

Suddenly Raven flung open the door and ran out into the rain. Rushing to the doorway, Marnie called him back; then realized the stupidity of it, and raced out after him. But he was running fast along the bank of the stream, heading for the hills, and she could not catch up with him. Drenched, she stamped back to the cottage, peeled off her soaking clothes, dried herself, and pulled on a clean shift.

"Fool, fool, Marnie Isherwood!" she said as she sat by the fire and rubbed furiously at her wet hair with a cloth. "Fool, to get him all inspired, and then to stop! He'll always be a step ahead, wanting another word, while you shilly-shally about and drive him half mad with impatience! You'll drive yourself mad as well, trying to keep up with him! You'll always come up against that great silence of his, and all the trying in the world won't make a road across it. You're a fool to think you could, Marnie. A flaming fool."

She threw the cloth on the hearth, and stood to go to bed. As she bent to blow out the candle, she hesitated, looking at the fragile flame. Thoughtfully she lifted her right hand, palm upward, gathered her fingertips close together, then flicked them slightly open and shut, imitating the flickering light. "Candle," she said. She smiled a little, pleased with the sign. Raising her hand high, she gathered her fingertips together in the same way, but flung them suddenly open, as if scattering a great light. "The sun."

Hours later she was still there by her table, unmindful of the rain that drummed on the oiled covering over her roof, or the dawn wind that whistled through the cracks in her door and rattled the latch; unmindful of anything save the hand-words she created, to cross a wilderness of quiet.

The next morning the rain stopped briefly, though the skies remained heavy and gray. During the break in the weather, Marnie took her food bowls and pots down to the stream to wash. She was still there when Raven came back. He was wearing a clean faded yellow shirt and patched leggings. Crouching by her on the bank, he made the hand-word for bowl.

I clean these, she signed, using some of the words she had invented in the night. *You help.* She gave him her pot to wash, showing him how to use sand to scour it. *Thank you,* she said when they finished, and he helped her take the things back to the house again, watching as she put them away.

When that was done, Marnie got the bucket of water from near the door and placed it on the table. "Bucket," she said, making a swinging motion as if carrying one. Raven looked alarmed for a moment, wanting to please but not knowing what was required of him. Then he noticed the action of her hands, and comprehension dawned. Marnie trickled the fingers of her right hand in the bucket, then repeated the action in the air, making the hand-word for water. Raven copied her. Moving around the cottage, she named the other objects for which she had created words last night, and Raven followed, his hands mimicking hers, his unearthly grunts excited and loud. *Bed,* they gestured. *Flowers. Chest. Clothes. Chair. Door. Table.*

Candle. Knife. Bread. Fish. Floor. Stone. Fire. Firewood. Pot. House. Man. You. Woman. Me.

Marnie stopped, elated, her eyes shining.

Drink, said Raven, with his hands. *Me, you, drink.*

"Aye," she said, smiling back. "You've earned it, Raven."

As she made them tea from marigold petals, he leaned against the side of the chimney watching her, his gray eyes solemn and inquisitive.

Sit here, drink, she said, putting the cups on the table, and indicating the two chairs.

Raven copied the signs, getting them confused. She made them again, and sat down. He sat too, though she was not sure whether he had understood her words, or whether he was simply copying what she did.

When he had finished his tea he made a hand-word. *Fish,* he said, and pretended to eat from his right hand.

The fish, you, I, will eat, she said.

She took the fish down onto the beach to fillet, and Raven followed her. He seemed to understand what she was doing, so she gave him the knife and watched him clean the fish.

Father Brannan, you, clean fish? she asked. He grinned at her, his dark hair across his eyes, then bent over his work again. Marnie sighed, and tried again. This time Raven's face lit up, and he nodded eagerly. But Marnie was still not sure he understood. She decided to talk to him all the time, to make up all the hand-words she could and use them constantly, whether or not he seemed to comprehend. Surely, she thought, after a time the meanings of words would dawn on him.

Gulls flew down, and Raven threw them the scraps. The gulls fought over them, shrieking. Marnie touched Raven's arm, so he would look at her hands. *The birds fight,* she said. *Hungry, want food.*

Raven watched her hands. He copied the sign for birds, making a beak with his fingers in front of his mouth, and pointed to the gulls whirling and screaming about their heads. Marnie nodded, thankful that he had understood even that much, and Raven smiled.

They took the fillets back to the house and cooked them, and ate sitting at the little table Isake had made. They could not talk with food in their hands, but their silence was easy and companionable. Marnie thought of her meal with Isake, with its awkwardness and irksome silence, except for the sounds the man had made as he ate. Raven also made sounds, not knowing that he did—moans and mutters of appreciation, and contented sighs. Marnie watched him over her bowl, her eyes amused and fond.

Afterward they went for a walk along the beach, and Marnie talked constantly with her hands, not caring that what she said would be trivial to anyone else. Raven copied her gestures, making noises with his mouth, and sometimes she thought he understood. But at the day's end, when he curled in a blanket by the fire to sleep, the only thing Marnie was certain of was that he was an excellent mimic, and that he wanted desperately to please her.

The next day it was raining again. Raven ate most of the food Marnie had, and still wanted more, trying to win her approval by picking up objects and naming them, hoping she would feed him as a reward. She struggled to explain.

No food here, she said. *Bread, gone. Eggs, gone. Fish, little here. Rain go, Father Brannan will come here, mend house. I will tell him, give food. Food inside Father Brannan's house. Eggs, bread, onions, cabbage, chicken.*

Raven watched her closely, his hands repeating the signs.

Marnie sighed. "You don't understand a word I'm saying, do you?" she said, without using her hands. "I'm giving up, Raven. You watch, and you mimic everything, but that's all. 'Tis all still a mystery to you, meaning nothing."

Suddenly Raven opened the door and rushed out into the rain. She watched him running up the hill toward Torcurra, his yellow shirt already plastered against him, his feet slithering on the wet grass in his mad haste to do whatever crazy thing had got into his head. Closing the door, she leaned against it for a while, biting her lower lip, her blue eyes sorrowful. Slowly, as if she were intensely weary, she went over to the fire and made herself herb tea. She sat at her table to drink it, looking about the dim room, and listening to the rain. Memories of home and family swept over her, and she covered her face with her hands, and sobbed. In front of her the tea grew cold, and the room darkened as night fell and the fire died down.

Suddenly there was a banging and scrabbling at her door. Before she could get to it, Raven burst in. He was beaming, exultant. In his hands was a bag, oiled against the rain. He opened it, tipping its contents onto her table. She could hardly see what was there, and got up to throw more wood on the fire. In the increased light she saw what he had brought. Proud, his hand-words excited and quick, Raven signed the names to her.

Eggs, he said. *Bread. Onions, cabbage, chicken.* He pointed out the open door and up the hill toward Torcurra, then made a cross on his chest, the sign for the priest. He tried to speak, choking in his eagerness, his hand-words frantic and too quick for her to read.

Marnie sat down, stunned. Raven sat down opposite her, leaning his dripping arms on the table, watching her face for signs of approval. Then he noticed her tears, and dismay flooded over him. Quickly, Marnie wiped her eyes, and smiled.

Thank you, she said with her hands. *I will cook food.*

Raven watched her hands, her mouth. He looked distraught, and Marnie knew he was concerned because she had been crying. She struggled to find words to explain.

You, gone. I . . . I hurt, want my house, my . . . But she had no hand-words for family, or mother or father or sisters.

Raven reached across the table and traced a cold finger down her cheek, where her tears had been, his beautiful eyes disturbed and questioning.

I want my house, she said, pointing outside several times, trying to indicate a great distance. *I want the man, the woman* . . . She stopped, frustrated at having no more words for him.

Seeing the word *man*, Raven copied it, scratching the light beard on his jaw; then he made motions as if digging, and pointed toward Isake's grave.

Marnie shook her head. Overwhelmed again with longing for people familiar and beloved, she started to cry and could not stop. "I'm sorry, Raven," she choked, burying her face in her hands. "I can't explain."

Confused, distraught, Raven went and stood in front of her. He drew her to her feet and tried to take her hands from her face, wanting her to talk to him in signs he understood. Sobbing, she shook her head. He murmured meaningless noises to comfort her, and tried again to take her hands, holding her by the wrists. She shrank from him, and he held her more tightly, his voice rising with frustration as he tried to communicate. Suddenly she wrenched away, and he saw her mouth gaping, her features distorted by fear. Grief and hurt swept over him. Howling, he wiped his arm across the table, scattering the gifts he had brought. The bowls shattered against the fireplace, and the food rolled on the floor. With inhuman cries, he upturned the table, then picked up a chair and hurled it at the door.

Marnie cringed against the wall, her arms over her head. She heard Raven panting, heard horrendous noises deep in his throat, as if fiends were trying to crawl out of him. Then there was silence, and she realized he had gone.

She staggered to her feet and went to the open doorway. The rain still came down in torrents. It shimmered about her door from the fire and candlelight, but beyond that was utter blackness, and only the sound of the waves crashing on the shore. There was no sign of Raven.

Marnie slammed the door and put the table upright again. The chair had been broken, two of its legs snapped. She set the chair and broken pieces beside the fire, and picked up the bowls, spoons, and precious food. Then she went over to Isake's box of tools. Straining, she dragged it across the stone floor, and wedged it hard against the door. She dragged over the other two chests as well, and placed them on top of the toolbox. Looking at the windows, she decided they were too small for anyone to climb through, even with the help of demons; but she sprinkled salt on the ledges, just to be safe. That night she slept with flints and a candle by her pillow, in case she needed light, and had the frying pan nearby, for protection.

Chapter 12

FIVE MORE DAYS it rained. Confined to a dreary room, severed from all that she had known and loved, Marnie suffered a desolation worse than anything else in her life. By day, unoccupied, she gazed at the rain on the lonely sea, and ached for human company. At night, the drumming of the unrelenting rain mingled in her nightmares with scrabblings at her door, unearthly cries, and the howls of the roaming dead.

In the afternoon of the fifth day the skies lightened, and a pale sun shone through the thin clouds. Marnie went out to wash in the stream, and to empty the bucket she used for a chamber pot. Isake had dug a hole behind the cottage, under the thickest canopy of the trees, to be used as a lavatory. Her ablutions completed, Marnie gathered up broken branches and driftwood, then stacked them to dry beside the hearth. Then she untethered the horse, pressing her face against its neck, cherishing the touch of something else alive and warm. As she took the animal down onto the beach, she tried not to look at the grave with its flowers flattened in mud, and its cross slipped sideways; tried not to think of Isake under it, with mud in his mouth and through his hair and in his laughing eyes.

She walked the horse to the far end of the cove, until a savage, rocky point made further progress impossible; then she turned and walked back the other way, facing Torcurra. Her cove was completely isolated, hidden from Torcurra by a rocky headland and high cliffs. As she looked at the headland, a little boat appeared around it, rowed by a brawny figure in a brown habit. He saw her and called out.

She waved and called back, overjoyed to see that he rowed toward her beach. Hurrying back to the trees, she tethered the horse in a fresh place, then ran to meet Father Brannan, in time to help him haul his boat up onto the sand.

"It's fair work rowing here, but quicker than walking," he said cheerfully, puffing a little. "Have you rowed before, Marnie?"

"No, father."

"I'll teach you, sometime. Or Raven will." Reaching into the bottom of the boat, he dragged out a little sack and held it out to her. Whatever was in the sack moved, and she shrank from it. "Lobster." Father Brannan smiled. "Take it. It'll be our supper tonight. I'm inviting myself, if that's all right."

"It's fine," she said, smiling, opening the sack and peering inside. Then she gave a cry of alarm and astonishment. "How do I skin the thing?"

Father Brannan laughed, and pulled another sack out of the bottom of the boat. "You don't," he said. "I'll show you how to cook it. And I've brought some more bread and vegetables for you, and some dill to make a tempting sauce to go with that ferocious little feast you're holding. You're in for a treat, Marnie lass, to be sure. My cooking, and Torcurra lobster. You'll think you've died and gone to heaven."

Marnie laughed, and they walked up toward the cottage. "I thank you for the food you sent, father," she said. "It was much appreciated. Raven eats like a horse."

"You're welcome. I suppose by now you're preaching sermons to him, and listening to his arguments."

"What do you mean?" she asked uneasily.

"Well, I've not seen him for a week, except when he rushed in that night and grabbed some food for you. Very determined, he was, about what he wanted. Then he pointed over the hill to your house. I presume you've spent all this time working your wonders on him."

"He's not been here," she said, reddening, her eyes on the ground.

"You've not seen him at all?"

"Only that one night, when he brought those things from you."

Father Brannan stopped walking, and looked up past her cottage and the trees, to where clouds still clung about the bleak surrounding hills. "Then where's he been all this time?" he asked. "I've not fed him. The villagers don't. Have you put out food for him?"

"No," she said guiltily, thinking of the barricade against him, the scrabbling on her door at night, the husky voice, gibbering and desperate, and her own terror.

"Oh, Marnie, I'll have to go and look for him. 'Tis the longest he's gone, without coming to me. He could be hurt somewhere. If only I'd known! I thought he was with you."

"I'm not his keeper!" She said it with such vehemence that Father Brannan stared at her in surprise.

"I never said you were, child."

"I'm glad we've agreed on that, then!" she said, striding ahead of him up to the cottage.

"I'm not blaming you!" he said, running after her, and following her inside. "Lord knows, if anyone's to blame, it's me. I'm the one he comes—"

He stopped, seeing the heavy chests just inside the door, and the marks on the floor where she had dragged them across to keep Raven out. Groaning, the priest sat on the chair nearby. "Oh, Marnie, child!" he whispered, his face colorless. "What's he done to you?"

"Nothing," she replied calmly, taking the sack he had dropped on the table, and putting it with the lobster sack on a peg on the wall.

"He must have done something if you've barricaded yourself against him."

"Do you want a cup of mint tea, father, or do you want to go and search for him right away?"

"The madness came on him, didn't it?"

"Shall I put my boots on and come and help you? It will be dark soon."

"Did he hurt you, Marnie?"

"No. I don't want to talk about it, except to say that you were right and I was wrong. He has a gentle spirit, but there is a madness comes on him as well. I was a fool to think that he and I could understand each other, a fool to ever think that we could talk. Please forget I mentioned such a thing. I'll mind my own business, and not meddle in his life again. Now, do you want me to come and help you look for him?"

"I don't think that'll be necessary," he replied. "There are one or two places I know about, where I think he hides. Maybe we'll give the lobster a reprieve tonight, and I'll come tomorrow instead. Put the creature in a bucket of seawater, and it'll keep." He stood up, and began to leave. In the doorway he turned. "By the way, Marnie, that boat's for you. Make sure that you keep it high on the beach, above the line of seaweed. Otherwise the sea will creep up and get it, and you'll not see it again."

"Father," she said, suddenly afraid, "do you think the sea has Raven?"

Father Brannan chuckled. "Not likely. He swims like a fish. He'll be in a little cave somewhere up in the hills. Don't you go worrying; he's my responsibility."

He gave her a cheery wave, and went.

Marnie stood in the doorway and watched as he went up the slope to the left of her cottage, following the stream. Leaving her door open, she went inside and moved the chests and the box of tools back to their places by her bed.

A short time later she was sitting eating soup and some of the bread Father Brannan had brought her, when a shadow darkened her doorway, and she looked up and saw Raven. He leaned against the door, his body narrow and dark against the evening sky. She could not see his face. Lifting his right hand, he traced the shape of a cross on his chest. He pointed over the hill to where the priest lived, and made a roof of his hands, which was the word for house; then shook his head.

Marnie too made the gesture for the priest, then put her hand above her eyes, as if searching, and pointed at Raven. *Father Brannan, looking, you.*

Raven groaned and slumped lower in the doorway, his head leaning on the wood. He breathed as if he were in pain. Moved to pity, Marnie got up and went to him. He was filthy, covered in grit and mud, and his hair was matted. There were welts on his wrists, where he had been bound, and Marnie noticed, when she put her arm about him to help him inside, that the back of his shirt was slippery with blood.

Chapter 13

SHE HELPED HIM to a chair, and Raven slouched with his head in his arms on the table, making hoarse and anguished sounds like sobs. Even the back of his neck bled from the lash, and the blood on his shirt came up in vivid stripes. He was shaking all over.

Marnie touched his arm, and he lifted his head. His eyes were full of torment and confusion and pain. Several times he made the hand-word for houses, meaning Torcurra; then groaned and pretended to eat from his hand.

Marnie made the signs: *You, looking, bread?*

Raven nodded. *Hungry*, said his hands. Then he made the signs for man and woman, repeating them to signify a crowd, and shook his fists, yelling terrible, incoherent sounds full of hate. Pointing to himself, he made violent motions of binding and whipping. Distressed, Marnie took his arms and made him stop.

She put some water over the fire to heat, and placed soap and cloths on the table. Seeing them, Raven made the sign for Father Brannan. He also signed the word for water, and made motions as if wringing out a cloth and washing skin. He touched his own shoulders, and made the sign for the priest again.

Marnie pointed to herself. *I will clean you*, she said with her hands.

Wearily, Raven nodded and staggered to his feet, gripping the table for support. Marnie took his arm and helped him over to the bed. Unselfconsciously, he began to undress, and Marnie returned to the hearth. She stood facing the flames, waiting for the water to heat, listening to Raven's groans as he peeled off his shirt and removed his leggings, and there was a relieved sigh as he finally lay down. When the water was warm she tipped some into a bowl, picked up the soap and the cloths, and went over to the bed. In the dimness she saw only the pale slenderness of him, his skin glimmering gold against the dark blankets. He was lying on his front, naked, his head buried in his arms. The marks from the lash crossed his shoulders, and made dark red welts all down his back, down across his buttocks and the backs of his thighs.

Placing the bowl on the floor beside the bed, Marnie picked up his clothes and put them in the bucket of water near the door, to soak ready for washing in the morning. Then she lit a candle and took it over to the bed. Raven lay so still, she thought he must be asleep. But he turned his head when she put down the light, so she knelt, wet the cloth in the bowl, soaped it, and gave it to him to wash his face and hands. He did, awkwardly, still lying on his front, and moaning every time he moved. Then he gave her back the cloth and rested again, his head on one arm, his eyes hidden by his tangled black hair.

Marnie rinsed the cloth in the clean water, and began washing his back. He groaned and sobbed, his face turned to the pillow, his body rigid with pain. Marnie wet his back, then soaped the cloth and carefully but firmly wiped away all the dried blood and dirt. The white cloth changed to pink, and the water in the bowl became stained deeper and deeper with crimson.

When his back was clean, Marnie went to her own chest of belongings, and took out a jar of oil her mother had given her. It was healing balm made from the herb called Saint-John's-wort, soothing for abrasions and burns. Marnie poured some of the precious liquid into her palm, smoothing it over her hands, warming it. Across the skin marked by the lash, she spread the shining oil; over his shoulders and neck and upper arms, along the curve of his back, down all of him. Comforted, Raven sighed deeply, and slept.

Marnie drew a blanket over him, placed the stopper back on the jar of oil, and put it away. Picking up the bowl and bloodied cloth, she went outside. She emptied the red water into the stream, and rinsed the cloths and the bowl. Before she went back in she stood facing the beach, breathing in the calmness of the night, and looking at the silver path of the moon across the sea.

Inside, the house was filled with the fragrance of the oil and with the serene breathing of the young man asleep. Moving quietly from habit, though it was not necessary, Marnie broke some bread and put it with a piece of smoked fish onto a platter, with a few of the pickles Isake had brought from the manor. She put the meal on the floor by the bed, placing the cross from Father Brannan beside it, so that, if Raven woke, he would know where she had gone. She piled more wood on the fire and placed the candle in a shallow dish of water. Then she got her cloak, checked one last time that Raven was asleep, and went out.

The houses of Torcurra stood dark and ominous against the moonlit sea. Unlike the houses of Fernleigh, there were no trees about them, and they seemed hostile and bleak. Lights burned inside, and she could smell the fragrant smoke from their peat fires. She passed the graveyard, and looked into the church. On the altar burned candles for the souls of the dead; but Father Brannan was not there. Neither was he in his house. Marnie worried, thinking he must still be out looking for Raven. She went to the house nearest the church, and knocked on the door. A woman answered. She had a kindly face, and was carrying a baby on her hip. But when she saw Marnie, her eyes widened in alarm, and she stepped back.

"I'm looking for Father Brannan," said Marnie. "Have you seen him?"

The woman did not answer. Without taking her eyes off Marnie, she called to someone in the house, "Come here, Terrell! Be quick!"

A man appeared, obviously her husband. He put an arm protectively about the woman's shoulders, and glared at Marnie. "What is it you want, she-devil?" he asked.

For a few moments Marnie was too shocked to speak. At last she stammered, "I—I'm looking for Father Brannan, sir."

"Aye, and you'll be needing a priest soon enough, if there's any justice in the world!" spat the man.

Marnie's heart thumped. "What do you mean?" she asked.

The man grunted and said nothing, but the woman cried, "We all know what you did to your husband! You cursed him, and he died!"

Marnie shook her head. Everything seemed to be spinning around her, and she felt as though she were falling, spiraling downward into an awful void. From somewhere far away came the man's voice, shouting and full of hate, "Get out! Out of our village! Get out, afore we hang you!"

Dimly, she was aware of doors being flung open in nearby cottages, and other people coming out. There were more shouts, and a stone was hurled at her, striking her chest. Marnie turned and fled.

She did not stop running until she burst through the doorway of her own home. Then she slammed the door shut and leaned against it, breathing hard. Raven remained asleep, the candle burning low beside his bed, his meal untouched. Marnie pushed the wooden chests across the floor to the door, forcing them against the wood. She selected a large, sharp-ended piece of firewood, and placed it on the table, along with the knife she had brought, used in her old life to skin rabbits and kill pigs. Then she lit three more candles, and threw extra wood on the fire.

She made herself a cup of chamomile tea and sat by the fire to drink it, facing the shadowy room. Raven looked so peaceful. She knew, now, how he felt when they went after him, to whip him; how he felt to be hated and rejected and despised. And he had no home to flee to, except that of a priest who was not always there.

"You have my home now, Raven," she said quietly. "I'll never close you out again, I swear, nor turn you away. This home is ours, I swear it on Christ's holy blood, and I'll never let it be taken away from us."

The candles burned low, and Marnie removed a folded spare blanket from under Raven's feet. He stirred, but did not wake. Going back to her chair by the fire, she wrapped the blanket about her for warmth, and sat facing the barricaded door, and waited for the dawn.

A fitful wind got up, and a corner of the covering on the roof flapped against the remaining thatch. In Marnie's dreams she was threshing wheat in the manor barn, getting out the grain; but she was the only villager there, and she was alone but for the man Isake, who watched her through the golden dust, his eyes black and burning. The barn melted, and she was running through a field, pursued by a man in a long cloak. He was close behind her, and when he breathed her name, she smelled the garlic on his breath. Then it was Isake, his body heavy on hers as she lay face down in the dark harvest field, her body paralyzed, and he took her while the villagers danced and the fiddlers played their frenzied music, and she could not breathe, for shame. Then she was bound tight, lying in a wagon, and they were hauling her to a tree for hanging. She was raised to her feet, and the rope was about her neck, its other end fixed high in a tree; and they were moving the wagon out from beneath her. Then it was gone, and she was swinging helplessly, choking, choking—

She jerked upright. Her eyes flew open and she saw the cottage full of sunshine, pouring in through the roof where the cover had blown back; and the knife on the table by the burned-out candles, the chests against the door, and Raven asleep in her bed. She had almost fallen off her chair, her neck was stiff, and there was a strand of her long hair caught tight across her throat. Almost laughing with relief, she slumped back, rubbing her hand across her eyes. And then she heard it, rumbling like low thunder as it came down the hill toward her house: the wagon to take her to her hanging.

Chapter 14

FROZEN WITH HORROR, Marnie listened while the wagon rumbled to a stop outside her door. She heard someone get down, heard footsteps, and then a banging on her door. Raven slept on, unaware. Marnie's heart thudded painfully, and she tried to speak, to pray, but could not. Neither could she move to go and wake Raven. Whoever it was knocked again. The latch rattled, and someone pushed on the door. They pushed again, harder, grunting and puffing. The chests moved, bumping against one another. Someone called her name, and pushed at the door again. Marnie picked up the knife.

A face darkened the window beside her.

"Sweet Jesus, lass!" cried Father Brannan, shocked, still scarlet from his exertions against the door. "What do you think you're doing? Put the knife down! 'Tis me, myself! The priest! What's the matter? You're whiter than a corpse!"

Marnie put down the knife, and tried to push aside the chests. She felt so weak, it took her a while, and Father Brannan finished the work for her, leaning his shoulder against the door and shoving so hard that the last chest shot aside, knocking over the chair.

Rushing in, the priest glanced about the room, and saw Raven asleep in the bed. He gripped Marnie by the shoulders. "What's going on?" he cried. "I swear, you're the most contrary soul I ever met! One day you barricade him out, the next you keep him in!"

"I was keeping *them* out," she whispered.

"Them? Who? Sit down, you look dreadful." He picked up the chair for her, and she sat down, her head bent and her hands trembling on her lap. Father Brannan pulled up a stool and sat in front of her, taking her hands and chaffing them between his, to comfort her. "Tell me what happened," he said softly.

"Raven came here last night. He was hurt. They'd whipped him again. It was bad, father. When he was asleep I came to see you, to tell you that he was here, and not to be worrying. I couldn't find you."

"I was still out looking for him. I didn't get back till cockcrow."

"I asked at one of the houses. I wanted to leave a message for you. The people . . . they . . ."

"Tell me, child! What did they do?"

"They said I cursed Isake, and that was why he died. They said they would hang me."

"Did they hurt you?"

"They threw a stone, that was all. But when I heard the wagon just now, I thought they were come to get me, to—" She turned her face away, trying to control the shuddering that went through her.

"I'm sorry, child," said Father Brannan. "I thought I'd talked sense into them."

"Tell me truly, father, can they hang me?"

"Not while I'm alive, they won't, I swear it. Oh, don't worry, Marnie. They'll settle down, soon enough. But if I were you, I wouldn't go into Torcurra again, not until they're calm. You caught them at a bad time, still wrought up after their dealings with poor Raven."

"Are they always like this, father? Always thinking the worst, always suspicious?"

"I think it's their nature to be hard. It's their life—the ungentle land, the indifferent sea. They have to be hard to survive. They can't help it."

"Why are you different, father?"

"Am I?"

"Of course you are. You're the only one who's helped me. The only one who helps Raven."

He sighed deeply, released her hands, and went and stood in the doorway, looking out at the sea, his kindly face pensive and sad. "Once, I was harder than anyone," he said. "Full of dreams I was, ready to thrash people's souls into gentleness, and transform human nature. I was going to clean the world up, make it a fit place for the kingdom to come, and God help anyone who stood in my way.

"One night I was preparing a sermon, and there was a storm outside. The sermon was about love, the heart of everything Christ taught. I was late getting it done, for some reason, and anxious that it wouldn't be finished in time. And it was an important sermon, because it was going to help set the world aright. While I was writing it, there was a knock on the door. It was an old beggar looking for a place to sleep the night. He looked awful sick, and I sent him off to one of the other houses, since I was busy on important work. Then I forgot him. All night I worked on that sermon. Oh, it was a fine discourse, Marnie! Christ himself would have been proud of it! I decided to go out early to pray in the church, since it was the Sabbath. I opened my door, and found the beggar still on my step. He was dead.

"Well, my sermon was a great success, and after it I buried the beggar in the pauper's ground outside the churchyard, and thought no more about him. That night I had a dream. I dreamed I was preparing a sermon on love, and it was a stormy night, and there was a knock on my door. It was just as things had really happened. Except that when I opened my door, it wasn't a beggar. It was the Lord Christ himself. And

I wanted to fall at his feet and bring him in out of the rain, and put him warm in my own bed, and have him a beloved guest in my home. But you know, Marnie, for all the longing in my heart, my tongue would not say those words. I said the same to him that I said to the beggar, and I sent my blessed Lord away, out into the storm. And in my dream I found him the next morning on my step, wrapped in rags, and dead. And I remembered the holy Scripture: 'Whatsoever you do to the least of these, my brethren, you do it unto me.'

"You reminded me of all this the other day, when you said our Lord didn't have a home. You were right. He was forsaken, hated, misunderstood, wrongly accused, betrayed, whipped. Oh, he knows all about these things, Marnie, all about places like Torcurra, and the pain of people like Raven and yourself. The least of his brethren. I've learned to love them, these least ones. It's the other kind I find hard to love, now—the so-called worthy ones, who do everything right; the self-righteous, the proud, the narrow-minded, the intolerant. The ones most like myself."

"I'd hardly call you intolerant, father. Not while you stand in a witch's house, and keep company with a mad boy and a murderer."

Father Brannan suddenly chuckled, and passed a hand over his eyes. "You're good for my weary soul, Marnie. And, talking of your house, I've brought some timber to replace that broken rafter, and some straw for thatching in case you haven't got enough. I've got a good strong board too, and I'll fix it so you can put it like a bolt across your door, instead of hauling over those heavy chests. And I've got some fresh bread and flour for you, more candles, and a few vegetables from my garden. There's also some peat for your fire, since you've used nearly all the wood nearby. All I need from you is a cup of peppermint tea, and some hot water to wash that strapping lad over there, if I can wake him up. He'll be needing a wash and ointments, after the whipping."

"I've done that," she said. "I washed him last night, and put oil on his wounds."

Father Brannan looked astonished, strode over to Raven, and lifted the blanket. Raven grunted and nestled further into the bed. Father Brannan dropped the blanket over him again, and came back to Marnie.

"That was brave of you, lass," he said, a strange expression on his face.

"I used to look after my little brothers and sisters when they were sick, and I helped my mother look after my father. I'm used to pain. It doesn't distress me."

"That wasn't my meaning. He's sixteen, or thereabouts. Not a child. There's been some pretty frantic things in his head sometimes, and I'm afraid there'll be frenzy in other places too, before long. He's unlearned, he doesn't know what's decent. Sometimes he runs around naked like an animal, not caring who sees. You have to be careful not to lead him on."

"I didn't lead him on!" Marnie cried, leaping up from her chair, and banging the table with her fists. "I cleaned his back for him, father, that was all!"

"But he slept in your bed."

"Aye, on his own!"

"I'm only telling you to take care, Marnie, that's all."

"Oh, I'll take care, father! I'll take so much care, that the first man who dares put his hand on me will lose it, along with other parts I wouldn't like to mention! No man will ever make me do again what Isake made me do! I'll slit his throat first, or—"

"Marnie! You don't know what you're saying, child! That's holy matrimony you're talking about!"

"Holy? *Holy?* If that's holy, I'll go with the devil and be burned in hell!"

Father Brannan turned and went outside. Walking quickly, he passed his wagon and horse, and went down to the beach.

Marnie sat at the table, her head in her hands. After a while she got up and went outside. The priest was sitting by the sea, leaning against the boat he had brought yesterday. He had one hand over his eyes, and Marnie thought he must be praying. She sat by him to wait.

"I'm sorry, Marnie," he said, without moving his hand. "I've got a remarkable lot of book-learning, and not a lot of sense when it comes to actual dealings between men and women. I didn't mean to judge you, and I hadn't forgotten what you said about your husband. All I was trying to say, and getting it out all wrong, was that no one has shown Raven kindness, excepting for myself. And kindness from a crusty old priest is one thing, but it's quite another from a comely young woman. I hope, if he ever mistakes your friendly interest for something else, you can make him understand the meaning of the word *no*."

"I'm sorry too, father. I should never have said those things. I can say them to God, maybe, but not to you."

"You say such things to God, do you?" he exclaimed, removing his hand from his eyes, and half smiling at her, astonished. "If ever I hear thunder in clear blue skies, I'll know 'tis Marnie saying her prayers, and the Almighty falling off his throne in shock!"

Marnie laughed, noticed that the priest had been crying, and looked away from him, toward the sea. She had never seen any man cry, except her father in his worst sufferings.

After a while she said, "I want Raven to live in the house with me, if and when he wants to."

Father Brannan thought about that, then said, "It goes against all the holy teachings, Marnie. I have to condemn it."

"If you condemn me, father, you make me do to Raven what you did to the beggar. There's no sin in my helping him, only charity, the way Christ meant us to show it."

"You're a hard woman to argue with, to be sure! I know what you're meaning, and I know there's no sin in your intent. But as your priest, I have to advise you most strongly against this. You'll be misunderstood. The people of Torcurra will judge you terrible hard. A woman living with a man, and not being wed to him, is a wicked kind of sin."

"I won't be sinning, you know that. And I don't care what the villagers think."

"I had a feeling you'd say that. But don't say I haven't cautioned you."

"Would you like a cup of peppermint tea now, father, then I can help you mend the roof."

Father Brannan did not answer; he was looking back at the cottage, his expression a mixture of worry and amusement.

Raven had woken up, and was out inspecting the supplies in the wagon Father Brannan had brought. He had found the priest's wide-brimmed hat on the seat and put it on. He caught sight of his friends down on the beach, and his face broke into a wide smile as he began running toward them. Apart from the hat, he was stark naked.

Laughing, scarlet with embarrassment, Marnie covered her eyes with her hands.

"Well, I did warn you." Father Brannan chuckled as he stood up. "Now we'd better go and find some clothes for him—that is, if you can open your eyes enough to see your way back to your house. Oh, lass, you'll fall and do yourself an injury, if you walk with them shut tight, like that. Here, give me your hand. For someone who's just said she wants to live with that magnificent spectacle of burgeoning manhood, you're mighty bashful. You're going to have to learn to turn a blind eye to a lot of things, while you're keeping a sharp lookout—if you get my meaning, Widow Isherwood."

Chapter 15

OPENING THE LID to Isake's toolbox, Father Brannan surveyed the orderly tools inside, selected a strong chisel, and glanced at the young woman standing straight and still beside him.

"You're sure about this, Marnie?" he asked.

White-faced, she nodded. "Aye, father. He said I was never to open it, but since he's dead now, and you're the one doing the opening, I suppose it's all right."

"These things are yours now, by law," he said, going over to the locked chest of Isake's belongings. He had lifted the chest onto the table, where the sunlight pouring down through the open roof showed clearly the intricate carving on the wood, and the lighter-colored woods inlaid around the lid and about the lock.

"'Tis a pleasing piece of work," muttered Father Brannan. "I'll do my best not to damage it. A pity we buried the key with him."

Raven, standing beside Marnie with a blanket wrapped about himself, mumbled and pointed out the window toward the grave. Marnie nodded, and pointed to the chest again. *Clothes, you,* she said with her hands.

Raven pointed to his own clothes, still soaking in the blood-red water in the bucket near the door.

Marnie smiled and shook her head. "Different," she said, putting both her palms together vertically, then sweeping them down quickly in opposite directions. She made the sign again. *Different clothes. Clean clothes.* She spoke aloud as she signed, as she always did when the priest was present.

Holding the blanket with his elbows, Raven repeated the hand-word for different, his face puzzled. Marnie thought for a few moments, then ran outside and scooped up a handful of sand from the beach. Coming back in, she sprinkled the sand over the table, beside Isake's chest; then she drew two lines in the sand, one line crooked, the other straight. Then she made the sign again. *Different.* Smoothing the sand across the crooked line, she drew another straight line beside the first, then placed her palms vertically again, and pressed them firmly together. "The same," she said. Then she drew a circle and a square. *Different,* she signed, speaking the word at the same time. Then two circles. *Same.*

Excited, Raven pressed the sand flat, and drew two squares. *Same,* he said with his hands. He pointed to himself, then to Father Brannan, who stood watching them in bewilderment.

Man, two, said Raven. *Man, two, different.* He pointed to his own clothes in the bucket. *Clothes, mine.* Touching Marnie's sleeve, he said, *Clothes, yours. Different. Yours clean. Yours woman clothes.*

Marnie nodded, and patted the chest containing Isake's things. *Different clothes, you.*

Raven nodded, and looked expectantly at the priest, waiting for him to open the chest.

Shaking his head, Father Brannan bent over the lock. "I don't know why you bother," he muttered. "That was a serious lot of fluttering just to tell him he has clean clothes coming. It'd be easier just to throw the things at him, when they're available."

"I'll never have to explain those words again," said Marnie, flinging the sand outside. "He'll remember them now. And I can't ignore him when he wants to know things."

"He's been ignored most of his life; I doubt a few more moments will harm him." Carefully, he worked the chisel into the keyhole and tried to turn it. For several minutes he worked, muttering to himself. "I have to confess that I'm not very skilled at thievery," he said at last, straightening his back, and wiping the sweat off his face with his sleeve. "Where's that drink you promised me? I could do with it. It's hot in here, with the sun and the fire. The sooner we get your thatching done, the better."

Marnie went to heat some water, and pretended not to hear when Father Brannan swore. At last there was a satisfied grunt, and he said, "Well, lass, you can come and open it now."

Marnie went over and stood beside him, her hand on the carved lid. For a few moments she hesitated, undecided and guilty; then, very slowly, she lifted the lid and pushed it back.

The smell of Isake rushed over her; the odor of his sweat in his folded shirts, and the reek of ale he had spilled on them. There were, as well, more pleasant smells: the warm fragrance of his fur-lined cloak and leather belts, the scent of wool, and the lavender and woodruff scattered through to keep out moths.

Seeing her distress, Father Brannan asked gently, "Do you want Raven and me to wait outside while you do this?"

Marnie shook her head and began taking out the clothes. She put aside the first garments, the ones she had seen Isake wear, his old working clothes, finer than anything her father had ever owned. Underneath were his best clothes: silken shirts, rich tunics with padded shoulders and quilted sleeves, soft pointed shoes, velvet jerkins, and a brimless hat of beaver felt. No doubt his first wife had made many of the clothes for him, though some would have been given as part of the tithes the people paid, for living on the manor land. The fur cloak and best tunics had been bought elsewhere. He must have traveled far, Marnie thought, holding up a quilted jerkin of dark blue velvet trimmed with white fur. She took out some fine linen, all embroidered with the Isherwood family emblem, the lily and the bear. And under the linen, more wonders: two books, with pages edged with gold; a silver comb; a hairbrush with a silver handle, and with Isake's hair still caught in the bristles; some sheets of fine parchment, kept flat between painted wooden boards; and a beautiful leather case containing quills and an inkwell. Under it all was a sheet of rolled parchment with a blue satin ribbon around it, and a broken yellow seal. Marnie looked at Father Brannan. "Do you think I could have the ribbon, father?" she asked.

"It's already yours, Marnie. It's all yours," he replied.

She undid the ribbon, and smoothed it between her fingers. "I wanted a ribbon," she said, "but not the red ones he gave."

The parchment unrolled on the bottom of the chest, and she noticed flowing script, embellished with long fine curls and elegant dashes. Father Brannan reached into the chest and took out the parchment, rolling it again. He handed it to her. "His family said there was no will, but this looks like one," he said. "I think you should read it, Marnie. Though it's already been opened, for some reason."

"I can't read, father. Will you read it to me?"

Unrolling the parchment, the priest glanced at the signature on the bottom. "It's not Isake's," he said. "It's his father's." Glancing up, he read the first few lines. Then he rolled the parchment again, and put it in the chest.

"Is it bad news?" cried Marnie. "Do I not own the cottage?"

"It's not a will, Marnie. It's a letter, a private letter, from Isake's father to him. I don't feel I have the right to read it. Not unless you really want me to."

Marnie shrugged and began sorting through the last few things in the chest. There were some pieces of round soap, Isake's purse containing gold and silver coins, his sheathed knife, and a small, shallow box made of ebony and gold. Opening the box, Marnie discovered a rare glass mirror, clearer than a pond on a windless day, and worth a fortune. Wonderingly, she held it up to her face. Smiling a little, amazed, she handed the glass carefully to the priest. "Have a look at yourself, father," she said.

"I don't know that I could stand the shock," he replied, though he peered curiously.

Raven leaned close, almost knocking the mirror out of the priest's hand. "Careful, lad!" Father Brannan warned. But Raven pulled on his arm, trying to see, then tugged at Marnie's hands, wanting her to explain what the object was.

"I don't know, Raven," she said. *No hand-word.*

He nodded, and pressed his fingers across her lips. Then he pointed to the mirror and signed, *Hand-word. You. Me. Hand-word. Different hand-word.*

"I don't know one," she said, and he slapped his hand roughly across her mouth to stop the talk he could not understand.

Shutting the ebony box, Father Brannan put it back in the chest, then took Raven firmly by both arms and dragged him outside.

"Don't do that, lad!" he shouted, bringing his hand hard down across Raven's mouth. "Not to her—all right? It's not a good feeling, is it, being slapped? Don't do it again!"

"Leave him, he doesn't understand!" Marnie cried, rushing to the door. "He can't hear you! Don't!"

Raven bit Father Brannan's hand, and the priest boxed his ears. Raven howled and ran off up the beach, in the opposite direction to Torcurra, leaving the blanket in the priest's hands. Father Brannan went back inside, breathing hard and swearing to himself. Dropping the blanket on the bed he said angrily, "There's no good going to come of your trying to help him, Marnie. He'll always have that wicked streak in him, that sudden flaring of rage and violence. You'll end up being hurt, that's all."

"Then I'll have no one to blame but myself," she said. "There was no need to punish him. He was only wanting me to show him the hand-word, that was all. He was trying to stop me talking, so I would use my hands."

"Well, he's not doing it, lass. He'll not slap you again like that, not while I'm here. I'll not stand for that."

"But *you* slapped *him*. I suppose that's all right?"

"Are you criticizing me, Marnie?"

"No. I'm just saying that what happens between Raven and me is our business. I'll thank you not to interfere."

"Oh, I'm interfering now, am I? Am I to take it you don't want my help around this place, after all? Because if you don't, I'll take my wagon and go. I didn't come here to be scolded and tongue-lashed. I've got better things to do than watch you and Raven fight over half-hatched hieroglyphics neither of you can understand."

"Well then, go and do them! Go and write another precious sermon on love, since that's your special subject—so long as the love doesn't hurt you, or test your patience too much, or overstretch your kindness!"

Father Brannan strode outside to his wagon. Marnie waited to hear it rumble away. It did not. Trembling, she bent over the chest of Isake's things, trying to look uncaring. Her eye fell on a little box once used to hold bone toothpicks. It had been given to Isake by Marnie's parents, as a wedding gift to their son-in-law. It was silver, and had been the most precious thing Micheal had owned. Marnie picked it up, stroking it between her hands, and grief went through her like a sword.

A shadow fell across her from the doorway, and she bent low over the chest of Isake's things, her hair concealing her face.

"I'm sorry, Marnie," Father Brannan said huskily. "I'm a blind old fool who hasn't any idea what you've been suffering."

"I'm sorry too," she said very low.

"We seem to be saying that to each other a fair bit, today. Is it the weather, do you think?"

Shaking her head, trying to laugh, and failing, she wiped her nose on her sleeve.

"Oh, lass, don't cry." He went over to her and drew her close, and she turned her face against his shoulder, and sobbed. Choking, she tried to talk; but he told her to hush, and stroked her hair while she wept out the last night's terror, and a week's cruel loneliness, and a winter's worth of pain.

Marnie sucked the last flesh from the red lobster claw, dropped the shell into her dish, and sighed contentedly. "That's the best meal I ever had in my life," she said to Father Brannan. "Thanks for cooking it, father. And for helping me and Raven mend and thatch the roof, and for fixing the broken chair. You've been good to me, and I don't deserve it."

"I'm thinking you deserve every morsel of it," he said, grinning, "especially the lobster. It does my soul good to be appreciated. I told you my cooking would transport you to heaven."

"I hope that doesn't mean your cooking's full of deadly poison," she said, and he laughed.

"I was speaking metaphorically. And I think it's time you did a bit of flutter-talk to Raven there, and told him that it's not decent for a guest to eat a whole loaf of bread himself. I brought that thinking it'd last you a week."

"I don't know all the words to tell him that, father."

"Then you're going to have to get busy and invent some, aren't you, else you'll starve, and he'll get mighty fat."

Raven studied their faces while they talked, his eyes puzzled and inquiring, his mouth still crammed with food. He was wearing a russet tunic of Isake's, a gilt leather belt, and soft woolen leggings. All the clothes were too big for him, but he wore them with pride. Sometimes, while Marnie and Father Brannan talked, he touched Marnie's wrist, wanting her to talk to him in hand-words, but he never dared put his hand over her mouth again. He finished the bread on his plate, and tapped her arm. *Bread*, he said. *Bread*.

Marnie shook her head. *You*, she signed, and puffed out her cheeks to indicate fatness. Putting her hands flat on her stomach, she moved them slowly out, suggesting rapid expansion. Alarmed, Raven frantically felt his own lean torso to see if what she said was true, and Father Brannan chuckled till he choked.

Realizing it was a joke, but taking the point, Raven selected a small pickle instead. Marnie made up a hand-word for pickle and showed it to him. Raven copied the sign, then pointed to the pickle jar, and repeated the sign several times. Then he pointed to himself.

No, Marnie said. *Two pickles, you.*

Nodding, Raven put his hand in the pickle jar, but took out only one more pickle. When he had eaten it he licked his fingers clean, and stood up. Then he touched Marnie's arm. *You,* he said, *water drink?*

She smiled and nodded. Then he asked Father Brannan. The priest shook his head. Raven got two cups, filled them both with water, and gave one to Marnie. Keeping the other drink for himself, he sat down again.

Father Brannan watched, shaking his head in wonderment. "I never thought I'd see the like!" he said. "I used to have a hard time just getting him to eat like a human being at my table. And here he is taking one pickle when he's told, and even asking if you want a drink, and getting it for you. If ever I asked him to fetch me anything, he just stared and made his mad noises. Even if I yelled at him, he'd just ape me or run away or start throwing things around."

"It's only because he can't hear, father. I'm giving him a language he can see, that's all. But, to be honest, I think I've bitten off more than I can chew. There's an awful lot of words yet I have to make up. It scares me to think of it."

"At least you're trying. You're a saint, Marnie, and that's a fact."

"You'd better tell that to the people of Torcurra, father, and change their minds about me."

"They'll come right."

"When can I go into the village? I want to get some chickens and a goat. And some seeds too, so I can grow my own vegetables. Where will I get them?"

"I can give you some seeds and chickens. And when I go and dig you some more peat for your fire, I'll ask the farmer if I can have a goat for you, as well."

"I'll buy it all, father. I have Isake's purse. I don't want charity."

"You're a widow, lass. You won't survive without charity."

"I don't want to be a widow! Widows are dependent and poorly off. I've got money. I'll buy everything I need."

"Oh, you don't want to be a widow?" said Father Brannan, surprised, his blue eyes dancing. "Well now, that'll cause the Almighty a bit of consternation, seeing as he's already made you one. I don't want to be an old fool either, lass, but that's an accomplished fact as well. Sometimes we don't have any say in these matters. And your money's not going to last forever, and then what'll you be doing? It'll be dependence on charity then, or starvation. While I'm here, let me see that you have all you need. Save your coins for a time when you might have to deal with the folks of Torcurra on your own."

"Are you planning to leave the village, father?"

"Only by way of a hole in the church ground. Just take my advice, and save your money until you need it. And don't go into Torcurra for a while. I'll bring you all you need. If there's anything in particular you want, you can always send Raven to tell me, since he's getting so clever."

"I can't depend on you for the rest of my life to bring me everything I want. How long before they forget what they think they heard me say?"

Father Brannan did not reply, but took a small flute from the bag in which he had brought supplies, and started to play. It was a jaunty tune, and after a while Marnie forgot her troubles, and tapped her feet and clapped her hands in time to the music. Raven watched them, and clapped his own hands in time too, mimicking Marnie.

"We danced to that tune on winter evenings," Marnie said when it was finished. "All my family, and our neighbors, on a clear night. Out in the lanes between our houses we'd dance."

"Well then, dance again. Teach Raven, since you want to make a regular human being of him."

He played another tune, more joyful than the last, and Marnie could no longer resist. Jumping up, and clapping her hands again, she moved easily into the lively rhythm of one of the folk dances she had loved since childhood. Raven watched, fascinated by the beat of her hands together and the movements of her feet, and the graceful sway of her body as she danced. He had seen dancing in Torcurra, and the synchronized movements of the people and musicians had always enthralled him; but he had never been allowed to join in. Now, stumbling and uncertain, he let Marnie take his hand and show him the moves. Gradually he learned to clap in harmony with her, and to move his feet when she moved hers, and the rhythm and joy got into him. Clapping, laughing when he made mistakes and they bumped into one another, he and Marnie danced while Father Brannan played; and the little house grew warm with the liveliness and the music and the fire.

At last Father Brannan stopped playing, and Marnie and Raven dropped onto their seats, panting and laughing, their faces aglow.

"Play us something peaceful, father," begged Marnie.

So he played a haunting melody, an old song about journeys and half-forgotten lands. Marnie listened, entranced, her elbows on the table, her chin resting in her hand; but Raven was soon bored with the inactivity. Retreating to his inner world, he got up and went out. They did not try to stop him.

Father Brannan played four more tunes, each one familiar to Marnie, beloved and beautiful. At last he put his flute away, and they were quiet together for a while.

"Our musicians at Fernleigh never played like that," Marnie said. "It was wonderful, father. The loveliest thing I've ever heard, excepting for some of the Scripture in church."

"That's high praise," he said, smiling. "My music and the Almighty's word, spoken of in the same hushed breath."

"It's true," she said. "It's a gift you've given me, your music, and

I'll hold it in my heart, and think on it in lonely times. You don't know what a comfort you've been to me."

The priest studied her face, seeing the tiredness there, the shadows of pain that still remained. But he saw too the clear sapphire eyes glowing in the semidark, brimming with simple honesty and gratitude and affection. Her small face, pensive and tender, was altogether lovely.

Abruptly, Father Brannan stood up. "I have to go now, Marnie," he said. "I have prayers in an hour or two, then a church full of grim-visaged souls waiting for a sermon to cheer them up. It's the Sabbath in the morning."

"What'll your sermon be about?" asked Marnie, standing with him.

"Well now," he said, grinning as he scratched his head. "That's a good question. The truth is, I haven't quite figured it out yet, seeing as I've been occupied with thatching and mending and cooking. But I'll think about it on the wagon, on the way home."

"Won't you have a drink with me, before you go?"

"Thank you, lass, but no."

"Are you sure?"

A moment he hesitated, then he said, "I'm sure it's time I went."

The night was clear, and cold after the warmth of the house, and Father Brannan pulled his hood over his head for warmth. He got his horse from where it waited under the trees with Isake's horse, and hitched the empty wagon to it again. Then he put his ladder on the wagon, to take home. Marnie helped, then stood back while he climbed up onto the wagon and picked up the reins.

"Thank you for a grand day, Marnie," he said. "Don't you be worrying about Raven if he doesn't come back for a day or two. He's like that; arrives to fill his belly, then goes away again. He's used to the hills and freedom."

"I know, father. And it's me should be thanking you, not the other way around. I don't know how I'll ever repay you."

"You already have. God bless you." He made the sign of the cross over her, then went away, his wagon blending into the darkness of the hill. Marnie watched until it reached the summit, where she saw it outlined clear against the stars. He turned and waved, and she waved back. Then he was gone, and there was only herself in the cove.

For a while she stood in her doorway facing the firelit room, listening to the silvery sea washing on the sand behind her, and the lonesome call of an owl in the windy trees. She looked at her roof, mended and whole, and the board that could be fixed across her door, to bolt it; and she felt safe. The little alcoves in her walls bore boxes of candles and jars of honey that Father Brannan had brought, and sacks plump with oats and flour hung from the rough roof beams. Bacon and fish smoked on hooks in her chimney, a cauldron of stew warmed over the flames, and there was bread on her table. And all the room smelled sweet as the earth in summertime, from the peat fire burning in her hearth.

Smiling, she lifted her fingertips to her lips and blew a kiss heavenward; then she went inside, leaving the door open a little for Raven.

Chapter 16

THE BOAT ROCKED gently on the sea, and Marnie leaned on the side, her head on her arm, and watched her fishing line through half-closed eyes. The water was clear blue, pierced by streaks of sunlight, shot through sometimes with silver fish. Winding her line about her forefinger, so she could tell if a fish nibbled the baited hook below, she turned her head and gazed at the distant beach. She could see the horse drinking from the stream, and the goat grazing on the tough grasses near the edge of the sand, where Raven had tethered it earlier. Chickens pecked in the shadow of her house, and she hoped they were not in her garden. Already her vegetables were finger high.

Closing her eyes, she listened to the placid lapping of the water on the hull, and the soft grunts Raven made behind her as he baited his hook and threw it over the side again. She heard the plop as the bait hit the water, and felt him settle down in the boat, his bare feet smooth and warm against hers. The day was lazy, hot, and the sun seeped through her clothes to her very bones.

Her line suddenly pulled taut, and she woke startled, crying out in alarm. Raven crouched beside her, grinning, his own fingers yanking at her line. *A big fish,* he said with his hands.

She laughed and prodded her elbow in his ribs. *A bad fish,* she said. *No good to cook. I will throw it away.*

It will swim back, he replied, *up to your house, and jump in the pot.*

Stupid fish, she said.

He smiled, the light dancing in his eyes and on his skin moist from the heat, and in his blue-black hair. The lines of suffering were gone, and he had lost the wariness and fear. In the month he had lived with Marnie he had put on weight, and he looked no longer gaunt, but serene and complete. As he smiled at her, Marnie thought again how excellent he was, shining and irrepressible. He seldom made his meaningless noises now, except when he expressed surprise or pain or anger. Once, when Marnie happened to speak with her voice as well as her hands, he had watched her mouth and made a sound that was almost a word. Astounded, inspired by new hopes, she had decided to speak aloud every time she communicated with him; and now Raven often tried to imitate the movements of her mouth. But always Marnie talked to him with her hands, never only with her voice.

Fish! he signed suddenly, frantically grabbing for his forgotten line. Too late, he watched as the line, and the little piece of wood it was wound to, suddenly shot up over the side, and was pulled away by a fish. Without a thought he dived after it, swimming strongly after the bobbing piece of wood. He got to it and grabbed it, winding the line about it while he trod water, all the time making wordless sounds of triumph. When he was sure the fish was hooked, he swam back to the boat and gave the line to Marnie.

You get the fish, he said, and gripped the side of the boat to pull himself back in. In his wild efforts to clamber aboard, he almost capsized the boat, and Marnie laughed so much she could not help him, nor see to wind the line about its bit of wood. Safe on board at last,

Raven took his line from her, and knelt in the boat with water streaming off him, to pull in the fish. It was longer than his forearm, worth the effort he had gone to. As it lay flapping in the bottom of the boat, Marnie removed the hook from its mouth. Then she got her knife and hit the fish sharply on the head with the handle until it lay still.

Supper tonight, she said. *Go, swim again and get us one more.*

You go swim, he said, stripping off his wet clothes and spreading them to dry across the bow. They were Isake's clothes, which Marnie had altered. Naked, Raven crouched in the bottom of the boat and sliced off a piece of the fish they were using for bait. He fixed the flesh to the hook, then stood up to cast it out again. Marnie looked away from his clean, straight limbs, and watched the sunlight on the water. Several times Raven had undressed in front of her, as naturally and unselfconsciously as now, and always to dry his clothes if they were wet or to wash himself or to swim. Struggling with old attitudes, she had been tempted to tell him that what he did was unacceptable; but then she considered the innocence of him, his natural enjoyment of the sun and wind and water, and she did not try to change him.

But her own modesty bewildered Raven. Once, when they were walking by the sea, she had been soaked by a sudden wave rolling in, and Raven had told her to take off her dress and spread it on the sand to dry. When she refused without explaining why, he had shaken his head in bafflement, and made the word *why* extravagantly with both hands instead of one, signifying his total perplexity at her lack of logic. His gesture had become their hand-word for *stupid.* He had created many of their words himself, when Marnie was at a loss, and was as inventive as she was. Anger still overcame him sometimes, when their hand-words ran out and he wanted to understand, or to make himself understood; but mostly the breakdowns were overlooked, and sentences begun again, revised, using known words, or else new words were created on the spot.

Raven did not live all the time with Marnie. Often he went away, without explanation or farewell, and slept somewhere else for two or three nights. Marnie never knew where he went, but she guessed he craved the solitude of the open fields that had been his home. She longed to go with him sometimes, but he never invited her, and she did not ask to go. His existence was a strange balance between wildness and ordinary life, and she honored both.

As he waited now for the next fish to bite, he signed to her: *I will cook fish tonight, you cook onions and potatoes.*

Marnie nodded, smiling. *I like the way you cook fish,* she said, teasing him, *black all over, and hard.*

He shook his head, gently kicking her, and she laughed and looked away again. They fished without talking, while the boat rocked on the tide. Looking past Marnie, Raven glanced at the beach, and lifted his head, suddenly alert. A man stood outside their house. It was not the priest. Puzzled, Raven reached over and tapped Marnie's shoulder. She was resting her head on her arm again, her line wrapped about her finger, her eyes closed. He tapped her again, urgently. Sleepily, she looked at him.

A man, he said, scratching the darkening shadow on his jaw, and pointing to her house.

Marnie looked at the beach, and fear went through her. It was a lone man, wearing fine clothes such as Isake had worn, and high boots that gleamed in the sun. He was on a splendid thoroughbred, unlike the common draft horses the village folk owned.

"Isake's brother!" she cried. "It's Isake's brother!"

Raven touched her hands, wanting her to sign. But she was pulling in her line, quickly, not winding it onto the stick, but hauling it up and throwing it in tangles in the bottom of the boat. Raven stopped her. *Who?* he asked. *Who?*

Holding her left hand flat, palm down, she made the sign of the cross on her middle finger, signifying Isake's grave. She had no word for brother, so signed *friend* instead. Raven frowned, not understanding her trepidation.

We must go to the house, she said, her gestures frantic and quick. *Now. Fast.* She grabbed the line out of his hands, and he scrambled into the seat and took up the oars. *No—put your clothes on! Fast!* she signed, and he obeyed, making weird yelps against the clamminess. Marnie sat trembling in the stern, her eyes on the man by her house. She saw him tether his horse by Isake's, and walk about looking at the ground. He stopped by the grave. Then he went into the house, and she wanted to scream at him to keep out.

Raven rowed strongly, the sweat trickling down his face, and he breathed hard, catching Marnie's fear. The boat moved swiftly through the water, until at last they felt the sand scraping on the hull. They both leaped out, up to their thighs in water, and dragged the boat above high-tide line. Raven grabbed the fish, and they raced up to the house.

In the doorway Marnie stopped. The man was searching through Isake's chest. Clothes lay strewn across the stony floor, and the books had been thrown on the table.

"What are you doing?" Marnie asked.

The man turned around. It was Isake's younger brother, Pierce. She had met him only once, at the wedding, and had thought then how like Isake he was, with his dark eyes and long hair curling on his shoulders. Only Pierce was smaller, less imposing, with lines of meanness about his mouth. He looked her up and down, noting her eyes angry behind her tousled dark hair, the hem of her dress hitched up into her girdle, her white shift underneath wet and clinging about her legs, her bare feet covered in sand. Seeing his look, she unhitched the hem, covering her legs. A sardonic smile crossed Pierce's lips—until he saw Raven, then the smile vanished.

"It didn't take you long to find someone else, did it, Marnie?" he said.

"What are you doing?" she asked again. "Your brother's grave is outside, and you're welcome to visit it. But this is my house, and I'll thank you not to touch my things."

He laughed, a mocking sound more like a grunt. "*Your* things?" he said. "Nothing here is yours. I've come to get them, and to claim the house."

Marnie's throat went dry, and she gripped the door for support. Vaguely, she was aware of Raven tapping her arm, wanting her to explain, but she shook her head. At last she managed to say, "It's my house, sir. It's mine by right. I'm his widow, and it's mine."

The man crouched by the open chest, and she heard him rifling through the parchments. Marnie turned to Raven. *Get Father Brannan,* she said. *Fast. Run fast!*

Raven dropped the fish on the step, and fled up the hill.

Marnie went into the cottage and stood beside the man. He was holding the letter that Isake's father had written to Isake, which had been bound by the blue ribbon. Pierce stood up, his eyes scanning the lines. Very slowly, he smiled. Then, startled, as if suddenly remembering she was there, he looked at Marnie.

"You can go now," he muttered, returning his attention to the letter.

"It's my house!" she said again, barely able to speak.

Pierce said nothing, while he stared at the parchment in his hands. Then he looked at Marnie again, half laughing to himself, his face flushed. "What did you say?" he asked.

"I said 'it's my house!'"

The smile faded from the man's face, and it became cold and relentless. "No doubt you'd like to think it is," he said, "but you're wrong. It's mine. It's my family's. You can go back to your parents. They're still in their house. They can keep it, since the arrangement was they could have it while you lived. We should have said, while the marriage lasted."

"But this is my home! I thatched the roof and whitewashed the walls and cleaned the fireplace and the floor, and I've made—"

"That's not what we're talking about, woman, and you know it!"

"What do you mean?" she cried. "It *is* my house! It was terrible

☙❧

when we came here, all broken and filthy and wet. I've fixed it. Father Brannan and I, and Raven. And Isake, when he was alive. He was—he was fixing the roof, when he fell and died. I was his wife, his lawful wife. It's my house now."

A bewildered expression crossed Pierce's face. "You haven't read this, have you?" he said, tapping the letter with the backs of his fingers. "You don't know."

"I don't know anything, excepting that it's my house! The priest said! He said it was mine, and no one else's, and that you couldn't take it from me!"

"Have you read this?" he shouted, gripping her arm. "Have you read it, Marnie?"

"No!" she screamed, trying to drag free.

"Are you sure?"

"I can't read!"

He released her, and she collapsed in the nearby chair, shaking uncontrollably, her hands over her face. "It's my house!" she repeated. *"It's my house!"*

Calmly, Isake's brother rolled the letter and placed it inside his tunic. "I'm sorry, Marnie, but it's not your house," he said. "It belongs to us, to Isake's family."

"It's mine! I was his wife!"

"Aye—you were his wife for two days, that's all! Two days! You think that gives you the right to take all this?"

"All this? A few stones, and some thatch? You have a manor house and a great farm! What do you want with this cottage? A hovel, that's what Isake called it! We weren't even going to live here long, he said! He didn't like it, not really. But I do. I love this house. Let me keep it, please, sir. I'll give you all his money, his mirror, his comb and brush and clothes, all the things he owns in that chest, but please let me keep the house!"

"I don't want his old clothes!" said Pierce. "It's this house I want, Marnie, this bit of land, and everything it contains."

"Is it his body you want, sir? It isn't in a coffin, and it would be—would be not easy, I think, to take it away, but if you wanted it, I'm sure the priest would let you—"

The brother swore, then laughed. "I don't want his rotting body, woman! What do you think I am—a ghoul? I want this house. Do you understand that? This house. Not Isake's old clothes or his watch or his hairbrush or his corpse. I want this house. Now take your things, and go. You don't deserve this place—not after two nights of pleasuring him, and then, while his body's hardly cold in the ground, taking another man to his bed. You don't qualify as Isake's heir. You're a hussy, that's all, and he was a fool to fall for you. Well, you're not getting everything you wanted, Marnie Isherwood. You got yourself a marriage to someone higher than yourself, and an honorable name, and a house for your family, but you're not getting what's here, as well. You don't have the right to that."

Quivering with hate and fury, Marnie stood up and went to the door. She looked up the hill for Father Brannan, but there was no sign of him. Behind her, the man's boots made soft footfalls on the floor as he looked around the cottage. She heard him moving dishes in the stone recesses by the fireplace, then a chair creaked as he sat down.

"Lord, what a dump!" he muttered. "I don't know how Isake stood it, living here. No wonder he wanted you, to make it bearable."

Marnie turned and confronted him. He was slouched in the chair, toying with the little cross that Father Brannan had given her. She always left it on the table, to think of him. She hated seeing it in Pierce's hands.

"If you despise this house so much, sir," she said, "why do you want it?"

"That is not your business, woman. Are you going to stand there all day haranguing me, or are you leaving? Because if you're going to stay, I'd like something to eat, and some ale."

"You'll have to go to Torcurra, to the alehouse."

Humming to himself, he got up and wandered about again, taking jars out of alcoves and peering at the contents. He put a few things on the table and sat down to eat.

"That's thieving," Marnie said.

He laughed scornfully and helped himself to some bread, slicing it with the jeweled knife he carried on his belt. "How can I steal from myself?" he asked. "If anyone's breaking the law, it's you. You're trespassing on my land. But, seeing as you're a comely wench, I'll let you stay."

"You're the one who's trespassing, sir."

"Well now, I don't know how that would stand up in a court, Marnie," he said, looking at her laughingly while he chewed. She thought again how like Isake he was, with those dark eyes and that same mocking smile. Only Isake never had that streak of meanness, that innate cruelty.

"Anyway," Pierce went on, with his mouth full, "you've never really wanted to take any matter to court, have you? You'd never be believed. You know what they say about you in Fernleigh, Marnie? They say you tempted Isake when he was drunk, and got yourself with child by him, so he would have to marry you. You always wanted Isake, didn't you? Always fancied marrying above yourself. But you still couldn't keep yourself away from the young rakes, from the likes of Jonty. And now you've got another boy. Perhaps 'tis just as well Isake is dead. You'd have broken the poor fool's heart."

"Get out of this house."

"*This* house now, is it? Not *my* house anymore? Well, I suppose that's an improvement."

"Get out."

"Don't you want to know what else they're saying in Fernleigh? How your parents are? I could give you a lot of news, Marnie, if only you'd be civil. Now, are you sure there's no ale?"

Without a word she went out to the stream, and got a pitcher of ale from a stony storehouse at the water's edge. She had last used the ale ten days ago, when Father Brannan had brought the goat. Going back to the cottage, she looked up the hill again. Still there was no sign of him. Suddenly the thought occurred to her that he might be visiting another parish somewhere, or out fishing with one of the Torcurra men. The thought panicked her, and her hands shook as she went inside and poured a drink for Pierce.

Smiling, he lifted the cup in salutation to her. "Aren't you drinking with me?" he asked. She got a cup and poured herself some, and sat down opposite him. The ale was bitter, and very cold.

Pierce cut himself some more bread, and placed some cheese on it. Slowly, without speaking, he sliced up a pickle and carefully placed the pieces on.

"How is my father, sir?" Marnie asked, trying to keep her voice calm.

Pierce took another mouthful of ale, then put the cup down, thoughtfully. "I did hear news of him," he said. "He took a turn for the worse, about a week ago. I have a feeling someone mentioned that he died. Or was that the new overseer's brother? I can't quite remember."

Marnie stared down at the cup clenched in her hands, and waited for the agony in her heart to ease. He's taunting me, she thought, like a barn cat with a mouse.

Pierce smiled, and added lightly, "Oh, I remember now. It was the new overseer's uncle who died. Your father's in good health, I think. Your brother, the oldest one, is working for us all the time, doing odd jobs about the manor. Don't look so upset, Marnie. All's well, after all. Sorry if I gave you a bit of a turn, getting myself mixed up, as I did."

"It's no matter, sir," she replied coolly, "since I don't believe a word you say."

His eyes glittered, and he drank more ale. "This isn't bad," he said. "Not brewed by you, I take it. Is it from the alehouse?"

"It's the priest's," she said.

"Oh, the priest's? Has his own little supply here, does he? He must visit you often. And what do the good people of Torcurra think of that, you being a bewitching young widow, and he being a man apart, and visiting you in this lonely place? And you've got a handsome boy as well, running about with you, half naked! The Torcurra folk must be a mite more tolerant than the people of Fernleigh, that's for sure."

She said nothing, and he added shrewdly, "Or perhaps they don't know, Marnie. Perhaps they don't know what their priest gets up to— or the enticing young widow. It would be troublesome, wouldn't it, if someone ever told them? They might—"

He was interrupted by footsteps outside the door, and the heavy breathing of a man who had been running. Father Brannan burst in, followed closely by Raven.

Chapter 17

THE PRIEST'S FACE was crimson from the long run, and sweat ran down his cheeks and neck. He saw Marnie sitting there white-faced but very calm, drinking ale with the stranger, and relief flooded over him. Still gasping for breath, and leaning in the doorway, he asked, "Are you all right, Marnie, child?"

"I'm well, father," she said. "This is Pierce Isherwood, Isake's brother."

Pierce stood up, and he and the priest shook hands.

"And this is Raven," said Marnie. Pierce held out his hand to Raven, but the youth folded his arms and leaned against the doorway, his eyes steely and watchful.

Father Brannan wiped his streaming face on his sleeve, and studied the stranger.

"I've come to claim my cottage, father," said Pierce, smiling broadly. "Only it seems our unlearned little woman here is mistaken. She thinks that two brief days of marriage gets her a goodly share of my brother's inheritance."

"Well now," said Father Brannan, "it's clear to me that marriage is marriage, whether it be for two days or twenty years. There's nothing in the law says it's less valid for being short."

Pierce gave an easy laugh, and went to get a cup for Father Brannan. He poured the priest an ale, and set it in front of him. "Sit down, man," he said. "Don't stand on ceremony. Let's talk this out."

From the doorway, Raven made hand-words to Marnie, and she explained, using her hands but not her voice. *The man says this house is his. Father Brannan will make it right.*

Pierce saw the strange gestures, and bewilderment colored his face. "What in Christ's name are you doing?" he hissed.

"I'm talking to Raven," said Marnie. "He can't hear, so I talk with my hands."

Pierce sat down, distrustful and appalled. "'Tis damned witchcraft!" he muttered.

"'Tis nothing more than talk," said Father Brannan, still standing, but leaning on his fists on the table, and glaring down into the stranger's face. "And it makes a good deal more sense than anything you're talking at the moment. It seems to me that you're under a serious misapprehension, sir. Widow Isherwood owns this house and all that's in it. If you have a problem with that, you'll have to take it up in a court—not come here browbeating a woman alone, and making out you have rights that don't exist. I'll thank you to go and not come back."

"You don't seem to understand the situation," said Pierce, standing up and confronting the priest. "I'm the youngest son of the deceased Lord William Isherwood. I don't think you realize that."

"Oh, I realize it, all right," said Father Brannan. "But you've got a few realizations to come to yourself, sir. I suggest you come to them in court, where you can be bothering someone else, and not us, with your ignorance and your arrogance."

Pierce picked up his hat, which he had thrown on the bed when he first arrived. "You'll regret crossing me, father," he said. "I have friends in high places."

"So have I," said Father Brannan.

Pierce put on his hat and strode out, and shortly afterward they heard him mount his horse and gallop away.

Marnie sank onto a chair. "Are you sure you know what you're talking about, father?" she said. "Sure about the law?"

"Aye, I am," he said. "There was no will leaving this house to anyone else. I checked. The gall of that man disgusts me. This dispute ought to be the other way around—you hammering on the manor door, asking for the rest of your inheritance. I don't believe that all your husband's earthly goods are in this little house. I'm sure there's a lot more that's due to you."

"I don't want any more, only what I have."

"Then Pierce Isherwood ought to be thanking you, not pestering you."

Raven pulled up a stool by Marnie's chair, taking her hands, making her face him.

The man says the house is his, she explained, speaking at the same time. *Father Brannan says the house is mine. The man is angry. He wants the house very bad.*

Why? asked Raven.

I do not know. She added, looking at Father Brannan, *He took one thing from the chest.*

"What was that?" asked the priest.

She replied, not signing, because she did not have all the words, "The letter that Isake's father wrote to him. He was looking for it when we arrived."

Impatiently, Raven touched her hands again, but she shook her head.

"Did he take anything else?" asked Father Brannan.

"I don't know. I haven't looked."

"Perhaps you'd better check."

Marnie got up and knelt in front of Isake's chest. Everything had been opened, even the little box from her parents, and the leather case of writing things. The parchments, once carefully stored between the painted boards, had been torn out and scattered, and the purse emptied. The copper coins were there, gleaming on the dark wood at the bottom of the chest, but all the silver and gold was gone, and the mirror. "He took my money," she choked, banging her fist on the edge of the chest. "I'll have to be a widow now, with nothing. Oh, the bastard! The bastard!"

"Marnie!" cried Father Brannan, shocked. "I didn't know you knew such a word!"

"'Tis no worse than what you've said at times, father."

"Maybe so," he said, "but I have the fortunate advantage of being able to swear and get the priest to forgive me, all in the same breath. Oh, lass, don't get yourself so wrought up! You were a widow afore he came here. Nothing's changed, in your own self."

"It is! I'm poor, now! I wish you'd taken the money when I offered it, for the chickens and the goat, and everything else."

"Aye, I wish I had too, then I could give it back to you," he said. "And I wish I'd read that letter. I'd give my back teeth to know what's in it—and what it is about this place that grips the interest of the Isherwoods. There must be something about this house, this land, that makes it valuable. I've been talking to the old folks in the village, the ones who remember Eilis, who lived here. They say she was the wife of an Isherwood lord, a commander in the king's army. It was in the days when the lords owned vaster lands than they do now, and were rewarded with more, for fighting for their king. But Eilis committed adultery with the king, and her husband threw her out with nothing but the clothes on her back. Shunned by her family, she came here to make a new life for herself. But she made no friends in Torcurra, either, and they say her life was hard. I thought maybe she was rich, and had her savings hidden here, and that was what Pierce Isherwood was after. But they say she was very poor, starving most of the time. They also say she put a curse on the Isherwoods, and they lost most of their lands, and have only the Fernleigh estate left. Have

Sherryl Jordan

you no idea, Marnie, why this humble place of hers might mean something to the Isherwoods, now?"

"No, I haven't, father."

Raven crouched by Marnie and touched her hands, wanting her to talk. Deep in thought, she ignored him, so he waved his hands in front of her face, until she took notice of him.

The man took things, she explained. Picking up a sheet of parchment, she added, *One he took, with words on. And the mirror, and gold.*

Why? he asked, but she shrugged and began putting away Isake's things. When she closed the chest she sat at the table facing Father Brannan, and asked, "Will he really take us to court, father?"

"I strongly doubt it."

Raven banged the table with his knuckles, but Marnie signed that she would talk to him later. He sighed and went and sat on the doorstep, facing the sea.

"But Pierce spoke true, when he said he has friends in high places!" Marnie continued. "He knows the judge who travels around in these parts, to decide about the most serious complaints. The judge came to Fernleigh once, when a man was accused of stealing an ox, and he stayed at the manor house, and feasted with them. He's Pierce's friend! He'll get him to judge against me, and I won't have a chance!"

"You've got more than a chance. Pierce Isherwood knows very well that the law will never support his claim, that's why he came here—to frighten you away. Clearly, he had no idea of the kind of challenge he was taking on." Father Brannan grinned, and drank some of the ale Pierce had poured for him. "Now, can I have a bit of this bread and cheese here? Raven fetched me all the way in from a fishing boat, and I haven't had a morsel since dawn, and my body's still trembling after running all this way, thinking you were being harmed. Raven's mighty eloquent when he wants to be. I don't understand a word of all your flutterings, but I knew there was a man here, and that you were needing help. This hand-talk of yours, it's ripened into something rather cunning, hasn't it?"

"We've made up a lot more words, since you were here last."

"So I see. Show me some of them? Slow, so I can see them properly."

She did, and he shook his head, astounded. "Some are almost the same," he said, "just a flick of a finger for one word, a flick of two or three for different words. How on earth do you remember them?"

"Remembering is easy; I use them all the time. The hardest part is understanding Raven's words, because I'm seeing them from the other side. And he's quick, and I miss a lot. Sometimes I get only one or two words out of a whole lot, and misunderstand him something awful."

"It's still a lot more understanding than he ever had in the past," said Father Brannan. "You'll be having proper conversations with him, next."

"That's what I'm hoping." She added, hesitantly, "Can I ask a favor, father? I know you've done a lot, but there's something else I'd really like."

"'Tis yours before you ask, you know that."

"Will you show me some letters? Will you write Raven's name for me, and my name, and Isake's? And the words mother and father, and sister and brother?"

"It would be a pleasure," he replied.

Opening Isake's chest again, Marnie took out several sheets of parchment, and the leather case with the ink and pens. Father Brannan finished his bread and cheese, and cleared a space on the table for the writing things. Almost with reverence, because he had never seen such a fine writing set, he opened the case and took out the bottle of black ink. He removed the stopper, set the ink by the parchment, and selected a quill.

"Now, then, Marnie," he said, pushing back his sleeves, and carefully dipping the quill in the ink. "What was it you wanted? Your name, and Raven's?"

"Wait a moment, father." She looked across at Raven sitting outside on the doorstep. There was a bowl of small pebbles on the table, and Marnie removed one of the stones and threw it softly at Raven's back. He turned around, and she signed to him to come in and watch. Then she noticed the surprise on the priest's face, and grinned. "It's the only way I can get his attention," she explained. "We've got wondrous deft at throwing things at one another. It saves a lot of walking. Though he can call me, if he wants."

Father Brannan shook his head. "And to think that I used to bellow myself hoarse, trying to make him come and do what he was told!" he said. "Oh, Marnie, I must have grieved the Almighty something terrible, the rages I got into, thinking Raven was just ignoring me, just being disobedient and contrary. I even hit him sometimes when he was a child, for not coming when I called. No wonder he got into such rages himself, and ran away. The world must have been hellish confusing for him, and I didn't help."

"You helped him a great deal, father. You were the only one who showed him any love at all. And I'm not exactly patient with him, all the time. 'Tis hard talking in hand-words, because we don't have enough of them. I have to think out everything I want to say before I start, or I get halfway through and don't have a word I need, and have to wipe that lot and start all over again. My head aches at times, having to think so hard. Sometimes I get mortal tired of talking with my hands, and I sit on them and won't say anything."

"Oh, don't tell me such things," said Father Brannan, with a twinkle in his eye. "You'll damage my notion that you're a saint." Then he bent his head over the parchment and wrote, in large clear letters: MARNIE.

"That's your name," he said, showing it to her.

For a long time Marnie studied her name. Then, very carefully, she made the sign she had decided on: the first letter of her name, traced with her forefinger over her heart. Then she said to Raven, *Marnie is my name. What people call me.*

You are woman, Raven said.

❧

THE RAGING QUIET
135

There are many women. Every one has a different name. My name is Marnie.

As always, she spoke as she signed, and Father Brannan observed Raven's reaction. He saw how Raven watched Marnie's lips, as well as the graceful movements of her hands; saw how the youth's face was solemn and attentive, comprehending everything. The priest shook his head, marveling, hardly able to believe that this was the mad Raver of Torcurra, for years flogged for his devils and mindless savagery.

Slowly, Raven lifted his right hand and traced the letter M on his own breast. Then he signed, with a tender smile, *Good day, woman Marnie.*

Father Brannan took the parchment from Marnie's hand, and dipped the pen in the ink again. RAVEN he wrote.

Again, Marnie studied the first letter, and made it over her heart. She said to Raven, *Your name is Raven. No other man is called Raven. Only you. You are Raven.*

For a few moments they stood gazing at one another, smiling, as if they had discovered something wonderful. It was then that Father Brannan realized the depth of the power that lay between them. It was an understanding that went far beyond the finite language of their hands; a soul unity, sacred and rare and beautiful.

Then Marnie leaned on the table again by Father Brannan. "Could you write some more words, please?" she asked.

He nodded, his eyes moist. "What is it you'd like next?"

"Mother, and father. And then Isake, if you don't mind. We talk of him, and it'll be easier if he's named. Perhaps you could write the name Pierce too. It gets confusing sometimes trying to explain different people."

"I'm sure it does," smiled the priest, bending over the parchment. "All your flutterings would try the patience of the Good Lord himself." For some time he wrote, and Marnie watched, entranced. Never had she seen the writing of letters, and it filled her with longing to have that skill herself. When he had written all she requested, Father Brannan put down the pen, blew the ink dry, and explained the words.

"Now, that word there is Mother. The first letter is the same as that of your own name," he said. "That's Father, next to it. Then Sister, and Brother. And here is Isake, and that is Pierce."

Marnie studied the parchment, repeating the words, remembering the shapes of the names. "Thank you, father," she said. "Thank you, with all my heart."

"You're welcome. Is there anything else you're wanting?"

She placed the sheet of parchment carefully on the table, smoothing it with her hands. "Actually," she said, "there is. There's something I'd like to do, if you'll agree."

"What is it?"

"I'm missing church, father. I went every Sabbath, in Fernleigh. I've not heard any of your fine sermons, yet. Can't I come to church?"

"Nothing would give me greater joy, than to see you and Raven there. But the people of Torcurra . . . To be honest with you, Marnie, they're still suspicious. I know you've done as I said, and left them time to come to their senses, but they still have bad feelings in their hearts. I've tried to explain to them about what you said in the church, but it's hard, seeing as you told me things I cannot tell to others. Folks still are wary of you. If you want to come to church, I'll not tell you to stay away, but it'll be hard for you, putting up with the whispers and the stares."

"I could abide them."

"No doubt you could. You're a brave soul, to be sure."

"I'll see you in church, then, father."

"I'll ring the bells early, and give you time to get there," he said, smiling. "And now I'd better go and start writing my sermon, since it's to have your critical hearing."

As he was about to leave, Marnie remembered something he had said earlier. She asked, "Father, when Pierce Isherwood said he had friends in high places, you said you did as well. Who's your friend? Someone higher than the judge?"

"Aye. Considerably higher."

"Who is it, then?"

"Can't you guess?" He chuckled, his blue eyes dancing. "'Tis the Almighty himself, Marnie! The Almighty himself!"

Marnie and Raven reached the top of the hill, and stood for a few moments looking down at Torcurra. People were already gathering under the trees in the churchyard, talking before they went inside through the beautiful little porch. Raven's footsteps dragged, and he touched Marnie's arm. His face was pale and strained, and his eyes wore the haunted look she had not seen all summer.

They will not hurt you, said Marnie. *We will sit in the big house, and I will tell you what Father Brannan says. All the people will look at him. They will not look at you, not hurt you.*

But Raven drew back, lifelong memories flooding over him, of all those people crowded there, and pain. Firmly, Marnie took his hand. He looked at her and shook his head.

At that moment they were seen, and all the people pointed at them. Raven turned and fled. Marnie watched him go, then, feeling incredibly alone, she faced the crowded churchyard. Slowly, but with deliberate steps, she went down the grassy slope toward them. They all stared; women whispered behind raised hands, and children asked questions and were hushed. At the edge of the gathering Marnie stopped. Every pair of staring eyes was cold, every mouth set grim, every face bitter with malice and accusation. The very air seemed thick with hate.

Marnie's heart hammered painfully. She wanted to run after Raven, but her feet felt rooted to the ground, and she could only stare back, her tongue dry in her mouth, her face ashen. It was almost a relief when a woman spoke, though her voice was harsh.

"I never thought you'd have the gall to show your face around here again, Widow Isherwood," she said.

Marnie tried to speak, but could not. She licked her lips, and tried to calm her heart.

"We don't want the likes of you in our church," said a man, stepping forward. "We don't want people who cast curses."

"I never cursed anyone," said Marnie.

"You cursed your husband, and he died. There be some of us what heard your confession," said another woman, holding tight to her husband's arm.

"You didn't hear a confession," said Marnie.

"What did we hear, then?" someone called. "A recipe for love?"

There was harsh laughter.

"Aye, she'd know all the recipes for *that*," said a youth, grinning, his face red and leering. "She was holding Raver's hand, when she came. Like lovers, they were."

"Jezebel!" shrieked a woman, and others took up the cry.

"Go back to your evil house, where you killed your husband, and took a mad boy to his bed!" shouted a man. "Go on—afore we hang you!"

Marnie stood her ground. "I'm going to church," she said.

"You'll not put a foot in this church!" cried an old man, spit dribbling down his whiskery chin. "This be the church of gentle and good folks! Not for the likes of you!"

"For gentle and good folks, is it?" roared a voice, and Father Brannan came around the corner, his prayer book and Bible in his hands. His face was red with anger, and his blue eyes were blazing. He stood on the porch step, and glared at them all. "Well then," he said, "let's sort out exactly who *can* come! Step forward all those who are gentle. In case you're wondering, gentle has several meanings: There's the meaning of the good birth, the noble family, which none of us belong to—excepting for one, who married a lord. Gentle also means kindly, tender, and mild. There's a softness about a gentle soul, a politeness, if you like. I don't see too many gentle folk about here. But if you'd like to argue with me, step into the porch. No gentle folk?

Oh well, then, we'll have to try for the good ones. Now, good's another interesting word. It holds a host of meanings. Fine, enjoyable, obedient, of moral excellence. Now, wouldn't you think that would cover just about everyone here?"

"Aye!" they yelled, warming to the idea. "We all be good, father!"

"Well now," said Father Brannan, looking worried, "there's just one little fly in the ointment. There's an embarrassing bit here in Holy Scripture, where Christ says no one is good, save the Almighty Father himself. I'm sorry to be the bringer of that bad news, but it wipes out every single one of us. So we'd best all sit down where we are, and I'll deliver my sermon out here, which is the only place we have a right to be."

There was a stunned silence, then a man asked, sounding bewildered, "But what are we going to do with our fine church, father, if we can't go inside?"

"I never said we couldn't go inside!" said Father Brannan. "You folks said that, when you said only the gentle and the good could go in there. Are you changing your blessed minds, now? Is the qualification different, now, for going in? The humble, maybe? The poor in spirit, the merciful, the peacemakers, the ones who love their neighbors—even if those neighbors happen to be a little peculiar? Are those the qualifications now?"

Silent, they stared at the ground.

Father Brannan added quietly, "I'm thinking we can all go in. All of us. And not because *we're* good, but because God is. Also, because I spent the last two days writing my sermon, and I didn't do it for nothing."

They filed in, very quiet, and would not look at the priest as they went past. Marnie came in last of all. "I was thinking that *was* your sermon, father," she whispered, smiling, and he grinned.

Marnie stood on the stone floor with all the people of Torcurra, and no one dared to move away from her, or to whisper or stare. There was hardly a murmur during the service, and Marnie listened to the sermon, more rapt than anyone. It was based on her favorite piece of Scripture: the story of the Good Samaritan, the true neighbor. Father Brannan did a fine job of it, and afterward two of the women actually said good morning to Marnie, though a smile was a bit beyond them.

Father Brannan walked some of the way back with Marnie. As they skirted the corner of the churchyard, they passed some broken headstones almost lost in the long grass.

"Whose are those?" asked Marnie, stopping to look at them.

"They're the graves of the unfortunate not judged worthy to be buried in the graveyard," said Father Brannan. "The graves of the unknown, the paupers, and criminals. Some call it villains' ground. It's unconsecrated."

Marnie said, "I suppose Isake's grandmother lies hereabouts."

"I think this is her grave," said Father Brannan, bending down and pushing aside long grass and daisies. There was a simple stone cross, with the name Eilis Isherwood. "Aye, this is it," he said, standing up again. "No dates, Marnie. Just her name. She died young, if I remember aright. One of the old women in the village told me about her, not long after I came here. I'd noticed the cottage on my walks, and wondered why it was empty, seeing as the cove it's in is so pretty."

"I wonder what she did wrong," said Marnie, "to be tried as a witch, and burned."

"Probably little, beyond being different," said the priest. "But being different is a terrible crime to be guilty of."

Marnie gathered up some daisies from the long grass and placed a bunch of them against the headstone. "I've been thinking about Pierce Isherwood," she said, "and why he wants Eilis's house. I'm thinking it's not the house at all that he wants, but the land it's on. He wants the cove."

"And why is that?"

"I remember hearing talk when I was working on the Isherwood estate. Before he died, Sir William talked of owning nothing but sheep—thousands of them—and shipping out the wool. I wondered about it because I didn't know what they meant by shipping out. But I think I understand now. Sometimes I see ships go by, their sails so fine and proud, and fast with the wind. A big ship like that would carry a mighty lot of wool, wouldn't it?—more than a team of wagons drawn by horses. Maybe if the Isherwoods wanted to sell a lot of wool, and owned the cove, they could get a ship to come here to pick the wool up."

"I think you may be right!" murmured Father Brannan. "There's no other port in these parts with easy access from their land, and the people of Torcurra wouldn't let ships in their bay, chasing out the fish and ruining their fishing business. But your little cove . . . If you're right, then the whole Isherwood business depends on their owning it! You could sell it for a fortune!"

"But I don't want to sell."

"Well, that's your choice. But if you change your mind, don't make a deal with Pierce Isherwood until you've talked it over with me. I'll do some inquiring, and find out what is a fair price."

"There's no fair price, father; I'm not selling."

Father Brannan shook his head and smiled to himself, and they began walking on.

"Why isn't Raven with you, today?" asked the priest.

"He saw all the people, and was afraid."

"And you weren't afraid?"

"Aye. I was terrified."

"But you still came."

"I wouldn't have missed it for anything, father. Even before we got in the church, you were grand. And your sermon I'll remember forever."

He laughed softly, and said, "There was someone grand there, Marnie lass, but it wasn't me."

Chapter 18

MARNIE PLAITED BACK her hair and tied it with the blue ribbon from Isake's chest. She was wearing the blue dress she had been married in, its long sleeves trimmed now with silver braid she had cut from one of Isake's jerkins. She wore one of his gilt belts about her hips, and had tucked into it a small twig of hazel, for good luck on the journey. On the table was a large basket of food, and a jar of water to drink because the day was warm.

She could hear Raven outside, talking in his husky noises to the horse as he hitched it to the wagon. Putting on her white linen hood, and carrying the basket, Marnie went outside and closed the door behind her.

The horse and wagon were ready, and Raven looked fine dressed in soft deerskin leggings of Isake's that Marnie had altered for him, and a knee-length purple tunic with a jeweled belt. He had even washed his hair, and it shone blue-black as it curled on his shoulders.

He took the basket from Marnie, checked it briefly to make sure she had put in some pickles, and lifted it onto the back of the wagon, just behind their seat.

Can I hold these? he asked, indicating the reins. *Can I? I watched people do it; I know how.*

Are you sure? Marnie asked doubtfully, imagining hair-raising gallops down the steep hills between here and her own village.

I know. I'm not stupid, he replied indignantly.

If you make the horse go fast, she warned, *I'll stop you. You must do what I tell you, and not argue.*

Crowing in triumph, Raven climbed into the seat and took up the reins, and Marnie got up beside him, anxiously biting her lip. But he proved a careful driver, though the horse was alarmed at times when he made his strange, excited cries. They did not go down the road through the village and along the beach, but went over the grassy hills, not minding the bumps, and met up with the road as it turned inland from the coast. The day shone, and Marnie sang to herself, until Raven thought she was talking and pestered her to say the words with her hands. She could not explain what singing was, so she hummed instead—a phenomenon Raven was unaware of.

In the basket with the food were gifts for Marnie's family: shells and sun-bleached bones of gulls and fish, for her brothers and sisters; a piece of seaweed Marnie had twisted into a wreath and threaded with lavender, for her mother; and, for her father, a graceful piece of driftwood shaped like a bird in flight. For several days she had walked along the beach, collecting the gifts. Tonight was Midsummer Eve, and she would spend it as she always had, with her friends and family, dancing in the fields by huge bonfires, celebrating the summer and the sun.

When she had first asked Raven to come to her far home with her, he had been unwilling, having suffered enough rejection without risking more from strangers. But she told him about her family and friends, and of the huge farm where she had worked for Isake's father, and he began to be interested. The idea of a mother and father intrigued him. And when she said they would be dancing at night, by

෨෩
Sherryl Jordan
144

moonlight and fire, the journey became irresistible, and he had counted the days until they could go.

That Raven was going home with her made Marnie's joy complete. His company was something she never took for granted. He still came and went as he pleased, sometimes returning late at night after days away, and making himself a meal before he curled up in his blanket by the fire. The wild part of his life remained a mystery to Marnie, but she knew he preferred the night to the daytime, probably because that was when people stayed in their homes and did not hurt him; and that somewhere in the hills he had what he called a hole, in which to live.

Dozing, wondering how he would fit in with her family, she leaned against him and let her body move with the wagon as it lurched and swayed. Suddenly the wagon stopped, and she woke. Raven was looking at the landscape to their left, his hand shading his eyes from the sun. There the hills rose to misty rugged peaks, wild and desolate and beautiful. They were the Mountains of Conara, Father Brannan had told Marnie; a place of ancient worship, where huge stones stood like gods, and spirits danced in the wind.

Raven touched her arm, and pointed to the mountains. *My faraway house*, he said, holding the reins between his knees, so he could talk.

You stay there sometimes? she asked, surprised. *Is that where your hole is?*

No. This house is different.

It's a long walk to there from our beach.

He nodded, smiling, his eyes wistful and longing. *In my house there,* he said, *I stand in the night, in moon-fire. I am strong. Alone, but it is a good alone. No people come and hurt me. I am me, not afraid. The moon is good. Under the moon, the sea, the fields . . . they all be . . . no word. What is the word? Good in the eyes, good in here.* He touched his heart.

"Beautiful," said Marnie, aloud.

Raven copied her lips, but the sound was incomprehensible. He made up a new sign; the sign for the moon, and the sign for good.

Moon-good, said Marnie. *Beautiful.*

It is a good word, he signed, pleased.

They went on, and the dust rose about the little wagon as the day grew hot. At noon they stopped under a grove of trees by a river. They were by a marshy field where peat was dug, and could see the long rows of rich turf laid out to dry in the sun. For a price the farmers let people into the fields to dig their own peat, but Father Brannan had always got Marnie's for her.

While the horse grazed and drank from the stream, Marnie and Raven ate the meal they had brought. They reclined in the shade to eat, and after she had finished, Marnie picked some of the daisies that grew in the long grass, and began threading them into a circle. Raven always took longer over meals than she did, eating twice as much, and noisily savoring every mouthful. A grasshopper crawled up Raven's foot, and Marnie signed the name to him. He laughed and nearly choked, repeating the sign, delighted with it. *Grass-hopper,* he said, watching it leap away. *Birds, they be sky-hoppers. Fish, water-hoppers. People, they be dirt-hoppers.*

You, said Marnie, *are a food-hopper.*

Raven grinned. Then he said, his face serious: *You, my one friend what gives me words. Father Brannan did not give me words. Only you. Why?*

I don't know why, she replied, dropping the daisies into her lap. *When I was little, I watched people whip a boy, the same way they whip you. I was sad about him. It was in my faraway house, over there, where the road is. The day I came to Torcurra, the people whipped you. I felt sad about you. I did want to help you.*

He was thoughtful, his eyes half-closed, silver bright under the lowered lids as he looked at the distant mountains. At last he signed: *Your faraway house, you like it?*

Yes.

Why come to the little house on the beach?

I came with the man Isake, she signed back. *To look after him in the house.*

He your friend?

She touched the gold band on her left ring finger; a new sign, for a new word. *Husband,* she said, speaking the words too, as she always did. *He was my husband.*

Your friend?

No. It is different.

In husky, guttural tones he asked the one word he could speak: "Why?"

Many friends, she said, *only one husband.*

You don't got many friends. Only Father Brannan and me.

In my faraway house I have many friends. You will see them tonight.

Why did you come here?

I gave you the words. I came with my husband.

Can I be your husband?

No.

Why? You look after me in your house. I help you, you help me. The same.

It is different.

Why?

Marnie smiled, and placed the circle of daisies across Raven's dark hair. *You are better than a husband,* she said.

Dedra tugged at the knots in the hair of her youngest daughter, while she scolded a son for dipping his fingers in the bowl of gravy that remained on the table. The meal was finished, and the older girls were washing the dishes, laughing and arguing over which lads they would dance with later, as if they had any say in it.

"Where are your aprons?" Dedra asked them, frowning at the water being splashed around. "You shouldn't have got in your best clothes, until later!"

One of the boys raced around the table, flapping his arms like wings. "I'm going to run through the fires!" he yelled. "Nathy did that last year, holding Em's hand! He said I wasn't big enough, but I am!"

"You'll do nothing of the kind!" snapped Dedra, tugging with the comb and making her daughter wail. "If you burn holes in your shoes, Barnaby, I'll not be buying you new ones—or even old ones. There's not enough to go around, now."

"Only sweethearts go jumping through the flames!" cried one of the girls washing the dishes. "No one would be your sweetheart, Barnaby, with your freckles and your teeth all missing in the front!"

"They're not all gone!" howled Barnaby. "I still got three!" And he pulled a heinous face to prove it.

Nathy came running in, sweating and red-faced, with wood chips in his black hair from chopping branches for the midsummer fires. "She's coming home!" he cried, racing around the table and gripping his mother's arms. "It's Marnie! She's almost here! In the wagon she is, with Sir Isake's horse!"

"Don't talk nonsense, and go and wash yourself," said Dedra. "There's meat I've kept hot for you, and—"

But Nathy raced out again, and tore down the dusty road between the cottages, yelling.

Marnie saw him coming, and leaped down off the wagon before Raven stopped it. She fell into her brother's arms, and they hugged, laughing.

"You look fine, Marnie!" cried Nathy, holding her away, and looking at her. "With a ribbon in your hair, and all! You've changed! You're happy! Oh, this is better than the way you were, when you went away! They said Sir Isherwood died. I've been waiting all this time for you to come home! I knew you wouldn't live there by yourself!"

"I've only come home for the night," Marnie said, noticing that he was taller than she was now, though he was three years younger. She added, beckoning to Raven, "I've brought a friend."

Raven got down and came over, holding out his hand toward Nathy. They greeted one another shyly. "It was good of you to bring Marnie here," said Nathy.

Marnie interpreted, and Nathy gazed at her hand movements, suspicious and afraid.

"Raven can't hear, or talk very well," Marnie explained. "We've made up some hand-words so we can understand each other. You can still talk to him, and I'll tell him with my hands what you say."

Astonished, Nathy asked, "Can I do some hand-words?"

Marnie gripped her left hand in her right, as if she shook hands with herself. "This is how we say hello," she said.

Nathy repeated the sign, and Raven beamed and made the sign in return.

There were glad shouts, and Marnie turned to see her mother and brothers and sisters running toward them. Dust rose about their bright forms, red-gold in the sunset. Marnie rushed to her mother and flung her arms about her, but Dedra pulled away, her face hard and shocked, her eyes on the road behind Marnie.

Raven stood in the middle of the road in front of the wagon, facing them all. He looked tall and unafraid, his lips slightly curved, his face vivid in the last golden light from the sun. He still wore the circle of daisies, and they glimmered white across his dark hair.

"This is Raven, Mama," Marnie said, disturbed by Dedra's expression. "He's my friend. I thought you would be pleased to meet him."

"Your friend?" repeated Dedra, faintly. "But you're a widow, Marnie! How could you bring a sweetheart here, with talk already what it is!"

"He's not my sweetheart, Mama! He's my friend. I thought you'd understand!"

Around them, silence fell. Marnie noticed her brothers and sisters, and they smiled, longing to run and embrace her, but hanging back because of their mother's disquiet. They looked clean and lovely in their best clothes and shoes, the girls with garlands of flowers in their hair. All Marnie's relatives lived in this small street, and her cousins and some of her aunts and uncles had come out too, when they heard Nathy's yells, to welcome Marnie home. But the welcome had turned uncannily quiet, and Marnie felt as if she had done something scandalous.

"Please be kind to him, Mama," she begged. "He's had a hard life in Torcurra. He can't hear and he speaks only a little, and the people there have been terrible cruel to him. And please don't be angry with me for bringing him. I've longed so much to come and see you, I can't bear it if you're cross."

Suddenly Dedra hugged her, kissing her cheek. "Oh, Marnie!" she sighed. "I suppose you can't help it, doing everything the wrong way, and making tongues wag! Sometimes I marvel that you're mine, you're so headstrong! But no matter what they say, I still love you, girl, and I've missed you too. I'm so pleased you've come home again, even if you have brought us an extra mouth to feed. But why on earth is the wagon empty? Where are your belongings?"

"I'm not here to live, Mama, only to visit. I wanted to take some things back with me, if you don't mind. Some more blankets, and a weaving for the floor. Also, if Nathy's got some shoes he's grown out of, I'd like them for Raven, if they fit. And if you don't want that little wooden pen we used to keep our dog in, I'd like it for my goat." Trying to ignore the confusion and alarm on her mother's face, she added, "Please come and meet Raven."

So Dedra walked on to Raven and greeted him, shaking his hand. Raven made the hand-word for good afternoon, and Marnie interpreted. Dedra's look of dismay deepened.

Suddenly Marnie's brothers and sisters swarmed toward her, screeching for hugs and kisses, and asking if she had brought them gifts. Warmly she embraced them, then turned again to Raven, and spoke the children's names while she explained a little about each one, their special idiosyncrasies and wickednesses. The children beamed, enthralled to see the magical gestures she made. The oldest of Marnie's sisters, Sheilah, learned the hand-word for hello, smiling shyly at Raven as she made it.

Marnie introduced Raven to her relatives, and some of the cousins, knowing what had been said about Marnie's sudden marriage and departure, whispered and smirked behind their hands. The aunts and uncles were reticent. Marnie ignored their coldness. When Nathy took Raven's arm and led him down the road, pointing out their house and gesturing toward the field where they would all soon dance, she took the horse's reins and followed after them, content. Dedra walked a little way ahead, worrying about gossip Raven would cause; but the children clung to Marnie's skirt, begging for gory details about Sir Isake's death. She told them instead about her little house by the sea.

While Nathy and Raven tended the horse, Marnie gave the children the gifts she had brought. Awed, they examined the seashells, small skeletons of fish, and bleached crab shells. While they fought over the skeletons, Marnie gave Dedra the little wreath.

"'Tis charming." Dedra smiled, taking it over to the window to look at it in a better light. Among the lavender flowers Marnie had woven little strips of parchment covered with kisses, and tiny hearts of love. Dedra put it on the mantelpiece, and gave Marnie another hug. "Oh, I've missed you, girl," she whispered. "I hope he was good to you, your Isake."

Marnie kissed her mother's cheek. "He was all right, Mama. We only had two days together, before he died. I want to see Father. Is he upstairs?"

"Aye. It will do him good to see your face again."

Marnie picked up the piece of driftwood that was Micheal's gift, and went up the stairs. Her father was sitting in a chair by the tiny window, the sunset illuminating his face. Marnie went and knelt by him, and he looked down at her, his mouth twisted in a smile, his right hand jerking roughly across her hair. She held his fingers and kissed them.

"I've missed you, Papa," she said. "I hated not knowing how you were."

He mumbled something, dribbling, and Marnie listened carefully, as she did when Raven tried to talk. Finally she realized he was trying to say the name Isake.

"He died, Papa," she said. "He fell when he was mending the roof. The cottage was a mess when we got there, but I love it now."

Micheal tried to say something else, but she could not understand it, and he looked out the window, his eyes wet. Again, she kissed his hand. "He was not a bad man, Papa. I can't say I was happy with him, but we only had two days together. I have two friends in Torcurra. The priest comes to see me often, and brings me supplies. He's very good to me. My cottage is in a little cove, apart from the village. I go fishing. I'm grand at fishing, Papa! And at rowing. You'd be so proud if you saw me! All those times you let me try things that were different, that women aren't supposed to do—I'm grateful for them, now."

Her father nodded and stroked her hair again, his hand heavy and uncontrolled.

"I've brought my other friend," she said. "You'll understand him, I think. He can't speak or hear. I've made up some hand-words, so we can talk." She showed him some, and tried to sign the line of a song he had loved. But she ran out of words and added, laughing, "It's difficult, sometimes, talking to him, because there aren't enough words. He taught me to row, and he built a little wall around my garden to keep out the chickens. I have my own goat, and Isake's horse, and I trap rabbits sometimes, though Raven gets cross with me for it. He's softer than I am, inside. We eat mainly fish."

She picked up the driftwood she had dropped in his lap, and showed it to him. "I found it on the beach," she said. "It's like a bird, see?" Then she told him about her house and her cove, and what the sea was like. He listened, nodding, his eyes bright.

Dedra came in, and Marnie realized it was dark.

"Your friend has gone with Nathy to light the fires," Dedra told Marnie, lighting a candle and setting it on the little table by her husband. "Do you want supper?"

"Later, maybe. We ate on the way here," said Marnie, standing up and kissing her father's cheek. "I'll see you tomorrow, Papa."

Marnie put Nathy's gift on his bed, then went downstairs with Dedra. She noticed how gray her mother's hair had become, and that she walked with a stoop, as if her back hurt.

"Are you managing all right, with Papa?" Marnie asked.

"Aye," replied Dedra, pulling her shawl about her shoulders. "The neighbors help when they can. And Micheal's improving, little by little. He can even walk a step or two, if a strong man bears him up."

"And the boys? They're managing our farm?"

"Of course. They're old enough. And Nathy works on the manor land now, all the time."

"Does anyone talk to Papa, tell him stories, or sing to him? He's not left alone all day, is he?"

"Are you thinking he's neglected, girl?"

"No. I'm just asking, Mama. And I'm thinking of Raven. People said he had no mind, that he was possessed, and they whipped him to get his devils out. Yet there's nothing wrong with him, excepting that he can't hear, and it makes him angry sometimes if he can't make himself understood. He has a fine mind, quick and willing to learn. He reminds me of Papa sometimes, locked inside a great quiet. Only Papa's worse off, because he can't talk with his hands nor his mouth."

"I talk to him all the time. And his brother carries him outside on the good days, to see what is going on with the planting or the birthing of the animals. The neighbors help with him, if I'm tired or the children are sick and needing me more."

"I'll come back and help, if you want me to."

Dedra went over to the table and started putting away the washed dishes the girls had left piled there. She and Marnie were the only ones in the room; the others had gone out to the fields for the dancing.

"Are you settled in Torcurra?" asked Dedra, her back to Marnie as she reached up to put the dishes on a shelf. Her voice sounded strained.

"Aye. I love my house, though it's small."

"Have you seen Sir Pierce?"

"I have. Why do you ask?"

Busily tidying the shelf, Dedra said, with forced brightness, "Go and get on with your dancing, Marnie, or they'll be finished afore you get there. I sent the others on, so you'd have a quiet time with your father. But they'll be waiting for you now, out in the field. I'll come home early to see that Micheal is all right, and I'll make up a bed by the fire for Raven."

Marnie kissed her mother's cheek, and ran outside. She was met by one of her little sisters, come back to fetch her. "Marnie! Davit Miller says he's wanting to dance with you!" shrieked the little girl, rushing up, her garland of flowers awry on her auburn hair, and her best dress already stained. "But I told him you've brought a sweetheart! He didn't believe me!"

Marnie laughed. "Raven's not my sweetheart," she said.

"But he looks like one! He's helping Nathy light the fires! The fiddlers are starting! You can hear them!"

The evening was balmy, glorious. The cottages were dark on either side of the road, their steep roofs black before the orange sky. Along the road people hurried in groups or pairs, out toward the celebrations in the fields. They all wore their best, with white flowers in their hair, and some of the men carried torches topped with burning tar.

They rounded a corner, and Marnie saw the field of fires. People leaped around the flames, and there were shouts and laughter. The children raced on, and Marnie followed more slowly, wondering where Raven was. Neighbors she had worked with in the fields walked past, greeted her briefly, and hurried on.

She found Raven standing near the biggest fire, watching the fiddlers and the young people already dancing. Marnie touched his arm, and he turned.

We can with the people dance, he said, his signs excited and difficult to read. Marnie told him to talk slowly, and he went on: *We can dance, the same we danced with Father Brannan. You and me, if you clap, and I will know when.*

Are you hungry? she asked. *There is food at my mother's house, if you want.*

After, he signed.

Nathy came up to them, a garland of creamy flowers in his hands. He gave it to Raven. "For Marnie," he said. "Put it on Marnie."

Raven watched the boy's lips, and recognized the shape of

Marnie's name. Solemnly, he placed the flowers across her hair. Then, gently, he wiped a smudge of dust from her cheek, and she blushed, because her brother was watching. Grinning, Nathy rushed off to find his friends.

Sheilah ran up, laughing, her face scarlet. "Oh, Marnie!" she cried. "Do you remember Dugal Fowler?"

Marnie nodded, and Sheilah went on, breathlessly, "He's asked me to dance with him! And to go to the wild woods with him, after! Oh, Marnie! What if he wants to kiss me? What shall I do?"

Marnie glanced at Raven, saw him watching their mouths.

"It's all right!" said Sheilah, giggling. "You said he couldn't hear."

"He watches our mouths," said Marnie. "He understands, sometimes."

"And I suppose he kisses you sometimes too," said Sheilah slyly. Before Marnie could say anything, Sheilah ran off, calling over her shoulder, "You're sleeping in your old bed with me tonight! We can talk until morning!"

Marnie waved to her, then signed to Raven, *My sister is happy, her favorite boy wants her to dance.*

Will a boy want you to dance? he asked.

Marnie noticed that people were watching them, and some were pointing and talking, their faces suspicious and disapproving. She remembered what Pierce Isherwood had told her about the gossip in Fernleigh. Did they all think the worst of her? Or was it Raven they disapproved of, with his different way of talking, and his silence? Or was it the fact that she was a widow, and had come here with a youth, tall and well made and handsome, and better than all the stupid Fernleigh boys put together?

Lifting her head, Marnie met the disapproving stares with her old defiance and boldness. Then she gave Raven a brilliant smile. *We will dance*, she signed to him. *We will show them all how to dance.*

Chapter 19

FIDDLERS SENT THEIR wild music over the fields, the fires blazed, and sparks flew high into the night air. Around the flames people danced, or stood singing and clapping, their faces aglow. Inspired by love and ale, young sweethearts ran, leaping, through the smaller fires, their hands clasped. At midnight a large cartwheel was set on fire and sent rolling down a hill, while the people watched to see if it would stay alight until it fell. If it stayed alight, that meant the summer would be long; but if the flames went out, it meant winter would come early. Tonight the wheel blazed gloriously all the way down to the valley, and the villagers cheered and celebrated, the music started up again, and the ale flowed.

Marnie took Raven's hand and led him over to the trestle tables and ale barrels. She helped herself to another drink, and they stood watching as Sir Gerard, the eldest of the Isherwood sons and now the manor lord, killed a bullock and went through the ceremony of offering it to the flames. It was an age-old rite, left over from the first midsummer festivals when pagan priests sacrificed to the ancient gods of the sun. Doubtless the village priest would disapprove, if he knew; but he was not around, and no one else would criticize.

Marnie looked for Sir Gerard's youngest brother, Pierce, but could not see him. She asked a young woman standing near, "Is Pierce Isherwood not well, seeing as he's not here?"

The girl looked at her, surprised, frowning a little, trying to think where she had seen Marnie before. "Have you not heard?" she replied. "He's gone to another village to live for a while. To Torcurra, so they say."

Marnie gulped the rest of her ale, hoping it might clear the havoc in her head. It did not. "When did he go?" she asked.

"A day or two past."

"Are his wife and children there too?"

"Nay, only him, I think. He's gone on business, he said, about a house. Did I work with you once, in the malthouse at the manor?"

Marnie turned away, but the girl gripped her sleeve. "I know!" she said, her eyes widening. "You're the former overseer's daughter, aren't you? The one who married Sir Isake." A smile crossed her face, half admiring, half malicious. "You were a clever one, weren't you!" Then her eyes slid to Marnie's waist, and she asked, "What happened to the babe? Did you lose it afore its proper time?"

"Aye," said Marnie gravely. "I put it down somewhere, but it were such a tiny mite, I clean forgot where I left it, and couldn't find it again."

"What did Sir Isherwood do?" the girl gasped, horrified.

Marnie replied, sweetly, "Why, the poor man died of shock!"

Aghast, the girl rushed off to spread the news.

Chuckling to herself, Marnie finished her ale, then turned to Raven. He was watching the dancers, clapping his hands to the rhythm of their feet. Seeing Marnie, he signed, *Can we again dance?*

She nodded, and they joined a group in a folk dance Marnie had learned as a child. It was a fast dance, growing faster near the end, but Marnie's reactions were slower than usual. Finally she collapsed against Raven, giggling. He put his arm around her waist and they started the next dance, managing admirably until Marnie began laughing and could not clap in time to the music; and then Raven, depending on her hands for the rhythm, gave up and walked off. She ran after him, catching him around the waist, begging him to come back. But she spoke with her voice, and he signed, angrily, *Hand-words. No more mouth, open, shut, open, shut, like a fish.*

She pulled silly faces at him, and they both laughed and sauntered off to watch the children dancing. Marnie's youngest brothers and sisters were among them, and she almost wept as she watched them, their little faces grave as they tried to remember the steps, the garlands of flowers slipping sideways off their heads. They were so fair. They were also rather blurred, and Marnie felt suddenly dizzy, watching the circle of children go around and around the fire. She tightened her arm about Raven's waist, and looked through the flames to the people on the other side. Her mother stood there watching them, her face shocked and disapproving.

Marnie tugged at Raven, and they walked away. She found five friends she had enjoyed working with in the happier days on the manor land, before her father's misfortune. They welcomed her with hugs and kisses, and she introduced them to Raven, showing them how to greet him in hand-words. Blushing, they talked to him, furtively looking from him to Marnie, and wondering what the relationship was. Then, laughing and chatting, they went walking through the fields beyond the fires, past the windmill with its huge blades dark against the stars, and the bakehouse where the bread was baked for those who had no ovens, and the rows of ripening corn. Marnie's friends were fascinated by Raven and the strange way he and Marnie talked. They learned a few more hand-words, and had some mixed-up conversations with Raven, which caused a great deal of mirth.

Marnie showed Raven where she had milked cows, the great barn where she had winnowed wheat, and the beautiful manor house where once Isake had lived. Raven's eyes bulged. Never had he seen a place so grand. The whole Isherwood estate entranced him, so differ-ent it was from the humble fishing village he had known all his life.

As they stood in front of the manor, one of Marnie's friends asked her shyly, "What was it like being married to him, Marnie?"

Marnie thought for a while, and they waited, silent and avid, for her reply.

Impatient, one of them said, "Well? What was he like? Was he kind?"

"Aye, kind enough," said Marnie. "But it was awkward, with him."

"You weren't awkward, dancing with him," said another.

"But it wasn't dancing she was doing, on her wedding night!" said someone else, and there were shrieks of laughter.

"Tell us, Marnie! What was it like on your wedding night?"

Silence fell, while they waited for her answer. Marnie turned away, looking at the manor house, her back to her friends. None of them were married, and they all had dreams, as she had once had dreams. From across the fields came the music of the fiddles and pipes, and rowdy laughter. Raven looked from Marnie to the girls again, and back to Marnie. He sensed their eagerness and her distress, and did not know what to do. "Tell us!" the girls prompted.

There was a shout, and they all turned around. Marnie welcomed the interruption, until she saw who approached. Four youths were walking toward them, swigging on pottery flagons of ale, and leaning on one another for support. One of them was Jonty, the plowman's son. Recognizing Marnie, he swaggered over, eyeing her up and down. Then he took another drink of ale, holding the large flagon up with both hands, and tipping his head back. The ale ran down his chin and neck, staining his shirt.

"Well, 'tis her ladyship back!" he said, wiping his sleeve across his mouth, and giving the flagon to one of his friends.

"Go away!" shouted one of the girls. "We don't need the likes of you tormenting us!"

"I'm not tormenting," said Jonty, his eyes still on Marnie. "I'm admiring, and I don't believe there's a law against that."

"There's a law against lying," said Marnie. "And you lied about me, Jonty."

Jonty tipped his head on one side, and scratched a spot on his chin. "Did I, now? What lie was that?"

"The one about us in the barn," said Marnie. "The lie your uncle, the overseer, paid you to tell."

"Oh, *that* one," said Jonty, and his friends sniggered. Swaying from the ale, Jonty walked right around Marnie, just looking. Raven watched from nearby, not understanding, but sensing the tension.

Jonty stopped in front of Marnie, his thumbs hooked into his belt, his head tilted back, looking at her through lowered eyelids. "Give me a kiss," he whispered.

"If you don't go," said Marnie, "I'll give you a black eye, and maybe worse."

"Oooh—I'm mortal scared," said Jonty.

"Come on!" called one of his friends. "There's more fun to be had elsewhere, than with her. She's too high and mighty for you, now. You haven't got a chance, Jonty. Besides, your betrothed might find out."

They laughed, and Jonty grinned. He stepped nearer to Marnie, but she stood her ground. Out of the corner of her eye she saw Raven move closer, and she held up a hand to him. *It's all right,* she signed, without speaking. *I'm not afraid.*

Jonty stared, and swore under his breath. "What kind of sorcery's that?" he gasped.

"None of your business," said Marnie. She glanced at her friends. "Come on," she added to them, "we'll go back."

She started to walk away, but Jonty gripped her arm. "I want to know what you were doing," he said, "because if you were putting a spell on me, Marnie, I'll make you sorry for it."

She tried to pull free, but he gripped her harder. "I've heard talk about you!" he hissed. "About how you want to keep the Isherwood estate in Torcurra, and how you're making trouble for Sir Pierce, because he's wanting it back. You're always making trouble, Marnie, always thinking you're better than everyone else, and getting your own way. Now you've come back here to laugh at us all, and brought your village lunatic too, who can't even talk. I suppose he suits you, because he can't be arguing with you. Does everything you want, does he? Must be nice, after an old—"

With her free hand Marnie slapped Jonty hard across the face. He lifted his hand to hit back, but Marnie's friends grabbed him and pulled him away. Suddenly they were all fighting, the six girls against Jonty and his friends. For a moment Raven hung back, too confused to move; but then he saw Jonty with his arms around Marnie, trying to drag her to the ground, and he flew, howling in rage, to her defense. He hauled on Jonty, his hands in Jonty's hair, jerking back his head. Jonty let Marnie go and he and Raven rolled on the ground, punching one another, tearing at each other's clothes and hair. Jonty was bigger and older than Raven, and well known for his cunning in a fight; but he had never met the likes of Raven, nor heard such bloodcurdling screams. The others forgot to fight, and watched, horrified, as Raven, howling like one possessed, wrestled Jonty down and smashed his head against the ground, again and again. Jonty's face was scratched, bleeding, and his tunic was ripped. The ground about his head was bloodied, and he was sobbing, choking, begging Raven for mercy.

It was Marnie who separated them, unable to move Raven, but repeating the same hand-word in front of his face until he saw it, and stopped. Raven staggered up, breathing hard, his hair over his face, blood and spit on his chin. At his feet, Jonty rolled over, retching, and tried to crawl away on his hands and knees. His friends helped him up, never taking their eyes off Raven. Supporting Jonty between them, they fled, stumbling over the broken ale flagons on the ground.

Marnie's friends stood about her, watching Raven, afraid. "Are you all right, Marnie?" one of them whispered. "Is he safe, your Raven? He won't attack you too?"

"We're all safe," said Marnie, straightening her clothes, and noticing that her dress was torn. When she looked up again her friends were walking quickly away, glancing uneasily over their shoulders.

Marnie turned to Raven. He was staring at the manor house but not seeing it, his shoulders stooped, his damp hair mixed with sweat and blood across his face. He had withdrawn into his own world, his gaze intense, as if he searched for something no one else could see. Marnie pushed back his hair, and saw that his cheek was bruised. His clothes were torn, and his knuckles bled from connecting with the bony bits of Jonty. Marnie touched his arm, and he looked at her, coming back from whatever place he had fled to in his mind.

Why fight, you and him? he asked.

He made bad words about you.

More than words. The way he looked at you. It was . . . a way, it made me afraid about you. Sometimes people's eyes show much. Sometimes I things see, and I don't know about them. I feel . . . they make big feelings, in here. He placed his palm on his heart. *Sometimes good feelings, sometimes bad. I feel alone. Bad alone. I feel different, like other people know something I do not know.*

We all have big feelings, Raven. You are not alone.

Why did he look at you the way to make afraid? What did he want?

I have no words.

Why?

She sighed deeply, her eyes on the manor house. *Sometimes,* she said, *feelings are too big, too . . . too strong, to have words about.*

Why?

Marnie shook her head. *Too many times you ask why,* she said.

Why? he asked again, grinning. She lightly punched his arm, and they walked on after their friends, back to the field of fires.

Chapter 20

MARNIE LAY IN the bed she shared with her sister Sheilah, listening to her father's snores. In the upstairs room there were five beds in a row along one wall. Four beds each held two children; the fifth bed was Sheilah's. The youngest children, both toddlers, slept in the room across the narrow passage, with Micheal and Dedra. A curtain hung between the other beds and the one Marnie and Sheilah shared, to give privacy from the boys.

"'Tis lovely to have you home again," whispered Sheilah. "I missed you when you went away. I missed our talks. Do you remember how we talked all night sometimes, and how we laughed, until Mama called out and told us to be quiet? I've missed you so much."

"I've missed you too," murmured Marnie.

"I danced all night with Dugal Fowler," whispered Sheilah, sighing blissfully. "His hands were sweaty and he left marks on my dress, but I do love him so. Do you want to know a secret?"

"What?"

"We went for a walk in the wild woods,

and he kissed me. Oh, it were wonderful, Marnie! His mouth, it were soft and hard at the same time, and his tongue, it tickled all over my mouth. I could have done it for hours. But Freethy Sopper came along with his friends, and they teased us, so we went away back to the dancing. But I can't stop thinking about it." She hesitated, then went on, still whispering, "Aunt Molly came home with her friends, and told Mama that you fought with Jonty, and that Raven went wild, like a madman, to defend you. Was it true?"

"Aye. Jonty said bad things about Raven, so I hit him. What did Mama say?"

"Nothing. She just made herself a cup of chamomile and went to bed. She does that, when she's the worst kind of angry. Oh, Marnie, you'll be in for it, in the morning!"

Marnie said nothing, and Sheilah faced her, leaning up on one elbow so she could see her sister's face. Marnie was lying on her back, her hands clasped on her chest, her eyes on the rafters just above her head. "Don't look so melancholy," whispered Sheilah. "We've got all night yet, before you're in trouble. Let's talk about nice things. Tell me about Sir Isake, and what it was like kissing him. Did his beard scratch?"

Marnie's eyes shimmered, and she whispered, so quietly Sheilah could hardly hear, "I don't want to talk about it."

Sheilah made an impatient sound, and collapsed back on the bed. "I hate it when you won't talk! You always used to talk. We talked whole nights, dreaming about what being wedded would be like. You promised you'd tell me. Why don't you?"

Marnie did not reply, and Sheilah went on, hushed and angry, "How else am I supposed to find out, unless you tell me? You're like Mama, not talking about kissing, or anything, like it's shameful. I bet her and Father kissed, to get the twelve of us."

There was a loud crash downstairs, and Marnie sat up. "It's Raven!" she whispered. "He hates being in the dark, not able to see or hear. And he doesn't know when he's making a noise. I'll go and light a candle for him."

She got out of bed and pulled her dress on over her shift. There was another crash downstairs, and a grunt, and the sound of a chair scraping on the stone floor. Marnie hurried downstairs.

It was only an hour or two before the dawn. The moon had fled the sky, and the fire in the kitchen had gone out. The room was so black, she could barely see Raven stumbling about. She touched his arm, and he yelped in fright. She clapped her hand over his mouth, felt his breath hot on her palm. Quickly she lit a candle and signed to him, without speaking, *You wake up all the people in the house.*

Why? he asked, speaking as well, and again she placed her finger on his lips.

When you move a chair, or touch anything, it makes a . . . She stopped, lost for words to explain noise.

Raven gave up waiting for her to finish. *I want a drink,* he said.

Marnie got him one, and he went to pull out a chair so he could sit while he drank. Marnie stopped him just as the heavy wood began to screech on the stone floor, and told him to get back into bed. His blankets were tumbled on a mat in front of the cold grate, and Marnie straightened them for him while he drank. He banged the cup down on the table, gave a loud, satisfied belch, and crawled back into bed. Marnie placed the candle on the hearth so he could see, with an extra candle and the flints.

Don't touch things if you walk about the house, she signed. *Be slow and careful. There are many people asleep here.*

I know, he signed, angrily. *I'm not stupid.*

Marnie sat on the edge of his blankets, her knees drawn up to her chin. *One day,* she signed, *I'll have words to tell you everything. Now I don't have words. You are not stupid. I no time say you are stupid.*

Tonight was good, he signed, trying to speak as well, until Marnie closed his mouth again, softly, with her hand. *The fires I liked, and the dancing. And your brother and your friends. They be good, making hand-words. The people in Torcurra no time made hand-words. I liked it, before came the boys and made a fight with us. I don't know why.*

I have no words, I'm sorry.

Why don't they like you?

They say I did a bad thing, when I was here before.

What thing?

I have no words.

Too many times, you got no words, he said, sighing. *In the morning, will we go to our house?*

Yes. Before we go, you will see my father. He is a little better now, but he can't walk or make words.

No hand-words?

No. His hands can't move. He can't make words, not with his hands, not with his mouth.

A profound compassion went across Raven's face, and he said, *He is like me, before you came. Do they whip him?*

No.

Did your mother stop them?

Before he was hurt, my father made words. He worked, made many things. Now he can do nothing. But the people do not hurt him.

Why?

Marnie sighed, and shook her head. *No words,* she said.

Like your father, Raven said. *No words.*

Outside, a cock crowed, and there was laughter in the street as people came home late. One of the children began to cry upstairs, and Marnie heard Sheilah crooning softly to her. Raven stared at the candlelight, unaware of everything else. His face was narrow, shadowed, his eyes so clear they were like violet glass in a church window, with the sun shining through. He looked incredibly sad, lost in thoughts for which he had no words.

There was a rustle on the stairs, and Marnie looked up to see her mother standing there, a shawl wrapped about her. Dedra's face was white with shock.

"Marnie!" she whispered. "What are you doing down there, with *him*?"

"Talking, Mama," Marnie said, standing up. "Raven was lost in the dark, looking for a drink. He was making a lot of noise without realizing, so I came down to help him. I'm going to bed now."

Quickly she signed to Raven: *I must go to bed. I'll see you in the morning.*

"I want him out of here," said Dedra, coming down the stairs, and staring at Raven with fear and loathing. "I won't have him wandering around this house, not with little children asleep."

"Why?" asked Marnie.

"Because he's dangerous!" hissed Dedra, her voice brimming with outrage and fear, but lowered in case the children heard. "I want him out of here! Now!"

"We can't leave now! He hasn't met Papa, yet! And I have some things I want to get."

"Didn't you hear, girl? I want him out of here! They told me you and Jonty fought last night, and that Raven went wild, like devils were in him. They're all talking about it, everyone! As if I haven't got enough to grieve over, with your father!"

"None of it was my fault, Mama! Jonty started it! He was saying evil things about Raven, and I—"

"You were well liquored up, from what I heard!" cried Dedra. "I heard you crawling up the stairs on your hands and knees, and giggling worse than Sheilah! You're a widow, Marnie! You should be respectable!"

Sheilah stood at the top of the stairs, a younger sister with her. "It wasn't Marnie's fault, Mama," she said. "It was—"

"Back to bed with you!" snapped Dedra. "Take your little sister. This instant!"

Sheilah fled, and Marnie sat at the table, her head in her hands. "Won't you listen to me, Mama?" she pleaded.

"No, I will not," said Dedra. "I can't bear any more trouble, Marnie. Just get him out of this house."

Raven had seen enough fear and rejection to know what was

being said. He got out of the blankets and began folding them, ready to leave. Marnie put her hand on his arm. *If you get the horse and wagon,* she signed, *I'll go with you.*

A long time you want to come here, he said. *You stay. I'll again see you in our house.*

No. We will go together.

Raven left his blankets folded beside the hearth, and went out.

"That's another thing," said Dedra, kneeling to pile kindling in the fireplace, and starting the fire. "I don't like that freakish way you speak to him. It's not natural. People were talking about it last night. And they laughed about you, saying how you'd gone from a lord to a lunatic. You've no idea how much it shamed me, to hear that."

"I don't care what people say," said Marnie.

"No, you don't—and it'll be your downfall one day," said Dedra. "You'll end up without a friend in the world. It can be terrible lonely if you don't fit in with people, Marnie. You're not better than everyone else, you know, just because you married higher than yourself."

"That wasn't my choice, Mama. I did that to save you all from poverty."

"And to please yourself."

"That's not fair, Mama! I never was in love with Isake."

"But you fancied him. And now you've got his grand house, and all the people of Torcurra bowing and scraping to you. Don't tell me it was a sacrifice, girl."

Shocked, Marnie stared at her mother's back. "Is that what you think, Mama?" she choked.

Her mother was silent, sweeping up the cold ashes on the hearth.

"I suppose you believe everything else you hear too," said Marnie. "I suppose you believed what Isake said, that night he came here and said I'd been found with Jonty. I suppose you believed that."

"Where there's smoke, there's fire," said Dedra. "And there's other things I've heard. I've heard talk that Sir Pierce wants the house back, and he's gone to Torcurra on business about it. You'll be living again with us before long, and working on the Isherwood land once more, with Nathy. So don't think of taking too much away with you now, because you'll only be hauling it all the way back again."

"And what about Raven?" asked Marnie.

"What about him?" said Dedra.

"I can't leave him in Torcurra. I'm the only one who can talk to him. Can he come and live here with us? He'll work well. He's strong, and has a wondrous way with animals. He—"

Very slowly, Dedra stood up and confronted her. "You're jesting, aren't you, Marnie?" she said, her white lips barely moving.

"No, Mama. I've never been more serious in my life. If I come back here, Raven comes too. I'll not live without him."

Dedra staggered a little, and put her hand on the mantelpiece to steady herself. She stared at Marnie, appalled. "Are you *living* with him?" she whispered.

"We share a cottage, that's all," said Marnie.

"That's *all*?" cried Dedra horrified. "Oh, Marnie! And to think I brought you up decent, and took you to church, and taught you what was right! How could you forsake it all, to live with a boy you're not wed to! If that's what you've been up to in Torcurra, I'll not have you back!"

"I wouldn't want to come back!" shouted Marnie, crying. "I gave everything I had, for you! For all of you! I even mated with a man I couldn't stand touching me, so that you could keep—"

"Marnie! I'll have no such talk in this house!"

"Why not? 'Tis the truth!"

Dedra stood up and slapped Marnie across the face. They stood staring at one another, shocked, both in tears.

Without another word Marnie went upstairs and finished dressing. Sheilah sat on the bed watching her, her eyes huge and frightened. "Was it true, Marnie?" she whispered. "Couldn't you stand him touching you?"

Marnie pulled on her shoes, then stooped and kissed her sister's

cheek. As she went around the curtain, she saw all the others standing there, their faces distraught. Crying, Marnie kissed each of them,
and they clung to her, sobbing. Then she went in to see her father. He
was still in bed, unshaven, his hair tousled. His cheeks were wet. She
leaned over him, and his arm bumped against her waist as he tried to
hug her. "Good-bye, Papa," she whispered. Then she ran down the
stairs, picked up her basket from the kitchen table, and left.

It was evening when they got back. It had been a slow journey, and
Marnie had been sick once, from the jolting of the wagon. Her head
ached intolerably, but it was not as bad as the agony in her heart.
With his usual intuition Raven understood, and when she moved
closer to him on the wagon and rested her head on his shoulder, he
bent his head against hers as if he shared her pain.

At home Marnie got down at the cottage door, and Raven took
the horse under the trees to tend to it and unhitch the wagon. But
another horse was already there. Raven gave a cry and raced into the
cottage.

The house was a shambles. Everything had been cleared from the
alcoves and window ledges, jars were emptied, boxes opened, and the
two chests and Isake's toolbox had been ransacked, their contents
strewn. Even the bed had been searched, the blankets thrown against
the wall and the straw scattered across the floor. Marnie was standing
by the table, her face full of defiance and rage. And standing by the
fireplace, leaning on the mantelpiece and smiling a little, was Pierce
Isherwood.

In a single stride, Raven was beside Marnie. *Will I get Father
Brannan?* he asked.

Marnie shook her head. She said to Pierce, "Get out of my house.
You have no right to be on my land, or in my house. Get out."

Pierce laughed. "That's a warm and friendly greeting, sister-in-
law! And I'm begging your pardon, but this is *my* property, and I may
be here if I wish." He took a bowl from her mantelpiece and emptied

the contents into his hand. They were the little pebbles Marnie used to get Raven's attention if he was across the room.

"You have no right!" said Marnie furiously.

Raven tapped her arm, wanting her to explain what was being said, but she ignored him and went on, to Pierce, "Father Brannan told me the laws of the land. This is my house. There was no will that said otherwise. That's the law, and you can't argue with it, not you nor all your fine judge friends."

The humor died on Pierce's face. "You're a stiff-necked woman, to be sure," he said. "I see there's no way but for me to buy this place."

"I'm not selling."

"Well now, that's a rash decision to make, since you don't know what I'll pay." He put the pebbles back in the bowl, replaced it, and picked up a jar.

"You can offer all the gold in the world, and I won't take it," Marnie said.

Raven tapped her arm again, and she shook him off, signing without speaking: *Stop touching me! I'll tell you after.* She said to Pierce: "Leave my things alone! Do you be looking for something?"

"Aye. A bit of justice," said Pierce angrily, peering into the empty jar and putting it back.

Raven tried to get Marnie's attention again, banging the table hard with his knuckles, and she slapped his wrists. Angry and hurt, he went and leaned in the open doorway, looking at the sea, but often glancing behind him.

"I'm taking this house, Marnie," Pierce was saying, his face hard and inexorable. "Will you let it go peaceably, or will you make me fight you for it?"

"I'll fight you to the death, sir."

In the dimness, Pierce's teeth glimmered. "It just might come to that. I've heard rumors in Torcurra. They say you confessed to murder."

"They heard me say something to Father Brannan. It was none of their business. Nor yours."

"It is my business, if you murdered my brother. Even if it was by speaking a spell."

"I didn't murder him, not by a spell nor any other way."

"Then why did you tell the priest you did?"

"I never confessed to murder. Isake fell from the roof while he was mending the thatch. That's the truth, and Father Brannan will tell you that."

"It seems to me that your Father Brannan will say anything you want him to say. It's not proper, the way he stands up for you against the whole village. He even holds meetings with the women, telling them that your mad friend there doesn't have devils at all, but is deaf, and those magic signs you use are only words made with your hands. He does a powerful lot, that priest, to defend your crafty ways. But he isn't the only one those village fools look up to, now that I'm here. Be very careful, Marnie. You say you'll fight me to the death, over this house. If it does come to such a fight, I know exactly how I'll win."

Pierce picked up his cloak from where he had left it on the back of a chair, and walked out the door, almost knocking Raven over as he passed. On the step Pierce turned around, his lips curved, though his eyes were cold. "Keep spinning words with those pretty hands of yours," he said, "and in the end you'll spin a rope to hang yourself."

Chapter 21

LAUGHING, **MARNIE** raced Raven up
the last hill, and stood, staggering, at the top,
her hands on her knees, her head bent as she
tried to get her breath. He was already there,
exultant because he had won, as usual.

I know why you are all times first, said Marnie,
standing up and wiping the sweat from her face.
You are big, and more strong than me, and more ugly.

Not ugly, he signed, grinning.

Marnie looked at him standing there with
the late summer sun in his eyes, his tunic and
shirt undone, his body tanned and muscled
from rowing around the cove; and she looked
away again, her cheeks pink not only from the
run. *No, you are not ugly,* she said. *Now show me
your cave, that I came all this way to see.*

A short way ahead stood a strange group of
gigantic stones, unnaturally straight and
orderly, marking the end of a long grassy
mound in the earth. Marnie hesitated, but
Raven took her hand and led her over to them.

The stones were twice Marnie's height, and
seemed at first to make up a solid wall. But
Raven squeezed through a small gap between

the last two, and Marnie followed. They went around several rocks and down dirt steps, and suddenly Marnie found herself facing an entrance to an underground tomb. It was lined on the walls and roof by huge stones, all placed there untold centuries ago. In the semidark Marnie glimpsed ghostly passages, low-roofed chambers, and secret crypts. She backed away, afraid.

It is where I sleep, said Raven.

It is where dead people sleep, she said.

Raven went into the first chamber, and Marnie followed cautiously, hardly breathing in the musty air, and gripping Raven's sleeve. The tomb was lined completely with massive stones, each shaped to fit the stone next to it. Some were pillars holding up the roof; some formed shallow recesses, while others made separate chambers where ancient chieftains were long ago interred. In a deep ledge was a moldy blanket, a broken bowl, a few gnawed bones, and several dirty cloths that perhaps had once enfolded food. Beyond the chambers the stones receded into the dark, so deep in the earth she could not see the end of them.

It is far inside, Raven said. *I stay here, near the sun and moon. Far inside, dead people sleep.*

Are you not afraid about them?

Why? They don't hurt me, not like other people.

Did you all times stay here?

In the rain I stayed here, said Raven. *And in the bad cold, when . . .* he hesitated, then made light fluttering movements downward with his hands, like snow falling. Then he went on, *Sometimes I stayed with Father Brannan.*

In the warm times, Marnie said, *did you sleep outside, in the fields?*

In the warm times, I stayed in your house. Many times I stayed in your house, before you came.

In my house? She looked surprised, and Raven grinned.

It was my house, before it was your house, he said.

It is all the time yours, Raven. Yours, and mine.

They sat in the sunny grass outside the burial chamber, facing the hills and the distant ocean. They could just see the cove, and the tops of the trees that stood beside their cottage. Marnie searched the hill on the far side, in case a figure walked there; but there was no one. Though two full moons had come and gone since that disastrous day she had returned from Fernleigh and found Pierce Isherwood in her home, she still feared him. She noticed heavy clouds rolling in over the sea, their shadows racing across the water toward the land. It would be a while yet, before the sunlight left the hills.

She lay on her back, thinking of Raven and the loneliness of his ancient sanctuary. *Tell me about your days, before I came,* she said.

Raven lay next to her, his shoulder touching hers, his hands dark and eloquent against the blazing sky. Marnie turned her head to watch, so that when his signs involved touching his own face or the upper part of his body, she could see them properly. Always now, when he made hand-words, he whispered, or semi-spoke, and the sounds were almost the beginnings of speech. "Far Brairn," he said, for Father Brannan.

When I was little, he said, *I was all the time hungry. Father Brannan gave me food, gave me sleep in his house. I don't know why I went away from his house and came here to my hole. He hit me, maybe, but not bad like the village people. Many times I stayed outside, in my hole here. I like being here, more at night, with stars and moon. The moon is a much beautiful thing. But under the moon I get hungry. In hungry times, I go and watch the houses in the village. The people get food, and laugh, are warm. I want to be with them. Alone is not good. Alone hurts. Alone is hungry and cold. When the people are outside in their boats or gardens, I go in their houses, get food. The people get me, and are angry. All the time their mouths open, shut, open, shut, like a fish outside water. All people have mouths like fish. I make fish faces the same, but I am bad. They are afraid about me, and I get angry, because I do only what they do. They are stupid. My anger, it is big like the rain and wind. In Father Brannan's house I am angry. He is angry. And he is stupid, makes fish faces too. I break things. Many things. And in different houses, sometimes. The people whip me. After, my angry feelings go, and I hurt. Many times, they whip me. After, Father Brannan washes me and gives me food. I come back here to my hole. Alone, I cry. Why? Why?*

Marnie sat up so he could clearly see her hands. *You feel that people are stupid when they open and shut their mouths?* she asked.

Raven nodded. *Very stupid. I do it, and they whip me. They are stupid, all them.*

When people open and shut their mouths, she said, *they make . . .* She hesitated, trying to think of a way to explain sound. Putting a fist to her right ear, she flicked her hand violently outward, all her fingers spread. "Sound," she said, as she did it.

Raven sat up, bewildered, suspecting a joke. *What?* he asked, repeating the sign for sound.

She took his right hand, and pressed his palm against her throat. "Sound," she said aloud, at the same time making the new hand-word by her ear. She spoke aloud again, her hand over Raven's, so he could feel the vibrations of the sound under her skin. Then she placed his hand on his own throat, and said, "Talk, Raven. Say something."

He shook his head, angry. *Make hand-words,* he signed. *Not the stupid fish face. I don't like that.*

It's not stupid, she said, using hand-words and her voice. She made the sign for sound again, and made him hold his palm flat against her throat, while she talked.

Do you feel . . . she began, and shook her hand slightly, like a trembling. *Do you feel that, in my neck?*

He nodded.

She put his hand on his own throat again, and talked to him aloud. He mimicked her, feeling the vibrations, annoyed because they made no sense.

You are making sound, she said. *That sound makes words in my ear.*

You are stupid! he signed. *Words are with the hands.*

Only with you, she said. *Only with you, and with me. All other people make words with their mouths. That is what they do, when they open and shut their mouths. They make a sound, make words. Like our hand-words, but different.*

Keeping her hands still, she said to him, clearly, so he could read her lips, "People make words with their mouths. They say words about work, about food, words about Father Brannan, words about you, me—"

Make good words to me! he signed, picking up her hands. He was upset, confused.

I am making good words, she signed, speaking as well. *I am making words about work, about food, and Father Brannan, and you and me. All people make sounds when they make fish faces. They don't have hand-words, like you. They don't have to see the words. They can hear.* She put a hand behind her ear, as if listening carefully, to signify hearing. *They can hear the sounds their mouths make when they open and shut. That is why they don't make words with their hands, only their mouths. But you are different. You can't hear the sounds. You have to see the words made with hands.*

Stunned, Raven shook his head. A bitter wind had sprung up, and it dashed his hair across his face. *I am the same like other people!* he said, his hand movements swift and furious. *The same!*

No. You are different.

The same! He leaped up and stormed off down the hill. Marnie ran after him, saw that he was crying, and tried to take his arm. He shook her off. She ran to keep up with him, signing, trying to explain, but he slapped at her hands, breaking the talk he did not want to know.

"I want to talk to you!" she shouted. They both were shaking, their faces and hands blue with the cold.

Go away! he signed. *You are like the whip on my back.*

He ran on, and she stared after him, anguished.

Above the sea huge clouds were banking up, and the sun vanished, and a violent wind was lashing the waves to white.

Raven flung open the door of the cottage, and went inside. A bowl on the table contained the last sweet-scented flowers of summer, and he swept it off, smashing the bowl on the hearth. Father Brannan's cross was on the table too, and he picked it up and flung it across the room. A cold wind blew in, and he slammed the door shut, then leaned against it, panting, his head in his hands. After a while he picked up the scattered flowers, putting them in another bowl. He was still picking up the pieces of the broken bowl when Marnie came in, carrying the clothes that had been drying on the trees. She dropped them onto the bed, and began folding them.

Raven touched her arm, and she stopped and looked at him. *Why do they whip me?* he asked. *Because I'm stupid?*

Marnie put down the shirt she was folding, and faced him. *You are not stupid,* she said. *You are no times stupid. You are different. When you try to make words with your mouth, when you make the fish faces, you say things people don't know.*

Stupid things?

No. Your things. Different sounds, not words. People are afraid. They are afraid about people who are different.

He turned away, leaning on the window ledge, looking at the sea. Marnie finished folding the clothes, put them away, then started the fire again. She looked for some potatoes to prepare a meal, and noticed their supplies were low. Soon she would have to go and see Father Brannan, and beg for food. Standing at the table, she began to prepare the vegetables. Raven turned around, rapping the opposite edge of the table to attract her attention, and she looked up to watch his words.

You are different, he said. *Are they afraid about you?*

Why am I different?

In Torcurra the people work together, fishing, looking after their gardens, fixing their nets or their boats. Their mouths make words, they are happy, laughing. All times they work two or three, maybe more, together. You are alone. You stay away from people. The man Pierce, the Torcurra people, all are angry with you. They don't come here to see you, only Father Brannan. And your mother, she is angry with you. You are like me. Different. Alone.

༺༻

Sherryl Jordan
178

His face was tender, sad, and Marnie looked down at the potato in her hands, and did not speak. Raven took the potato from her, putting it down on the table with the knife. Gently he touched her cheek, sliding his fingers down under her chin, and lifting her face so he could see her eyes.

"Ah, Marn," he said, with his voice. It was the first time he had spoken her name, and Marnie was so moved, she turned her face toward his hand, and kissed his palm.

A gust of wind forced the door open, swinging it back hard against the wall. Marnie rushed to close it. At that moment lightning flashed, so intense it struck everything it touched with lurid blue, and made the shadows purple. Thunder crashed, shaking the ground. The skies were livid.

The chickens! Marnie cried. *They must come in here with us. Them, and the goat. It's not good that they are outside. They will maybe get hurt.*

Raven nodded. *You stay here. I'll get them,* he said, and ran out. Lightning ripped across the skies again, and thunder boomed. And then came the rain, falling in solid sheets across the cove, streaming down over the cottage roof, and hissing on the ground outside. It seemed as if the very heavens cracked open, and floodwaters from another world were poured out upon the earth.

The cottage grew dark, and Marnie lit a candle and placed it on the table, then looked out one of the tiny windows. Raven was battling the wind down on the beach, his clothes thrashed to his skin by the wind and driving rain, as he pulled the boat to higher ground and turned it upside down so it would not fill with water. Then he moved the horse, tethering it close to the wall of the house, in the side sheltered from the storm. He spent a long time looking for the hens. Eventually he came in, saturated and blue with the cold, but with only one hen. *I see two more,* he said, *stupid and afraid, hard to catch.*

You must get them, and the goat, she demanded.

Sighing, he went out again. At last the goat was safely in the house, and three of the five hens.

I can't find the last two chickens, Raven told her, shivering, water flying off his fingers as he talked, his feet making puddles on the floor between the stones.

Go and look again! Marnie said. *Maybe they are hurt. If you won't look, I will.*

Muttering strange noises Marnie clearly guessed the meaning of, Raven went outside again. While he was out, Marnie began cooking their midday meal, putting the last of their precious bacon in a pan over the embers, with slices of potatoes.

Suddenly there was a crack outside above the roof, and the sound of something crashing over the house. Stones and grit and ancient mortar poured down the chimney and across the hearth, falling into the food, and filling the house with smoke. The hens flapped wildly, and the goat bleated in terror. Marnie leaped back from the fireplace, hot soot and ashes scattered across her bare feet. She rushed to the bucket of water by the door, and poured it over her burns. Raven burst in, almost knocking her over as he flung open the door. His face was pale, and he shivered from cold and fright.

You hurt? he asked.

My feet, she replied, and put down the bucket. Raven helped her to a chair. They both were coughing in the smoke, and already their faces were covered with a dusting of soot and ash. The tops of Marnie's feet were scorched, and Raven ran to fill the bucket again from the stream. He put a large bowl under her feet, and gently ran the cold water over them, again and again, to stop the burning.

Sobbing quietly with pain, Marnie looked through the settling dust at the devastation in the fireplace. The fire had been almost extinguished by the broken chimney stones that had fallen into it. Debris was scattered over the hearth and across the floor—bits of ancient blackened nests, shattered stones, embers still red-hot, and fragments of old mortar. Much of it had fallen in the cauldron, which fortunately had been almost empty. The frying pan lay lopsided in the ashes, the food ruined. Most of the soot swirling in the house went out the windows, or back up the chimney, and Marnie was thankful that at least the chimney was not blocked. If anything, it worked better for the clean-out.

Raven explained what he had seen from outside. *The high thing,* he said, meaning the chimney, *a tree came down over it. It's broke.*

All broke? Marnie asked.

This many, on top. He indicated a piece as long as his forearm.

All the tree came down? she asked, worrying about the thatch.

No. It broke, hit the high thing, and went on the grass.

Going over to the hearth, he picked the frying pan out of the ashes, and tried to take the stones and grit out of the bacon. *I'll wash it in the stream,* he said.

Will you get more water in the bucket, please, she asked.

He went out again into the pouring rain, and Marnie hitched up her skirts so they did not drag on her burns and, limping, began to sweep the floor and hearth. When Raven came in he made her sit down again, and cleaned the hearth himself. Suddenly he gave a surprised cry, picked something out of the debris, and took it over to Marnie. She polished it on her skirt, and discovered that it was a ring, very large and ornate, with several pieces of colored glass clutched in blackened claws. It was ugly, gaudy, the kind of bauble that Gypsies sold for a penny to eager children.

Marnie dropped the ring in her lap, and said to Raven, *Sometimes the black and white birds, they take things from houses, and hide them in their nests. When the nest came down, this came with it.*

What is it? he asked.

A child's plaything. It's not beautiful.

Can I have it?

She gave it to him, and he tried to put it on. It was too big, so he put it in an alcove by the fireplace, and went on with the cleaning. When it was done he got the fire going again, and put the washed bacon on to finish frying. He looked like a chimney sweep, his wet face and clothes grimy with soot. He took the soap outside and washed in the stream, stripping off his clothes and washing them too in the swift waters. Afterward he briefly looked again for the missing hens, but could not find them. Naked, and shivering so much that his teeth clattered, he went back inside, dropping his clothes in a pile just inside the door. Marnie was sitting in her chair, but she had put the bowls away, and there was a towel warming for Raven by the fire. Beside it were dry clothes from Isake's chest. Marnie sat with her eyes lowered while Raven dressed, though he never seemed to care whether or not she watched.

The cottage filled again with the tantalizing aroma of bacon, and Raven hung a fresh pot of water over the fire, for tea. When he was dry and dressed, he knelt on the floor in front of Marnie, and took her feet in his hands. They were blistering, but the burns were clean, the skin unbroken. With great care he patted them dry with his towel, making sure they were clean. At her instruction, he got the oil from her chest, and spread some gently on her burns. Then he crouched in front of her, his arms across her lap, and signed, *Do you want me to get you warm water, and you can wash? Your face is black, your hair is like an old woman's, from the dirt.*

Smiling, she nodded. *Thank you. I will wash my face and hands. Tomorrow I'll go outside and wash all over in the rain, like you.*

Your feet, they hurt bad?

Yes.

What can I do, to stop your hurt?

Nothing more, she said. *You do everything, and you make me all right. Thank you.*

Very gently, he touched her sooty cheek. *If there was a way,* he said, *I'd take your hurt, and carry it for you.*

The next day Marnie woke to the homely sounds of Raven building up the fire and making a drink. The smoke from the peat was fragrant, earth-sweet, the room warm. Raven's blankets were tidily folded in one corner. The hens clucked softly under the table, where he had scattered grain for them, and the goat was bleating plaintively by the door. It had gnawed on Raven's blankets in the night, so he had tethered it to the door latch where it could do no damage.

Outside, the tempest was worse, the wind a screaming gale. The waves pounded the beach, their crests streaming spray like tattered mist, their white fingers clawing at the very edges of the grass. Marnie got out of bed, wrapped a blanket about herself, and watched from her tiny window.

The sea, she asked anxiously, *will it come and take our house?*

Laughing a little, Raven gave her a cup of marigold tea. *The sea will no time come to your house,* he said. He leaned on the deep window ledge beside her, marveling at the fury outside, his face alight as if he exulted in it. Marnie tried to imagine what it was like for him, seeing the violence but hearing nothing. Surely half the world was lost to him.

She put down her cup and touched his arm. *The sea,* she said, *it makes sound. A huge sound, when it comes over the beach.*

Raven looked stunned. *What sound?*

Huge. I can't hear my mouth-words, when the sea and wind make their huge sound. Seabirds make sound; high, hard sound. My chickens make sound; soft, low sound.

Your chickens are not high in the sky, like seabirds, Raven said. *That is why their sound is low. It's on the dirt.*

Marnie half laughed, and shook her head. *It's different.*

Why?

I have no more words. Sorry.

Later in the day the wind dropped, but the rain did not abate. The pain in Marnie's burned feet eased, and she felt better, though she wanted to wash, and to use the lavatory hole under the trees. To Raven's amusement she limped outside wearing only her white shift, taking the soap with her, and washed her gritty hair in the heavy rain. Raven went out too, wearing nothing, and did a crazy dance in the edge of the foaming sea. He signed to Marnie to come into the water with him, but she stood with her hair plastered across her face, laughing too much to move, and pretending she was not looking.

Suddenly he raced over to her, swept her up in his arms, and carried her, screaming and laughing and struggling, down to the sea. He strode out into the edge of the breakers, and Marnie shut her eyes in terror, her arms clutched about his neck. Foam and spray flew all around, and the water surged about Raven's waist, flowing over Marnie's body to her shoulders. To her astonishment, the sea was warmer than the wind, its foam soft and bubbling, like apple cider. Raven danced with her, holding her firmly, the waves swirling and eddying about them. Feeling braver, Marnie opened her eyes, but when she saw the sea rolling toward her, white and thundering, she quickly shut them again, and pressed her face into Raven's neck. Her arms were so tight about him, he was almost choked, and they both were laughing, jubilant.

He carried her back to the house, not putting her down until they were by the fire. She stood shivering in the smoky warm, awkward, her face averted, too aware of his nakedness, of her thin shift plastered to her skin, of the overwhelming closeness of him.

Raven lifted his hand and touched her chin, turning her head so she looked at him. He was breathing hard, exhilarated, his face dripping with the water that ran from his hair, his long black lashes wet from the rain and sea. He was no longer the starving boy she had met on the beach outside the alehouse at Torcurra; he was a young man, strong and compelling. His beard was deeper, soft; and the duskiness of it, with his sleek hair and straight black brows, made his violet-gray eyes more vivid, more full of light. He was all shining, pure and unflawed. His hand moved on her face, caressing her, stroking the water from her skin, smoothing back her tangled hair. She was trembling, her eyes not meeting his. He moved his hand down, his fingers gentle on her throat, and slow across her wet clothes, across her breasts.

You are moon-good beautiful, he signed.

Briefly her eyes met his, and he saw the wariness there, the longing mixed with fear. He touched her again, and she shook her head and turned away. Confused and wanting, he took hold of her wrist. He did not mean to grip her hard, but when she tried to move away he held her more tightly. Suddenly she pulled free, turning on him, afraid and fierce. "Don't hold me!" she shouted.

Devastated, Raven stared at her. She stared back, as shocked as he was, realizing what she had done.

I'm sorry, she said, trembling. *I'm sorry, Raven.*

Raven picked up the towel he had used earlier and began drying himself. He faced the corner where he slept, as was the custom when he and Marnie were dressing or having a wash.

Sick with regret, Marnie found another towel and got dried and dressed, then sat on her stool by the hearth, dreading the sound of Raven walking out. But when he was dressed he came and sat with her, on the other side of the fire.

Why are you afraid about me? he asked, close to tears. *I see it in your eyes, in all you. It hurts me. I will no time hurt you. Are you afraid because I'm different, because I can't make mouth-words the way you do? Don't you like me? Am I stupid? Ugly? Am I bad?*

No. There is nothing bad about you, Raven. I know you will no time hurt me, but I am . . . Not afraid; that word is too strong. There are other words, but I don't know how to say them with my hands. I'm sorry. Maybe I'm stupid.

He smiled, though his gray eyes were solemn, and gentle on her.

Not stupid, he said. *I know the word.* Slowly, he put his hand over his face, his fingers slightly spread, so he could just look through. *Not bad afraid,* he said. *Soft-afraid. Like a little bird when I hold out food to it. It wants to come, and it wants to fly away. Soft-afraid.*

Marnie gazed into the fire, away from the look in his eyes.

A good word, she signed.

Chapter 22

FATHER BRANNAN STOOD with the other people of the village, gazing up at the tree leaning against the church wall, and the broken stained-glass window behind the battered branches. Beyond the fallen tree and the church roof, an insipid sun gleamed through vaporous clouds. The fisherfolk were somber, clutching their ragged cloaks and shawls close against the wind, their faces white and drawn.

"'Tis a fair bit of damage, all right," said the man nearest the priest. "And it were the pride of our church, that window."

"The pride of a church is its cross, Reilly," replied Father Brannan, pushing his cold hands further into his thick sleeves. "Though I must admit the window was a wondrous thing, as well."

"We'll never replace it, not with most of our boats needing mending, and all," said a woman, holding a little boy close in her patched skirts to keep him warm. "Our money won't stretch every which way, but we'll be helping all we can, father."

"We can put an ordinary window in its

place," said Father Brannan. "The colored glass was pleasing to the eye, but it wasn't vital in the saving of our souls. Nor as vital as mended fishing boats, in the saving of our bodies."

The group was joined by a man wearing a fashionable knee-length tunic, finely woven leggings, and costly boots. He sauntered over and stared up at the broken window.

"You're lucky the church wall wasn't damaged, as well," he remarked.

"Luck had nothing to do with it, Sir Isherwood," said Father Brannan, sharply. "The Almighty's quite capable of telling a tree where to fall."

"He should have made it fall the other way, then," said Pierce.

"Not if he wasn't particularly pleased with the window," returned the priest.

"He took a mighty long time making up his mind about it," muttered an old fisherman. "That window was there when my father's father were a weanling. It would be a great pity not to replace it. And it were lovely, the way the colors from it spread across our heads when we was praying, like light from heaven itself."

"Well, we've got no money for it," said a young mother with three children tugging at her skirts. "That window must have cost a king's fortune. We'll never afford another."

Pierce said, very softly, "I have a liking for old churches such as this. And I would like a fit memorial for my brother, in the village where he died. If I paid for the making of a new window, would you carve into the stone underneath, that it is in memory of Isake Isherwood?"

He looked at Father Brannan, waiting for an answer, but the priest was gazing up at the tree, frowning, as if he had not heard.

"That is a very generous and Christian thing you offer, Sir Isherwood," said one of the men, impressed. "And we would all be forever grateful to you, sir."

"Well, we shall have to pray about the matter," said Father Brannan gruffly. "In the meanwhile there's a tree must be cut up, and the wood given to those who need it for repairs. There'll be five days work in it, and I can't be doing it alone. Who'll help?"

Several youths said they would. And then Pierce Isherwood said, casually, "I'd like to help, if I may. I've a strong horse, and a good wagon. I could deliver the wood to those who need it. And I've a sharp ax I know how to use."

"But you're a lord, sir!" cried one of the elderly men.

"That's of no account," said Pierce, with an engaging smile. "I'm a visitor here, and I share your misfortunes and your work. I wouldn't be much help mending your boats, since I've no skill at putting wood together; but I'm a fair hand at chopping it up."

"Your brother was a carpenter, wasn't he?"

"Aye, he was the clever one at putting things together."

"It was a terrible thing, his death," murmured an old woman. "We were awful shocked, considering the circumstances, and all. It would be fitting to have a window dedicated to his name, to make up for it in a way."

"Well, I suppose he died doing what he loved best—mending things," said Pierce, his face suddenly sorrowful, though he still had a gentle smile. "It was a sad accident, seeing as he was not really old."

"Accident, was it?" said a man bitterly. "There's some of us have a different word for it."

At that moment Marnie and Raven came around the church corner. Unaware at first of the villagers gathered about, they smiled together and sometimes laughed, their dark heads bent close. As they walked they talked with their hands, and to the watchful village folk the signs seemed strange and mystical. But stranger still was the madman's transformation.

"Lord a'mercy!" breathed an old woman. "'Tis Raver, clean and mild and manly, and with all his demons gone!"

Noticing the village folk, Marnie and Raven stopped. Firmly holding Raven's hand, and ignoring the stares and sudden hush, Marnie went over to Father Brannan. "Good morning, father," she said.

"Good morning, Marnie," he replied, smiling, though his blue eyes were apprehensive. "As you see, we've had a mishap at the church."

She glanced up at the broken window, then turned to Raven. *Give Father Brannan the gold,* she said, speaking aloud as well. Gold was the only word they had for money, and Raven gave two copper coins to the priest. Seeing the mysterious signs again, and the way Raven obeyed, meek as a lamb, the astounded villagers began murmuring.

"I'm sorry to see the window like that, father," Marnie said. "We came to buy some food from you, but I'll go without a bit so you can have a coin to help with the church's mending."

"We don't want your money in it!" shouted a man.

"Her money's as good as yours," said Father Brannan. "And I'd be careful what else I'd say about it, since the money came in the first place from the estate of Sir Isherwood, here."

Marnie noticed the man Pierce, and her face went hard.

"Good morning, sister-in-law," he said cheerfully. "Did you get through the storm all right, in that worthy little house?"

"Aye, sir, I did," she replied coldly.

"So did I," he said, his eyes amused. "I'm renting the cottage that belonged to Widow Orley until my business here is finished. It's as well I am here; they need all hands to mend the damage from the storm."

Marnie turned to Father Brannan again. "If you're not too busy, father," she said, "I'd like some bread and flour, and some more candles, please."

"You should be lighting candles in the church, not in your wicked house!" shouted a man. "You should be lighting them for that poor soul you did away with!"

Father Brannan strode over to the man and hit him so hard he stumbled and fell. As the man lay on the ground fingering the bruise on his jaw, Father Brannan said, very quiet but so all could hear, "I'll not tolerate that talk. Old Finian's witness was very clear: The death scene showed it was an accident, beyond doubt. There's two of us testify to that."

"Aye—'tis true!" cried Finian, stepping forward. "I saw the man's corpse, and I'll swear it was an accident what killed him! I saw the roof all broke, and the straw all over the place, like he had clutched wildlike at it, to stop himself from tumbling down! I saw!"

"Finian's witness is true, before God and man," said Father Brannan. "I'll swear on my very soul that there was no curse that made Isake Isherwood die. And if I hear one more word of doubt, I'll break the head of the fool who speaks it."

Pierce Isherwood watched and listened, his black eyes narrowed, his face inscrutable.

Uncertain, wary, the village folk stared as Raven's hands made their curious signs again, and Marnie's hands replied. The air between them seemed alive, potent, filled with supernatural understandings and magical communion. Then the priest touched Raven's arm, and took him and the widow over to his house.

One old woman made the sign of the cross, and stared after them with streaming eyes. "I think I've seen a miracle!" she whispered. "It was Raver himself, a proper gentleman!"

"You're a fool, Mother Mor," said another woman harshly. "That's no miracle. It's uncanny, what she's done. You saw their hands. He's bewitched. She's working a power on him—and on us too, most like. We shouldn't be seeing things like that, lest *our* hands start a-twitching too."

Several people furtively slid their hands in their pockets, or put them in their armpits, pretending to warm them. Some of the mothers hurried their children away, back to the safety of their homes. Finian took his wife's arm and went away, shaking his head. Those remaining started to talk, and Pierce Isherwood listened, a smile beginning to curl his lips.

One of the men remembered he was there, and said, "You've lived here a while now, sir, and doubtless you've heard about your brother's widow, and how she admitted it was her fault that your poor brother met an untimely end. As you see, Father Brannan has taken it upon himself to overlook the matter, saying we're all sorely mistook, and it weren't murder at all; but it does bother the souls of simple folks like ourselves, seeing as three of our number heard her confess with their own ears. Will you be taking the matter further, sir?"

Pierce said nothing for a while, just stood frowning and thoughtful, as if more important things than murder were being considered in his head. At last he murmured, "Aye, it is worrying; but I'll not be doing anything about it. Old Finian is not a fool, and I accept his word on the matter." He hesitated, looking deeply troubled. Slowly he added, "To tell the truth, I'm more concerned about your village, and about you gentle folks."

"Why, sir?" asked a woman. "It's not us she's got, but Raver."

"It's not that simple, good mother," said Pierce, measuring his words carefully, as if reluctant to speak.

"Well, tell us what's on your mind, sir, seeing as we respect a lord," urged one of the men.

"I'm not one to spread alarm," said Pierce very softly, and the wind, blowing about his breathless audience, spread his words like wildfire in parched wheat. "In truth, it is your priest who should be warning you, but I fear he may be trapped in it too, and blinded. It's wisest, I think, not to speak of it to him, for it will only make him defend her more. But the words must be spoke; and though I'm loathe that they should come from me, you have a right to hear them."

He hesitated again, and a woman prompted him, her voice eager and dreading, "A right to hear what, sir?"

"I fear there's worse than murder, crawling in this place," said Pierce, his tones hushed. "I've seen this thing before, its evil shadow creeping over folks as pure and reverent as yourselves. You saw her talking with her fingers, spinning words in thin air, that only the madman could hear. It isn't just a simple skill that comes from out her hands, and weaves that power between her and her paramour. It's something far worse, something devilish and shameful and mortal dangerous."

They waited, hanging on his every word, and he looked around about them all, his dark eyes grave and full of warning, as he told them, whispering, "'Tis witchcraft."

Chapter 23

MARNIE OPENED THE leather case that was Isake's, took out a quill and the bottle of ink, and placed them beside the clean sheets of parchment. On the table nearby, propped up against a jar of salt, was the sheet of names Father Brannan had written for her. She took the lid off the ink, placed a blank page in front of her, and moved the candle so the light shone on it and on the page of Father Brannan's. For a long time she studied his writing, comparing the roundness of the letters and the angles of the strokes. Carefully, as if taking part in a holy ritual, she dipped the quill in the ink, wiping off the excess ink the way she had seen the priest do, and with breath held and her hand shaking a little, she wrote the first letter of her name. Then she put down the pen and sat back to study the result.

The letter was wobbly, without the flourish and smooth flow of Father Brannan's script, but it was passable. Satisfied, she picked up the sheet and blew the ink dry. She put the parchment down again and was about to take up the pen, when she heard a noise outside. Lifting her head, she listened, wondering if it was Raven back. He had been gone two days. She glanced out the window, and saw the sky full of stars. It would be a full moon tonight. He seldom stayed in their house when the moon was full; it was his favorite time for the fields and the wildness of his other life.

The noises came again, and the horse whinnied, disturbed. Marnie got up and peered out her window. The beach was deserted. She drew the bolt across the door, then sat down again. For several minutes she sat listening, then shook her head and picked up the pen. Three more times she wrote the letter *M*, each time improving it. Again she heard noises. It was someone down on the beach, dragging something heavy along the sand.

Foreboding swept over Marnie, and she forced herself to go again and peer out the window. But it was only Raven pulling their boat higher on the beach, away from the tide. Obviously Marnie had not brought it high enough herself, when she came back from fishing that afternoon. Breathing easily once more, smiling at her needless fear, she removed the bolt and went and sat at the table again.

Raven came in shortly after, making quiet, joyful noises to himself. Pulling up a stool close to her chair, he leaned his elbows on the table and looked at what she had done. There was never any greeting from him, or explanation of where he had been; always he picked up life with her as if only moments had passed since they were last together.

Yours? he signed, indicating the letters she had made. He was shivering, and his bare feet, touching hers under the table, were like ice.

I'm showing myself how to make parchment-words, she said. *One day I'll ask Father Brannan to show me how to make all the words, not only these.*

Why?

Because I want to know.

Why?

All times, why? Why? Why? It is Raven's favorite word.

He smiled, his eyes warm and brilliant in the candlelight. *Marnie is my favorite word,* he said.

She bent over her writing again, her hair covering her face.

Raven touched her wrist, so she would watch his hands. *It is huge beautiful out there*, he said. *I'm going to my far house, where the big stones be.*

To your hole?

No. To different stones, where I dance. Will you come with me?

Now?

Now is the most better time, with the moon big.

I'd like to come, she said. *Do you want to eat, first?*

We can eat and walk, same time. I want to be there before the sun.

Quickly, Marnie cut some bread, putting thick wedges of cold cooked bacon and cheese between the slices, and wrapped some cold baked potatoes in a cloth. Then she got her cloak, and Isake's fur-lined cloak for Raven. It was nearly autumn now, and the nights were chilly. Raven blew out the candle and made sure the fire was safe, and they left.

The path Raven took up the mountain was steep and narrow, winding between huge rugged stones wreathed in mist. Marnie breathed hard, her breath white in the darkness. Raven walked just ahead of her, his strides long and sure, Isake's heavy cloak slung over his shoulder. Marnie hurried to keep up with him, struggling to see rabbit holes and stinging nettles, too afraid to look at the shadowy rocks around. She was not used to walking in the dark. Raven was the only person she knew who willingly walked at night, unafraid of fairy folk or witches or the walking dead. Once she did dare to look behind her, and glimpsed a shadow melting into mist. Sensing her fear, Raven waited for her and took her hand, and they ascended the last hill together.

Beyond them stretched a great valley. In the center of it was a circular embankment, worn low by wind and time; and inside, on the plain of moon-drenched grass, stood a circle of stones.

Hand in hand, Raven and Marnie walked down into the valley and onto the sacred place. As they neared the stones, Marnie's footsteps slowed. Like ancient sentinels, the stones leaned dark and overpowering against the wheeling stars. The air seemed alive, the shining silence still ringing with the songs of bygone worshipers. Marnie shivered, remembering the warnings she had heard about these places; warnings of heathen gods, spirit forces, and forbidden rites. But Raven embraced the stones, stroking them, sensing their primal force. After a while he removed his clothes and began to dance.

Standing in the heart of the stone circle, he turned slowly, his head back and his eyes closed, his arms uplifted. He was singing in that husky voice of his, words and songs only he knew, his hands describing signs toward the stars. Rising between the stones behind him was the moon, thin like a slice of white melon, perfectly round and luminous. Its brightness spilled across the grass between the shadows of the stones, turning the earth blue and striking Raven's body with pure light. He danced in its silver silence, transfigured. Sometimes he cried out, almost words that Marnie imagined she caught the meaning of; but mostly he just made his hand signs, graceful and wide so the moon could see.

Marnie watched him, her eyes wet. Longing for lost innocence, for that oneness with the perfect earth, she yearned to dance as Raven danced—as surely Adam and Eve had danced—in newborn Eden.

"Marn," Raven said, smiling at her across the grass. His hands made the words: *Dance with me, in the stones.*

Shyly, she shook her head.

Why? he signed, coming over to her.

I don't know how, she said.

I'll show you. It's not hard.

Gently he removed her cloak, dropping it on the grass, then knelt and unbound her shoes. She was trembling, her eyes downcast. Slowly he unlaced the front of her dress and untied her belt, and the heavy folds slid down her to the ground. Shaking, she felt his fingers undoing the ties on the front of her shift. For a few moments she let him; then she shook her head, and he stopped. Taking her hands, he drew her toward the center of the stone ring. *I'll dance, you dance the same,* he said.

With joy, uninhibited and spontaneous, he lifted his arms again to the skies.

Hesitantly, Marnie raised her hands. Raven spun in slow, graceful circles, and she followed him, feeling the grass cold and wet beneath her feet, the night breeze deliciously cool on her skin. In and out of the shadows of the stones they danced, and after a while Marnie forgot herself, and did not care that her shift was undone, or that Raven might watch. In the end she danced as he did, with eyes half closed and her body at one with the moonlight and the night, unaware of self, unaware of everything but this freedom, this cleansing unity with the earth and sky and God.

At last Raven stopped, leaning against one of the stones to rest, his breathing deep and misty in the air. Marnie leaned next to him, her face half veiled by her windblown hair, her clothes awry and her body drenched in moonlight, perfect, beautiful beyond words.

"Ah, Marn," he said huskily, looking at her.

Turning her head, she saw the yearning in his eyes. For long moments she stood very still, wanting him to touch her, afraid that he might. But he sighed and went a little way apart and put on his clothes.

Marnie shook the creases from her damp dress and put it on, then pulled on her shoes and wrapped her cloak firmly about herself. For a few moments she and Raven stood in the center of the stone circle again, looking at the moon going down behind the awesome stones, and the eastern skies shimmering with the first hint of dawn. Raven kissed her forehead, so softly that she hardly felt his lips; and they began the long walk home. They did not talk, but walked with their arms about each other, their footsteps quick and in harmony on the dew-wet grass, their hair dusted with the mist.

The skies were blushing orange along the horizon, when they climbed over the last hill and saw their cove spread out below. They could not see the cottage or the beach; only the group of huge old trees, their branches black against the sea and lightening sky.

Heading toward the trees, they walked with their eyes downcast, because the ground was rough. In a shallow place behind the trees, they crossed the little bubbling stream, then went down beside the water to the house. As they rounded the corner they stopped, and Raven's arm tightened about her.

A crowd was gathered on the beach. Several men carried burning torches, the flames blood-bright against the dark blue sea. Silent they stood, grim and somber as they clutched their ropes and clubs. A horse and wagon waited outside the cottage, not too close to it.

For a long time they stood looking at one another, the widow and the madman on one side, on the other the crowd that had come with a solemn and holy purpose; and no one spoke. Then a man called out, "If you come quiet, Widow Isherwood, it will go easier with you. But fight us, and we'll burn your house, and you and your paramour with it."

"What do you want?" she called.

"You, witch!" called someone else. "We won't harm Raver because he's ignorant, and you've put a spell on him, and he can't help it. But you know what you've been doing, and it's against all the laws of nature and of God."

Marnie signed to Raven: *It's me they want. Not you.*

Why? he asked. He was shaking more than she was.

I don't know.

To the people, she called, "What have I done? What is it I'm supposed to be guilty of?"

There was no reply. Deathly quiet hung over the beach, broken only by the waves tumbling on the shore.

"I haven't sinned with Raven!" she cried. "I haven't done anything wrong! Ask Father Brannan!"

"We can't ask him!" yelled a man. "You've bewitched him, as well! You tempted him here to your very house, and put your evil spells on him!"

Horror washed over her. Was there no limit to their dreadful stupidity? She looked for Finian, remembering that once before he had spoken on her behalf, and might do so again; but he was not here.

Beside her, Raven signed: *What are they saying, with their mouths?*

But she shook her head, unable to tell him.

Where is Father Brannan? Raven asked. *He will help—*

The man was yelling again, and Marnie put her hand across Raven's, stopping his signs.

"You'll not use that magic talk again, witch!" cried the man. "Come to us quiet, or we'll burn your house, and force you!"

Run away! Marnie signed to Raven. *Go to the stones, hide! Fast! Don't come back.*

But he stood holding her tight, his eyes fixed on the crowd. They were all yelling now, screaming at the witch to surrender. A man stepped toward her house, and Marnie moved away from Raven. He walked with her, every nerve taut, ready to flee, or fight. *Father Brannan,* he signed. *I'll get Father Brannan.*

No, she said, signing quickly, urgent, because they were coming for her, hissing and shrieking and crossing themselves, and stumbling on the dark stones. *Run, Raven!*

Then they were all around her, clutching at her arms, spitting at her, dragging her toward the wagon. She pulled back, stumbled, and fell, and someone kicked her in the stomach. Retching, she tried to crawl away; but feet and legs surged about her, and rough hands were hauling on her clothes, dragging her by the hair, wrenching her arms and legs, and punching her. And somewhere in the turmoil were Raven's awful howls, wild and mad and raging. She screamed and bit, and a sack was yanked over her head and tied about the neck. Choking, gasping for breath, she clawed at the rope to loosen it. Darkness, and terror, and Raven still howling—and then his cries stopped. Fury overwhelmed her. Like a wildcat she fought, until they gripped her hands and forced them behind her, binding them so tight they ached. She felt herself lifted and thrown on something hard. Then she was moving, helpless, blind, half suffocated; and there was only the rumble of the wagon wheels, and the frenzy of the crowd, savage and triumphant and screaming for a hanging.

❦

Sherryl Jordan
198

Chapter 24

THE WORST PART WAS the darkness, the stifling heat of the hood over her head, and her own fear choking her. All the time the people howled and screamed, and she never knew whether at any moment she would be strung up to hang, or thrown in a fire, or drowned. It was the unknowing that tortured her, more than the bloodlust and the hate. She tried to pray, but the wagon rattled her to the very bones, and she had bitten her tongue, and there was blood in her mouth, and sweat running down all of her, and she could not think for terror.

At last the jolting stopped, and there was quiet. Hands took hold of her, and she was dragged off the wagon. She ached all over, and trembled so much she could hardly stand. They forced her to walk a short distance, and she stumbled, totally blinded by the hood. All around were men breathing hard, and people murmuring. Smoke wafted over her, and she smelled fire. She drew back, struggling against the ropes that bound her, but rough hands forced her on. Then she was grabbed and made to stop. Hands were about her neck, and she thought they were going to hang her, and sobbed as she began the Lord's Prayer. But they were only taking off the hood.

She was in the churchyard, facing the wall of the church where the window was broken. The sun had risen, but this side of the church was in shadow, the earth dim and the gray walls misty and indistinct. She could just make out the shape of the stump of the great tree that had fallen, breaking the window. People stood around, blurred on the edge of her sight, dark and silent and featureless like ghosts. On the ground in front of her a fire burned, and a rod of iron lay across it, heating.

Marnie's breath came in painful gasps, and sweat ran down her face into her eyes. She tried to speak, but could not. She looked for Father Brannan, but he was not there. Only these people, their blood-less lips half grinning, their eyes hollow and burning like the fire.

"'Tis a long time since we tried a witch," said an old woman, from behind Marnie. Her voice was eager, breathless. "You know what you have to be doing, Ultan?"

The man called Ultan stepped forward. He was middle-aged, large and strong, and the people respected him. "Aye, I know," he said, licking his lips. "When the iron's hot enough, it'll be done."

"We ought to be quick, afore Father Brannan gets back," said another man. "That's what his lordship said."

"No point, till the iron's hot," replied Ultan.

Marnie stood very straight and still, watching him, watching them all. She was thirsty, her throat so dry she wanted to retch, and she wished with all her heart that she would faint. But the morning air was icy on her cheeks, and she shivered from cold and terror, all her senses sharpened by fear. She looked at the fire, at the iron rod red-tipped in the flames. Then she looked at Ultan. He smiled, his eyes narrowed, leering.

"What will you do to me?" she whispered, almost choking. "What will you do?"

"Well now, witch, 'tis the judgment of the glowing iron for you," he said. "If it burns you bad, you'll be guilty, and if it doesn't, you'll be innocent." He went over to the fire, and spat on the iron bar. His spit sizzled, and he smiled again, almost satisfied. Then he came back. "But first, there's another thing to be done," he said to Marnie softly. "First, we be needing to examine your body for devil's marks." He grinned, looking her up and down, and passed his tongue across his lips again.

There was a bellow from across the churchyard, and Father Brannan burst into the startled gathering. In a moment his eyes took in the fire, the iron across it, and Marnie standing bound. He went and took her by the shoulders, and looked at her face, seeing the bruises, the blood on her chin, the terror. "Oh, Marnie, child!" he cried. "What have they done to you?" He went behind her, and unbound her hands. Several of the people moved back, but the man Ultan stood his ground. Father Brannan turned on him.

"I thought you had some sense, man!" he cried. "What is this—a witch trial?"

"Aye," said Ultan. "We were going to do it, father, good and proper. We know what to do. Old Mother Biddy told us."

"Oh, she did, did she?" shouted the priest. "And what sort of trial was that, done outside the church, without a priest, without the sacraments, without the judgment of the Almighty involved?"

"We were told not to have a priest," said Ultan, lifting his chin and daring to meet Father Brannan's fiery eyes, "since the priest too was under her spell, like the madman. We couldn't have you, father, that's why we waited until you was away, visiting another parish. You weren't coming back till tonight, father."

"No, I wasn't," said Father Brannan, breathing hard, his hands clenching into fists. "But the horse hurt its foot in a rabbit hole, and I had to walk it back. I reckon the Almighty must have arranged it to stop this wickedness."

"There's only one wickedness," said Ultan, "and you're

bewitched, and too blind to see it, father. I tell you with respect, and with my love, seeing as you've been my priest all these years, but we're all in danger, and so are you, and she has to be stopped."

"And what's she done that has to be stopped?" asked Father Brannan.

"She's a witch, father. She's laid a spell on Raver, and put him and his devils under her power. She makes magic in the air with her hands, and commands him in ways that aren't natural, and he obeys."

"She has his demons for familiars!" shrieked a woman. "She worships Lucifer with him!"

"'Tis true!" cried another woman, her voice shrill and frenzied and echoing in the still morning air. "They dance in the devil's ring, stark naked! My Tobit followed them and saw, this very night just passed!"

Emboldened by the rising evidence against Marnie, the people who had sidled away when Father Brannan arrived now came creeping back.

"Aye, father!" yelled someone else. "We were afeared she'd bewitched you too, father, seeing as you were there with her so many times in her house. We were worried sick about you, and that's the truth!"

"Well, you were worrying yourselves sick for nothing!" yelled Father Brannan. "I've a good mind to bang your stupid skulls together!"

"But that wouldn't bring her poor husband back, would it, that she killed with a curse?" said Ultan, very low, and the shouting and mumbling stopped. "You keep telling us all we're mistaken, father, in the matter of the curse. But it seems to me that it was only the beginning. And in this other matter, the one of witchcraft, we're not wrong. Sir Isherwood, who's living here among us at this time, and who is so kindly buying us a new window for our church, he says he's seen this kind of thing before, and recognizes all the signs. 'Tis witchcraft, he says, and for that the widow must be tried."

"The law is very clear in these matters," said Father Brannan.

"There's a proper ordeal in the church, only after three days of fasting, and with prayers and the Holy Eucharist. And you're not qualified to do that, Ultan. Not one of you is. And there's the end to it."

"I'm begging your pardon, father, but it's not the end to it," said Ultan. "She's a witch, and she's put all of Raver's devils under her power, and talks to him with magic in her hands. She has to go through the ordeal, father, she has to be tried. If you don't do it, we'll bring a priest from another village, or do it ourselves. If you won't try her, we can only believe that she's got you so far under bewitchment that you can't see what's going on no more. I'm sorry to be overriding you like this, father, but I've got the whole village behind me, excepting Old Finian, and it's nothing you can stop."

Father Brannan took Marnie's shoulders in both hands again, and made her look at him. "Are you all right, lass?" he asked gently. "Have they harmed you yet, beyond the binding?"

She shook her head, and he brushed her hair out of her eyes, and wiped the blood off her chin. She was deadly white. "Do you want a stool to sit down on?" he asked.

"I'll stand." It was barely a whisper. "Father, where's Raven?"

"He's not our problem at the moment. Do you understand what they're saying?"

"It's all wrong, father."

"And this wild talk that you danced naked in the devil's stones with him?"

She would not meet his eyes, and he shook her a little, impatient and alarmed. "Answer me! It's a lie, isn't it? Answer me true, Marnie, or I can't help you. Did you dance in the devil's ring with him?"

"It's not what you think," she whispered, white-lipped, and he released her suddenly and turned away.

"Oh, Marnie, lass!" he said, his voice angry and full of reproach.

The man Ultan stepped forward. "We'll not wait for the fasting days; she'll fly off, or do something terrible to us all," he said. "There'll be a trial this morning. Will you do it, father?"

"Aye," said Father Brannan, very low. "I will."

Marnie gave a wild cry, and several men rushed at her, and held her.

Quietly, his voice shaking, Father Brannan said to Ultan, "Take a brazier and make a fire in the church, and get another iron bar, and put it in front of the altar. It has to be blessed before it's heated. Choose another man to help you do it. And choose four witnesses. You're all to eat or drink nothing else until after the trial, and you must have men who kept themselves from their wives last night. I'll have no one in the church but the six of you, and Marnie and me. I'll not have her subjected to the stares of the whole village."

"Are you going to be searching her for devil's marks, father?" cried an old man eagerly.

"No, I am not!" shouted Father Brannan. "And if any one of you lays a finger on her, I'll excommunicate you and damn you to hell!"

Then the priest turned to Marnie, and told the men holding her to let her go. She refused to look at Father Brannan, and he took her arm and led her into the church. They passed down the timeworn stones of the empty nave, and Marnie knelt in front of the altar. Looking up, she fixed her eyes on the wooden cross, and tried to control the awful shaking that went through her. The church felt icy cold, and in the dim hollowness her breaths sounded loud and unnatural. Kneeling beside her, Father Brannan saw that she was very white, but her face was resolute. He picked up the crucifix he wore on his rope belt, and tried to press it into her hands. She knocked it aside.

"Listen to me, Marnie," he said. "There's no way out of this. If there was I'd find it for you, I swear."

"Judas!" she whispered. "Traitor!"

He put a hand over his face, and was silent for so long she thought he must be praying. "There's not much point," she said harshly. "Your praying, I mean. There's no God to listen. If there was, he'd not let this happen to me."

Father Brannan wiped his sleeve across his face, and looked up.

"There is a God," he said, and she could tell he was crying. "If the village folk had done this themselves, Marnie, they wouldn't have done it the proper way. They would have shamed you, and damaged you something terrible, and killed you. And if another priest did it, it would be twenty times worse than if I do it. At least you'll have a friend beside you."

"No, I won't," she said.

Behind them, a brazier grated on the church floor, and the smell of smoke filled the air. Ultan came up to the altar, and laid an iron bar on the floor by it. Then he backed out, his head bent, humble and reverent.

"You know what this trial is, Marnie?" asked Father Brannan, gently.

"Aye," she said. "A betrayal."

"Oh, Marnie. Don't hate me. I'm doing this because it'll go easiest with you. I could turn my back, and they'd all just say I was a poor bewitched fool, and another priest would come and try you, and afterward exorcise me for my folly in trying to help you. I was meaning, do you know what to expect?"

"No."

"This is only your trial, an ordeal, to discover the judgment of God, whether you be innocent, or whether you be guilty."

"And if they say I'm guilty?"

"Don't you be worrying about that yet, child."

She looked up at the crucifix again, her eyes full of agony. "They'll burn me," she whispered, "like they burned Eilis."

"I swear on my soul, I won't let them burn you."

"They'll hang me, then. If they do that, father, will you look after Raven? Will you let him show you the hand-words, so he'll have someone to talk to?"

"I'll do the best that I can for him. Now, do you want me to tell you what to expect in this ordeal, so you'll be ready in your heart for it?"

"Aye, father."

So he told her, and she listened, and for the first time that dreadful dawn, she wept. "I won't be able to talk to Raven after," she said.

"You'll still have one good hand, child."

"But we use both. Can't I have a different trial?"

"I'm sorry. This is the one they demand."

She leaned over, sobbing, choking in grief and fear and agony, and the priest listened, crying himself, not knowing what else he could do to help her. The church door banged shut, echoing in the smoky hollowness, and Ultan came, and said that all was ready.

"Come on, Marnie," said Father Brannan, standing up. Marnie tried to stand, but could not. She wept, begging him to give her time to prepare herself, to make the trial tomorrow.

"I can't," he said softly, lifting her by the arms and holding her, though six witnesses watched. "Be brave, Marnie, love. You'll be praying, and taking the Communion first. You'll be prepared. And Christ will be with you, and so will I."

And he helped her walk to the middle of the church, and stood with her behind the fire, and began the Judgment of the Glowing Iron.

Chapter 25

NUMB WITH SHOCK, feeling as if she were watching from a distance, observing something happening to someone else and not to herself, Marnie stood and listened as Father Brannan sang a hymn. He had a good voice, strong and true, though the high notes were tremulous this morning, as they echoed in the ancient stones. She watched as, with great care, he used tongs to pick up the iron bar and place it across the fire. Ultan and the other witnesses stood lined up on either side, their lips moving in prayer, their faces reverent and zealous. Holding his hands high above the flames, Father Brannan said a blessing over the fire.

"Bless, O Lord God, this place," he said, "that there may be for us in it sanctity, chastity, virtue, and victory, and humility, goodness, gentleness, and obedience to God the Father, and the Son, and the Holy Ghost . . ."

Watching his face, Marnie saw that it was streaked with tears, and his hands shook more than her own. After the prayer, he took her arm and turned her around to face the back of the church. The nave yawned before her, empty, endless.

"Stand beside the brazier, Marnie," he said, his voice gentle. "You have to take nine steps, and I'll make a mark on the floor where you stop. Take good steps, lass, or they'll say it wasn't a fair trial; steps such as you would normally walk. That's the distance you'll have to carry the iron bar."

Marnie looked at the stones, and thought of the grass where she and Raven had danced. Taking a deep breath, she paced out nine steps, and Ultan brought a little wooden stand and put it in the place where she stopped. Marnie turned and looked back at the fire, at the iron bar already smoking. So far . . .

"I'll walk beside you," Father Brannan was saying, "to make sure you don't run, that you make the steps as you made them just now. I'll show you with my hand, like this." With his hand flat and in a chopping motion, he made several downward moves, evenly spaced. "When I do this, every time my hand goes down, you take a step. Not before. Not after. Do you understand?"

She nodded.

"When you get to this end, place the bar on the stand here. Then you'll come to the front of the church, near the altar, and I will wrap your hand in holy cloths, and bind them, and seal them with a sacred seal. This must stay on, the wax seal unbroken, for three days. During that time you must fast and pray. Then you'll come back, and I will take off the cloths, and if your burn is clean and healing, you will be judged innocent. But if the burn is festering and bad, it will be God's sign that you are guilty. If the cloths are disturbed in any way, the seal broken, the ordeal will be void, and you will have to go through it again. Do you understand everything, child?"

Again she nodded, her head low.

Father Brannan raised his voice and said to her, as well as to the witnesses, "There's one other thing that must be observed. During this ordeal absolute silence must be kept. There will be no word, no sound, except the prayers in your own hearts. That includes you, Marnie. You must keep absolutely quiet, right through the ordeal."

Then Father Brannan was leading her back to the altar again, to the fire and the witnesses. Hardly hearing what was said, she watched as he sprinkled holy water over herself and the witnesses, and placed a drop on their tongues, and let them each kiss a book of the Gospels.

"We have Communion to take, first, before you do it," Father Brannan whispered to her, as she pressed her lips against the book. She trembled so violently she could hardly stand, and each breath was like a sob. Somehow she found herself kneeling, repeating the prayers, taking the tiny piece of bread, the sip of wine—the holy sacraments, symbols of all Christ's pain and love. She tried to think, to pray for courage and the strength to remain silent; but terror turned her thoughts to bedlam, and her strength flowed out of her like water. Stumbling, supported by the priest, she stood up and went back to the fire. With the tongs, Father Brannan removed the glowing iron, placing it across a stand similar to the one at the other end of the nave. Over the iron bar he sprinkled holy water, and the drops hissed and evaporated.

"The blessing of God the Father, the Son, and the Holy Ghost," he prayed, "descend upon this iron for the discerning of the right judgment of God."

Marnie wiped her hands across her face. Sweat ran into her eyes, and she could hardly see. Her bowels cramped, and she wanted to be sick. Anguished, she prayed she would not lose control. Father Brannan took her hands in his.

"Listen to me, Marnie," he said. "Which hand are you going to use, to do it?"

Unable to speak, she put out her left hand. It was the hand least used in her talk with Raven. Father Brannan removed the wedding band from it, and put it on the ring finger of her right hand. "Pick up the bar halfway along, firmly, across your palm, not in your fingers," he said. "Grip it hard, be sure. If you drop it, the ordeal will have to start again. And remember to keep quiet."

She tried to calm her breathing, the awful gasps that came rasping from her throat like sobs. "I'll keep quiet, father," she whispered. "Pray for me."

"I already am, child. Now, when you're ready."

Breathing hard, Marnie faced the glowing bar, and the way she had to walk. All else in the world became dim. The silent witnesses, the church, the priest, vanished; and there was only this iron, and her hand, and the nine steps. Praying, remembering what Father Brannan had told her, she placed her hand under the iron. The heat from it scorched her skin, even before it was touched. Compressing her lips so she would not cry out, she closed her hand around it. Pain exploded up her arm, rushed like wildfire through all of her, tearing through her bowels, her lungs, up into her mouth—

She clenched her teeth against it, defying it, fighting the screams that rose, gurgling and desperate, in her throat; and she lifted the bar and took the first step. Father Brannan was just in front if her, a little to her right, his hand held up. He moved it down, and she took another step. So much agony, she could not breathe or think or move—

The hand again, going down. Another step. Her mind, her body, withdrawing, enfolding into itself, separating. A nothingness, safe, beyond pain, beyond everything. On the edge of it, a hand. The hand moving down, urgent. Incredibly, her body obeyed. Another step. The stones soft, like mist. Sinking into them. A hand under her arm, steadying her, bringing her back from the edge of the dark. Then the hand, moving again. Step. Another step. And three more. And then a voice, faint, as if from a huge distance: "Put it down, child. It's over."

She stared at the glowing iron in her hand. Father Brannan shook her arm hard, and she dropped the bar. It crashed across the wooden stand, then tipped and rolled on the stone floor. The clangor echoed around the stone walls. Dizziness swept over her. Clenching her teeth, she locked back the sounds that still tore upward from her throat. She heard Father Brannan's voice, distant and broken, felt his arm supporting her, the roughness of his robe on her face . . .

Then, out of the dimness, a white cloth bound about her hand, wrapped carefully, sealed with holy wax across its joins and folds. Father Brannan was kneeling by her, crying, smiling. "It's over, Marnie. You were fine. You were fine."

She stood up and, staggering a little, went out of the church. The people were outside, gathered like eager crows among the tombstones. It was broad daylight. The world was new, shining. Father Brannan was beside her.

"Remember," he said, "don't break the seals on the cloths, or all this has been for nothing. And pray well, child; the judgment depends on whether or not the scar is healing clean."

Her lips were closed, her teeth clamped tight, her tongue stuck, immovable. She could not speak. Her soul was somewhere far.

"I'll walk home with you," he said, but she shook her head. She walked out between the little carved gates from the porch, almost falling, her limbs wooden and unwilling. Her skirt was damp and cold against her legs, and she realized, vaguely, that she had wet herself. Between all the people she walked, slow so she would not stumble, her burned hand resting in its sealed white cloths on her other hand in front of her. And it was while she passed among them, on her way to the grassy track to her cove, that her soul came back from wherever it had been, and the numbness passed, and the pain crashed over her. She ran then, sobbing, half blinded with agony; ran, stumbling and falling, until she was back in her own cove, safe; and she rushed to her home and threw open the door, and fell onto the floor inside, screaming and screaming and screaming.

Chapter 26

RAVEN SAT IN the burial chamber, rocking back and forth in anguish. His head throbbed, and blood ran down the back of his neck, from the blow that had knocked him unconscious. He hardly remembered crawling to the tomb. One name filled his mind, his world: Marnie. Marnie, bruised and bleeding, and dragged away by the people. Marnie gone, and why? Why?

The sun rose higher, and Raven's mind cleared. He staggered outside and along the hillside until he could see the cove. The people had not come back. In his heart he knew they would not. But something drew him down there, and he limped, groaning for the pain in his head, down to the house. The door was ajar, and he pushed it open.

On the floor there, half lying on her back, with her left hand strangely wrapped in a cloth, was Marnie.

Moaning, Raven knelt by her. "Marn," he wept. "Marn, Marn."

Across a vast darkness, she heard him. She tried to move, but her limbs would not obey.

Vaguely she was aware of his hands on her, touching her face, her hair; heard his voice calling her, heard the hoarse tones of his weeping. And then he was touching her hand, unwrapping the sealed cloths, and she tried to call out, to stop him, but the darkness kept sucking her down, and her tongue would not move, and all she could see was the iron bar, white-hot, spinning out of the blackness toward her again . . .

The dark, turning red as blood. And pain, her hand on fire. Someone doing something to it. Scraping off the skin? Fire again, someone holding her arm, forcing her hand into a cauldron of molten metal. People jeering, Father Brannan's hand going down again, and again, over and over until she had walked so far the iron was burned through to her bones, fixed forever into her flesh. So much pain . . .

Water, cool and refreshing, on her face, on her lips and tongue, over her burning hand. Ease from pain. Sleep.

A fire in the darkness, blurred and distant. Someone in front of it, building up the flames. She groaned, fearing more torment. The person came over to her, and gentle hands touched her forehead. "Marn?"

She was lying in bed, her fouled and bloodied clothes removed. Her face was washed, and she felt clean. The pain in her burned hand had eased a little.

I put oil on your hurt hand, Raven signed, *the way I mended your feet when you hurt them. It's better, your hand. The hurt is clean, good.*

He smiled, his face full of concern and love, and wondered why she looked at him as if he had done a terrible thing, and why she wailed and howled and clawed the wall as if to escape, leaving trails of blood on the stone.

Distraught, Raven lay down and held her, his front curled against her back, his arms across her chest, his hands holding her wrists so she would not scratch the walls. She fought, sobbing, and he cried with her, knowing her pain; but he would not let her go. At last she slept, exhausted by terror and suffering, and he slept with her.

Dawn glimmered in the little windows, and Father Brannan

knocked softly at the door. No one answered, so he went in, and saw them sleeping there together on the bed, with Marnie's burned hand outstretched before the wall, and the sacred cloth trampled on the floor.

The priest picked the cloth up, as well as every piece of the broken wax that had sealed it, and threw them on the embers in the fireplace. He stayed until they were totally destroyed, then he went out and tramped wearily back to the church.

Marnie opened her eyes and stared at the wall in front of her. Dancing across the dim stones were colors, vivid like fragments of rainbow. She watched them, wondering what they were, and thinking perhaps bits of the glowing iron had traveled through her body to her head, and altered the way she saw things. Marveling, she looked at her left hand, saw the burn red and raw, but clean. Her palm still throbbed, but it was bearable. The nails of her right hand were torn and had been bleeding, and she noticed blood marks on the wall beside the colored lights. There were bruises on her wrists, and they mystified her. Then she remembered Raven lying with her, curled against her back, holding her so she would not hurt herself. She could hear Raven now, banging something sharp on the table, and could smell broth cooking. Blankets felt rough against her skin, and she realized she was naked. Who had washed her? "Mama?" she sobbed, rolling over.

But there was only Raven, sitting at the table in the sunlight from the window, playing with the ring he had found in the fireplace. The sun flashed on the bits of colored glass, and it was those reflecting on Marnie's wall. He saw her watching him, and smiled. Getting up, he put the ring away in an alcove, poured a bowl of soup, and took it over to the chest by the bed. Kneeling, he pushed her hair back, and wiped away her tears. Then he signed, *Your hurt, is it better?*

It's only a little hurt now, she signed back, awkwardly, because she could not use her left hand. Then she remembered she was wearing nothing, and pulled the blankets up to her chin. *How many days have I been here?*

Three, he replied.

Will you get my clothes?

Why? You must eat; I cooked soup.

I must go.

Outside? I'll bring you the bucket. I'll help you.

It is not that. I must go away. They will hurt my other hand.

Why? Why, Marnie?

They say I did bad things. They will hurt me again if I stay. Please bring my clothes. The signs confused him because they were one-handed, and she asked him again, moving her burned hand painfully toward her chest, to signify the word *bring.* Then she waited while Raven opened her wooden chest, and brought back her clean shift and a dress. Sitting up, trying to keep the blankets covering her, she reached for the shift. Raven tried to help, but she pushed his hands away and told him to turn around. He did, but she struggled with the fabric, getting caught up in the long folds, hurting her burned hand. In the end she broke down, weeping with frustration and pain. Raven turned around and helped her, finding the neck of the garment, and gently pulling it on over her shoulders. He was about to draw together the front, to tie the ribbons for her, but she covered her breasts with her arms, and shook her head. So he sat at the table, his back to her, and waited.

After a long time he turned and saw her lying in bed, the blankets kicked off, her shift on but still undone because she could not manage the ties with one hand. Her right arm was over her face, and she was crying.

Raven knelt at the edge of the bed, and tied the ribbons for her. She let him, her arm still over her face. He stroked her wrist, and she peered at him from under her arm, her eyes swollen and red.

Do you want me to help you put on your dress? he asked.

She shook her head, her body racked with sobs.

What can I do? he asked, near tears himself. *What do you want?*

She signed, as well as she could with one hand, *I want Mama.*

Raven gazed at the closed door, his eyes despairing and full of grief. After a while he signed, *I'll go and bring her.*

But Marnie shook her head, signing, *No.*

Raven picked up a bowl of soup, and placed it near her pillow. *I'll help you eat,* he said.

I'm not hungry.

Three days you have no food. It's a long time for you.

I'm not hungry.

Leaning down, Raven stroked her hair, feeling her skin hot and feverish. He sighed, wanting to help her but not knowing how. Behind him the door opened and shut again. Feeling the rush of cool air, Raven leaped up, his hands clenched into fists. But when he saw that it was Father Brannan, he rushed over and grabbed his arm. "Elp Marn!" Raven pleaded, his voice broken by tears. "Elp Marn!"

Father Brannan put down the basket he had brought, and embraced the distraught youth. "Aye, I'll help her, Raven," he said.

But when the priest approached Marnie, she cringed from him, trying to hide her burned hand with its sealed cloths removed. "He didn't know!" she cried. "He didn't understand, and I couldn't tell him! I'll not go through it again, father! I'll run away first, I swear!"

"You don't have to go through it again, child," he said. "I've brought another cloth, and more sealing wax. I'll wrap your hand, just like before. No one will know, except we three and the Almighty—and I'm hoping he won't mind."

"Are you sure they won't know? Ultan, and the others?"

"I wouldn't be doing this if I thought they'd find out," he replied. "Can you get up now, and let me see your hand properly, in the sunlight?"

"Aye. But don't look at me, father; I'm not dressed yet."

He went and stood by the window, his back to her, and Marnie struggled out of bed and picked up the dress. With infinite patience Raven helped, though she slapped at his hands sometimes, frustrated by her own weakness and vulnerability. Carefully he put the dress on her, brushed her hair with the silver brush that had been Isake's, and helped as she washed her face. Then he took her to a chair, and she sat down.

"I'm ready, father," she said, stretching out her burned hand on the table. Father Brannan turned around and came over to inspect her palm. Unspeakable relief showed on his face.

"It's healing remarkably well," he said. "We have nothing to worry about. The Almighty himself has acquitted you. And because you're guiltless, I know he won't be pouring brimstone down on my head, either, for this felony I'm about to commit. Can you ask Raven to keep a sharp lookout, and tell me if anyone comes?"

With difficulty Marnie signed with her right hand to Raven: *Father Brannan wants you to watch, and tell us if people come from Torcurra. If they come, you must tell us.*

Raven opened the door and stood on the step, looking toward Torcurra. He kept the door open so he could see Marnie too, and they could talk if they wanted to.

Sitting down, Father Brannan removed the cloth from the basket, and took out bread and vegetables, a bag of flour, and some wheat for Marnie's hens. "I thought it best to have something ordinary to show, if I was stopped on my way here," he said, opening the bag of wheat. He felt around in the grain, and eventually drew out a new white cloth, a piece of sealing wax, and the sacred seal from the church. He added, with a grin, "I was afraid I might be stopped, since the village folk are a mite suspicious of my godly and guileless self, now."

The shadow of a smile crossed Marnie's pallid lips. Father Brannan shook the wheat from the white fabric, spread the cloth on the table near Marnie's hand, and said a prayer. Then he lit the candle that was on the table, ready to melt the wax. Marnie noticed that his hands shook, and his face was pale and strained.

"Put your hand on the cloth," he said. "That's right. I'll try not to hurt you as I wrap it. I don't suppose you remember much of the first time this was done."

"No, father. What will happen to you, if they find out you've done this?"

"To be sure, 'twill be something I won't find boring," he said lightly, though there was apprehension in his eyes. "Could you put a finger on the cloth here, and hold it while I melt the wax, and drip it over the joins? That's the way. When this is done, it might be an idea for you to get it a bit dirty, since you're supposed to have had it on for three days. And this afternoon, get Raven to bring you to the church." He stopped, looking sharply at her face. "Are you all right, lass? You look white."

"I'm mortal tired. Father, why are you doing this for me?"

Using a small spoon, he melted a piece of wax over the candle flame, then poured it over a join in the cloth. Before the pool of wax was hard, he pressed the seal into it. Melting some more wax, he sealed another join, and another, each time marking the congealing wax with the sacred insignia of the church. "We'll wait a bit longer," he said, still holding the cloth, "until all the wax holds firm."

Feeling faint, Marnie slouched in her chair, putting her head down on the upper part of her outstretched arm. Her eyes were half closed, two bright spots of blue behind her tangled hair.

"Do you want me to send for your mother, Marnie?" the priest asked. "You need someone to look after you."

"Raven's doing that. Besides, my mother . . . She doesn't approve of Raven. And she has my father to look after. I'll be all right. I'm tired, that's all."

"It's the shock of the trial."

"Had you ever tried anyone for witchcraft, before?" she asked.

"No, I hadn't," he replied.

"How did you know what to do?"

"As I told you once before, I've a great deal of book learning."

"I wish I did. I can't read a word, excepting those names you wrote for me."

"It's passing strange," he said, with a grin, "me with all the book learning, and you with none, and you a whole lot wiser. 'Tis hardly fair, and I'll have a word with the Almighty about it when I see him."

"What will he say about you doing this for me?"

"I'm hoping he'll overlook it, seeing as you're innocent."

Sherryl Jordan
218

"What if I'm not? What if the village folk are right? Are you committing a wicked crime, helping me?"

"The village folk are not right. You've had your trial, and your hand's clean. Almighty God himself has made the judgment."

"My hand's clean because Raven put oil on it, and looked after it. 'Tis nothing to do with God."

"Everything's to do with God, Marnie."

One of Marnie's hens came in, clucking softly, and pecked the grain by the priest's feet. Marnie looked at the bird, thinking how pure and white it was in the sunlight from the door. Her eyes moved across the floor, over the step, to Raven, leaning against the wide door frame, his profile strong and beautiful as he kept vigil. Beyond him glittered the sea she had grown to love, and the dark shape of their little boat drawn up on the sand.

"You told me something, once, father," she said. "You said all things work together for our good, and that God always has our happiness in mind. I didn't believe it, then."

Father Brannan tested the last pool of wax with his thumb nail, saw that it was completely hard, and lifted his fingers from the cloth. The folds held firm.

"If I'd known you didn't believe everything I said," he muttered, "I'd never have cooked you all those lobster suppers. Now, if you'll excuse the irreverence of it, I'll just be hiding this sacred wax and spoon and holy seal in my boots, in case I'm questioned on the way home. I don't normally carry things this way, but seeing as this is one of those mysterious events that's working together for good, I'm trusting the Almighty won't mind the sacrilege."

Murmuring a prayer for forgiveness, he poked the sacred instruments into his boots, and stood up to go. Marnie moved as if to stand up too, but Father Brannan put his hand on her hair, briefly caressing her. "Rest for a while," he said softly. He made the sign of the cross over her, adding, "And while you rest, you might pray for us. For both of us. And for that cloth there, that it looks as the witnesses remember it."

"Thank you for everything, father," she said. "I'm sorry I called you Judas, the other day."

"I'd already forgot." He smiled, picking up his empty basket. He said farewell, blessed them, and left.

Halfway up the hill he turned and looked back at the cottage. Raven and Marnie were standing together on the step, watching him. Marnie was leaning with her back against Raven, and he was holding her, his arms about her waist, his cheek against her hair.

Father Brannan waited at the edge of the churchyard, looking anxiously up the hill toward the cove, his lips moving in prayer. Finian stood with him, his old face creased in lines of apprehension. Behind them stood the villagers, restless and muttering.

"She's not coming, father!" someone said, and the priest turned around.

It was Ultan, dressed in his best Sabbath clothes, and swaggering with self-importance, since he was chief witness in a witchcraft case. He came up to the priest, the other five witnesses with him.

"We'll have to pronounce the ordeal null and void," Ultan went on, stopping by Father Brannan, "if she doesn't come for the final part. We've all done our bit, father, and fasted and prayed these three days, while the judgment of the Almighty is being made. But my patience is wearing mighty thin, like my stomach, and I'll not be over-lenient if the ordeal's not finished properlike. And I'm begging your pardon, father, but if there's another ordeal, 'twill be done with a priest from another village."

"And why's that, man?" asked Father Brannan, testily.

"Well, father, it's something Sir Isherwood said. Something to the effect that maybe you, being her friend and all, mightn't be the right priest for the ordeal. You've done it once and you did a good job, father, we're none of us questioning that; but the next time it will be different. She's a cunning woman, is Widow Isherwood, and we're having to be very careful."

Sherryl Jordan

"You seem to be setting great importance on these words of Sir Isherwood," said Father Brannan quietly, his eyes still on the track from the cove.

"Aye," said Ultan. "It was him put us onto this witchery thing, in the first place. If he hadn't warned us, father, God knows what would have happened to us. She'd have had us all bewitched, and not just Raver."

"And what if she isn't a witch, Ultan?" asked Father Brannan, turning on him. He looked past Ultan to them all, his voice rising with fervor. "What if this witchery thing was all a mistake, and she's vindicated by the Almighty himself? What then? Are you all going to accept that, and love her as the Almighty commands, like good neighbors, or are you going to cling to your wild notions, and find other reasons to hate and reject her? Because if her hand's clean, then she's as guiltless as you and I—maybe more so. And you'll all be committing the most dreadful sin, by holding her still guilty in your hearts."

"And if her hand's not clean?" cried an elderly woman. "If the Almighty's judgment is for her guilt?"

"Aye—what then?" they shouted.

Father Brannan looked on them all, his face full of grief and agony, and he said, very low, "If she's guilty, then you'll hang her, and God have mercy on us all."

At that moment a wagon arrived on the brow of the hill. Raven held the reins, but one arm was about Marnie. They stopped near the churchyard, and Raven got down and lifted Marnie to the ground. Father Brannan hurried over to them.

"Thank God you've come!" he said.

Marnie looked past Father Brannan at all the people, saw the eagerness in their faces, the bloodlust and fear; and she took a deep breath and stood very straight. "Let us get this done with, please, father," she said.

Holding hands, she and Raven followed Father Brannan across the ground and through the beautiful little porch into the church. The people parted to let them through, and several spat at Marnie, though only behind the priest's back. Then they all crowded in behind the priest and the accused, for every soul in the village was here to witness this miraculous judgment of God upon a witch.

In the church Marnie walked down the stone floor where she had walked three days ago, with the glowing iron in her hand. The mark where she had dropped it was still there, ash white on the floor. She passed the place where the fire had burned in its brazier, and where the iron had heated. Her steps faltered, and Raven's hand tightened about hers. He wept, being in this place, because she had told him what they had done—what she had done—and he knew well her voiceless pain, the raging quiet within.

At the altar they stopped. Father Brannan lifted his hands, and all the people fell silent.

"Have you fasted and prayed, these past three days?" Father Brannan asked Marnie.

"Aye, father," she whispered.

He said a prayer, and the witnesses stood close on either side of Marnie. Then, in absolute silence, the cloth was unbound.

In the back of the church, unnoticed, a man stood tense and listening. It was Pierce Isherwood.

Marnie stretched out her hand, and the witnesses examined it. Father Brannan said, very loud and clear, "The hand is clean. There is no festering on the track of the iron. Do the witnesses agree?"

"Aye, father," said Ultan, sounding disappointed, and all the witnesses agreed.

"Then Marnie Isherwood stands acquitted, in the sight of man and God," said Father Brannan, smiling as he held out a cross to Marnie to kiss.

In the back of the church, Pierce Isherwood swore quietly, and went out.

Chapter 27

QUIETLY, SO HE would not wake Marnie, Raven got out of his bed by the hearth, stacked more peat on the embers, and hung a pot of water over the growing flames. Then he slid the bolt on the door, and went out.

The dawn was breathtaking, the sun a red-hot orb shimmering on the edge of the molten sea. Half blinded, Raven looked away, and noticed that their boat was not on the beach. Bewildered, he walked to where he had left it after fishing yesterday, and saw the sand churned where the boat had been. Footprints made by boots covered the imprints of his own bare feet, and a deep groove in the sand showed where the boat had been hauled down to the water.

Muttering in anger, Raven ran along the beach to the cliffs that separated the cove from Torcurra. He scanned the rocks, his eyes narrowed against the rising sun. Then he saw it; the bow driven half up on the rocks, broken, battered by the waves. While he watched, another wave lifted the boat, covering it with foam and spume, and crashed it down again on the rocks. Frantic, howling with anger, Raven raced along the beach, leaping over the rocks to the boat. It was shattered beyond mending, its finely curved planks like broken ribs against the sky. A fishing line lay in the battered hull, and Raven tried to get to it, but another wave crashed over the wreck, hurling him back against the rocks. Gasping, he felt the violence of the water rushing over him, then he clung to a rock as the waters receded, sucked out again to the sea. Choking with rage, drenched and defeated, he went back to the cottage.

Marnie was making porridge, and she looked up, startled, as Raven burst in.

Our boat, he signed furiously, *it was put in the sea. The sea threw it up on the big stones. It's broke. All broke.*

He went over to the fire and began peeling off his soaking clothes. Marnie went to Isake's chest and took out some clean leggings and a shirt, and also the fur-lined cloak. She gave the garments to Raven, and he dried himself and pulled them on, shivering and groaning with cold. Without another word they sat by the fire and ate their bowls of porridge. Afterward Marnie signed awkwardly, with one hand: *We must get rabbits to eat. Maybe birds.*

Maybe Father Brannan will give us a different boat, Raven signed. *I don't want to hurt rabbits dead.*

It's only like making fish dead.

It is not. I stayed with rabbits in the fields.

We can't ask Father Brannan for a different boat.

Ask him for bacon and other food.

I'll not ask him to give us everything, Raven.

Why?

Because we are not his children. He does not have to look after us. He helps us much now, giving us food and candles and peat for the fire. I'll not ask him for more. If you are afraid to make rabbits dead, I'll do it.

I am not afraid! He stormed outside, leaving the door open. As Marnie got up to close it, she saw him striding off down the beach, the cloak billowing behind him in the wind. Sighing heavily, she began to tidy the cottage. It was difficult with only one hand, and many times she muttered and cursed. It was eight days since the ordeal, and her hand continued to heal, though the shrinking scar made full extension of her palm and fingers impossible. It was also impossible to completely close her hand, and she grieved the loss of its use. As she hung the sack of oats back on its hook, she felt how light it was, and checked the rest of their supplies. There was very little. And there was no money.

Despairing, she stood by the little table Isake had carved, and banged her good fist down on it, hard. "Damn you, Pierce Isherwood!" she cried. "Damn you!"

She was sitting mending a tunic for Raven, holding it clumsily with her burned hand, when a shadow passed her window and there was a bold knock on the door. Throwing the sewing down on the table, she opened the door. Father Brannan stood there, a large basket hanging from one arm, a bundle of clothes under the other.

"'Tis good to see you, father!" she said. "Come in! It's warm in here."

"Aye, that it is," he said, entering, and putting the basket and bundle on the table. "This wind means autumn's on its way, to be sure!" Glancing around, he added, "Where's Raven?"

"He went out for a walk."

"Perhaps it's just as well. I wanted to talk, without your stopping every other word to do your flutterings. You still manage them, I hope?"

"Aye, though they're difficult when I need two hands."

"And yourself? You're keeping all right?"

"I'm well, thank you."

"I brought you some things. A basket of food, and a lobster. There are candles there too, and one or two other things I thought you might use. And this bundle here, 'tis clothes for you and Raven. You'll need them with cooler weather coming on."

"You have to take them back, father. I can't pay you for them."

"I don't expect you to."

"You don't have to supply us with clothes."

"I can supply you with whatever I have in excess."

Marnie opened the bundle and pulled out a white dress, soft wool, with leaves embroidered on the bodice. "I see," she said, with a sly look at him. "Since when have you had too many dresses in your clothes chest, father?"

"Ah—I've been caught out!" he chuckled. "'Tis a secret sin of mine, collecting women's garments. Actually, there was a market yesterday, and I bought them from one of the women. They've been used, but they're clean and need only a little mending, which I see you can manage. I hope they fit."

"I can't take your charity, father."

"How are you going to manage, then? Besides, it isn't charity. If you're so bent on fair exchange, you can cook a few dinners for me, including your divine puddings."

Suddenly distraught, she sat down. "I don't know what to do, father!" she cried. "I don't know how we're going to manage! Someone dragged our boat into the sea last night, while we were asleep. Raven found it this morning, broken on the rocks. We can't fish now, and Raven doesn't like killing rabbits, or anything that lives in the fields. I don't see how we can survive. I can't ask you for everything. You have yourself to look after. If I could earn some money, it would be all right. If I could take in some mending, maybe mind children . . ." Her voice trailed off, and she looked down at her hands. "But I suppose they wouldn't let me do that, would they, even though I've been proven guiltless?"

"Well, that's something I need to talk to you about," he said, sitting very straight, and not quite looking at her. "The people, they know you're not guilty of witchcraft, but there's something else that's bothering them. And I have to tell you the truth, child, and say it's bothering me, as well. It'll cause dissension still, between you and the people of Torcurra, and while it's there they'll never let you do work for them, nor accept you, nor give you their charity. And if I let you do work for me, I'm thinking I wouldn't be their priest much longer. I've already stretched their loyalty to the limits."

"I know that, father, and I'm grateful. But what is it that bothers you?"

Father Brannan hesitated. Then he took a deep breath, and said, "Well, it's Raven. I'm not asking what's happening between you, and I'm not judging. But you've been judged already by other folks, and you know the agony they can cause. And they can do it again in other ways, if they get it into their minds that you're breaking the law of God. No—don't interrupt. Listen to me, lass, I have to finish. There was a woman in Torcurra who lived in sin with a man only for a week, and they drove him out, and did not talk to her for forty years. I know, because when she died, she told me of it on her deathbed. They don't tolerate such a sin, Marnie. I'm only saying this because I don't want to see you hurt again. You're a woman of spirit, and that's a fine thing, but you've cut yourself off from an awful lot of folks, including your own family. There comes a time when you have to start heeding what others think, when you have to try walking in step with other folks, instead of always being against them. I want to see you living in peace for a change, Marnie. I want to see you doing right."

Marnie reddened. "Right? Doing *right*?" she said. "And what's right, father? You gave a very good talk on that once, as I remember, and I loved you well for it, and for standing up for me when they were all against me. But you're as bad as they are, knowing me as you do, and still wondering about me and Raven. We're not sinning together. And even if we were, it wouldn't be as much a sin as that misery you call holy matrimony. I'm learning a lot of things, father, and one of them is that sometimes there's more sin in what people call lawful and right, and less in what they call wrong."

"I wasn't thinking you were sinning with him, Marnie," he said, his own face reddening. "I was going to offer . . . Oh, it's no matter, lass. Whatever I say, 'twill be the wrong thing."

"You may as well say it now, since you've started."

"I was going to say, if you wished for it, and Raven did as well, I'd join you both in hol—I mean, I'd make you man and wife, Marnie."

For a long time Marnie did not speak. She got up and put more peat on the fire, and filled two cups with hot water. She set them on the table, saying, "I'm sorry it's only hot water. The goat got free and ruined the herbs in my garden."

"I believe water's better for my complexion," he replied with a faint smile. "Well, lass, what do you say? If you and Raven were married, you'd be accepted—if not here, then somewhere else. I know a priest in Killacureen, a town about sixty miles away. He was visiting me once, and met Raven, and was sympathetic to him. Killacureen's bigger, and there's work to be had there. I'm not telling you to go, for if you do it'll break my silly old heart. But I'm thinking it'll break yours, if you stay here. The people of Torcurra don't forget things, never in fifty years. You'll always be the witch, and Raven will always be the madman. If you can be happy with that, then stay, and I'll help you all I can. But you won't be able to refuse my charity, because it will be all you get. Just think about it. I'll go now, and leave you in peace. I'll come back this evening for supper, if that suits."

She nodded, and he stood up, his face sad as he looked at her bent head and the tears dripping off her chin. "And there's something else for you to consider, while you're thinking," he added very gently. "I may be a crusty old fool, but I've seen a lot of life, and I know one or two things. I've seen the way Raven looks at you. He loves you, lass. You might think, as well, on what he wants."

He went out, closing the door quietly behind him.

Chapter 28

CROUCHING IN THE long grass on one of the hills behind Torcurra, Raven bent over the rabbit. It was still alive, weakened by terror and pain, its hind leg caught in a trap set by one of the Torcurra people. Tenderly, Raven released the animal and bound it firmly in his cloak. Then, with difficulty, he ripped a piece off the hem of his shirt, bandaged the rabbit's injured leg, bundled it up in his cloak again, and carried it home.

The sun was going down as he neared Marnie's cottage. His strides faltered, though his face became set and determined. Pushing open the door, he went in. He was met by the delicious fragrance of lobster simmering, and the scent of fresh-baked bread. Marnie was setting the table for a meal, and it was a scrumptious feast she had laid out. But she barely looked at him when he came in, and he could tell she was upset.

What hurts you? he signed, using his right hand, since his left arm held the bundled cloak.

Nothing, she replied. *What have you got?*

Kneeling by the hearth, he gently unfolded

the cloak. The rabbit lay quivering, its eyes large with fear. Keeping his left hand on the animal, Raven signed, *It's our supper.*

Marnie crouched down by him, and stroked the soft brown fur. *You mended its leg,* she said.

I wanted to stop its hurt, he replied.

This will stop its hurt. She handed him the knife.

Holding the rabbit's shoulders firmly in his left hand, Raven held the blade over its throat. The rabbit gazed up at him with black liquid eyes, and he felt its heart rapid under his hand, like his own heart when he was afraid. Suddenly he dropped the knife on the hearth. *It is beautiful,* he signed. *I can't make it dead. It's like making dead my brother.*

Maybe your brother is hungry, Marnie said, smiling. *Give him cabbage and water. He must get strong if he wants to run in the fields again. Father Brannan came with much food for us.*

Together they emptied Isake's toolbox and placed in it some cabbage leaves and a bowl of water. Then they put the box by the hearth and placed the rabbit in, so it could rest secure.

I must say big things to you, Marnie said. She looked nervous and tense, and Raven worried as he sat by her at the table, the gifts of food from Father Brannan spread between them.

I am going away from this house, she said. *The man Pierce can have it, and give me gold. He said he will do this. I'll go away, far from here, to a big village Father Brannan knows about. I'd like you to come with me, but you must ask your heart if you will come or stay. If you stay in Torcurra, you can't stay in this house. Pierce will be here.*

Raven went and knelt in front of her. *I don't want to stay here without you,* he signed. *I can't be without you. You are me. We are the same, in our hearts.* He stopped, searching for words, frustrated and near tears. He went on: *I feel . . . feelings too big, I have no words. If you go away from me, I will lie down and sleep, and not wake up again.*

Still kneeling, he put his arms around her waist, and pressed his face against her neck. He was crying, making strange, hoarse sounds of longing and love. He seldom wept, and Marnie put her arms about his shoulders, her lips against his hair. When he was calm, she drew gently away, so she could talk to him.

I want you to come with me when I go. But maybe you will not see your cave again, or the stone ring where we danced. We will maybe not stay near the sea. Will you be happy?

If I can see your face, he signed, *I'll be happy.*

He embraced her again. For a long time they stayed with their arms about each other, and Marnie did not notice that the potatoes in the embers were burning black, or that the rabbit had jumped out of its box and was drinking the cup of ale she had placed on the hearth to warm for Father Brannan.

Father Brannan sat and sipped his ale, his blue eyes thoughtful and sad as he regarded his two friends across the table.

"Well, I'm sorry you're leaving," he said, "but a new beginning is a good thing. I'll give you a letter to take to the priest in Killacureen. He'll arrange for a house for you to rent. You'll have money enough, seeing as Pierce Isherwood is so keen to buy this property."

Marnie interpreted his words for Raven. Using hand-words as well as trying to speak, Raven said to Father Brannan, *Will you come and see us, when we are there?*

"Aye," nodded the priest, smiling. "I'll come."

Watching his mouth, Raven understood, and beamed. Then he signed to Marnie: *I'll go on a walk, and come back after. I'll not sleep outside all night.*

You can sleep under the moon if you want to, said Marnie, speaking as well. *The people will not come for me again. I'll be all right.*

I'll dance near the stones one last time.

Marnie smiled. *Dance there for me too,* she said, but only with her hands. Raven got Isake's thick cloak he had worn in the afternoon, and shook Father Brannan's hand. Then he went to Marnie, and lovingly stroked her cheek. It was a caress more eloquent than words, and she blushed at his touch, knowing that the priest watched.

"He's sleeping in the hills," she explained, when Raven had gone. "He still loves being outside. The hills are home to him. He wouldn't kill that rabbit over there, because he said it was his brother. I love that wildness in him, and will not change it."

"'Tis more than his wildness you love," said Father Brannan softly. "You will marry him, won't you, lass?"

Marnie looked down, and toyed with the spoon on her empty plate. "I was going to talk to you about that, father," she said. "I've decided I won't. I'll not marry to please you, or to stop people's tongues wagging. I've a lot of things to forget, before I vow I'll live the rest of my life with a man in wedlock, with everything that means. I love Raven, but you're asking me to make a solemn promise on something I know nothing about. It'd be like buying a wagon without seeing if the wheels worked. And there's another reason. Raven has another life, out there in the hills. He's free, and I haven't the right to shut him in. He says he wants to be with me, but being pledged forever is an awful powerful thing. I've been thinking about Isake and me, and what would have happened if he didn't die. I'd still be with him, as miserable as a rabbit in a trap, and stuck there for life. I don't want Raven to ever feel like that."

"I won't argue with you, Marnie; I have a strong suspicion you'd win. But I'm disappointed, and not because I'm a priest and what you're doing is against everything I preach. I'm disappointed for your sake. You're flying in the face of custom, and you'll be spurned for it."

"I'll call Raven my brother. I'll say we're both orphans. It wouldn't be so great a lie; my mother will never accept me back, not with Raven. Not for a while, anyway."

"But if you say he's your brother, and folks believe you, what happens if you decide to marry him, after all?"

"I'd move to another place."

"You can't be always moving, Marnie."

"I don't see why not. Maybe we'll be Gypsies, roaming everywhere and taking work where we find it."

Father Brannan sighed, and gave up. "When are you planning to start this roaming?"

"I'll see Pierce tomorrow. As soon as I have the money, we'll go. It will be better traveling now, in the autumn, while the days are fine. I'll give you back the goat, father, but I'd like to keep the three chickens that are left, if you don't mind."

Father Brannan poured himself another ale, and one for her. "Mind, Marnie? You can take anything you like. All that's mine is yours. I'll pray every day for your happiness, for both of you, and I'll miss you something terrible." He raised his cup, trying to smile, and failing. "So here's to you and Raven, then, wherever he is at this moment: to the least of Christ's brethren, and the best loved of mine."

Marnie raised her cup, then put it down again, and went and wound her arms about the priest's neck. "I'll miss you, father," she said. "You've been a truer friend than any I ever had, excepting for Raven."

He kissed her forehead, and told her to sit down again. "You're making me cry," he said, gruffly. "Now stop it, or we shan't be having a celebration at a new beginning, but a lamentation. And I think you'd better dish me up a second helping of that pudding you made, so I'll have the strength to walk back home again. Mind you, many more of your puddings, and I'd be rolling home. Maybe it's just as well you're going, Widow Isherwood; I'm not at all sure you're good for my stomach."

Marnie placed another bowl of pudding in front of him, and sat down in Raven's chair, so she faced him. "You're good for my stomach, father," she said. "I'd have starved without you. I don't know how to thank—"

"I hope you're not starting a sermon on gratitude," he said, "because I'd just find it embarrassing. Besides, sometimes your sermonizing is better than mine, and then I'm annoyed, as well."

"No words, then," she said. "Just this, for you to sell and make some money from." She removed the golden wedding band from the finger of her right hand, and placed it on the table between her and the priest.

"I can't take your gold, Marnie. It's all you have."

"It's the only gold I don't want. If you won't take it for yourself, at least use the money to help someone who needs it. But I'd rather you kept it, as payment for all you've given us."

Father Brannan picked up the ring. "I'll sell it, and get the best price I can," he said. "But I won't spend the money. I'll hold it for you, and all you ever have to do is ask me for it."

"Why are you so stubborn, father?"

"Me, stubborn?" cried Father Brannan, nearly choking on his pudding. "Listen to who's talking! The most mulish, argumentative, contrary woman I ever met! And you call *me* stubborn!"

"Call me any more names, father, and I'll take away your pudding."

"In that case, I'll eat my words, along with my plum pie. I do apologize. I was speaking from the depths of mortification and shock."

Marnie giggled. For a few moments she sat looking at her left hand, where the skin of her palm and the underside of her fingers was thickened by ugly scars. "I'm glad you put the ring on my other hand," she said. "I'd never have got it off, now. I suppose you thought of that, you crafty old fox."

Father Brannan choked again. "I don't much like the terms you use to describe my sublime wisdom," he said, when he had got his breath. "And I was thinking that one day there'd be another ring going on, and not just the old one coming off."

"I'm begging your pardon, but that's being crafty," she said.

"Not crafty enough, or we'd be having a wedding in the morning," he muttered, slipping the ring into his pocket, and standing up. "Now, what did I do with my scarf? There's a cold wind out there. Make sure you lock yourself in, since Raven's not here to protect you."

"I can protect myself, father," she said, giving him his scarf, and opening the door for him.

"No doubt you can," he grinned.

She smiled and kissed his cheek, and he trudged off into the night.

"Don't forget to see me before you sell your house!" he called back. "Pierce Isherwood's a craftier fox than I am!"

"I won't forget!" she promised, laughing, and he turned and went on. Marnie blew a kiss to his vanishing back, and went inside, her eyes sad.

Marnie did not bolt her door that night. She had told Raven she would never lock him out, and would not break her word. But she slept with her knife nearby, and was glad of the company of the rabbit, which had jumped out of the box again and was stretched out by the hearth. It was the first time she had slept alone since her ordeal in the church, and she was afraid that someone from the village might still hate her, still want her dead. But, more than her fear of the people, was her terror of the dreams.

As always they came just before the dawn, when she thought she was safe: the shadows gathering on the beach outside her house, and the rumble of the wagon wheels filling the sky, and the hood tight over her head. Only this time they did not take the hood off; they left it on, and she did not know where they would burn her, or how; and there was pain all over her, and suffocating smoke, and—

Gasping, she woke up, and threw the blankets off her head. Raven was crouched by the fire, blowing it back into life, and quietly placing on more peat. He had taken off the cloak and put it over a chair. The dark folds glimmered with silver mist, and the hem was wet from long grass. With great gentleness he lifted the rabbit in his arms, lying it on its back. It was very calm, its eyes half closed. Raven bent his head and sniffed its fur, rubbing his cheek along its ears, stroking it, loving it. Marnie watched, smiling to herself, the terrors of her nightmare slipping away. The rabbit was utterly relaxed, trusting, finding in the youth's presence the same consolation and peace that Marnie found.

Gently, Raven placed the rabbit in the box, and began making up his bed in front of the fire. As he spread out the last blanket, Marnie threw a tiny pebble at him, hitting him on the back. He came over and crouched by her bed.

I came back before the sun, he signed, his hands golden in the growing firelight. *I was afraid that maybe you are afraid. I wanted to be with you.*

It was good near the stones? she asked.

Yes. I danced two dances, one for me and one for you. I danced like the little birds in the sky, fast and beautiful. But I danced on a prickle, and came down hard on the dirt. It was a stupid stop on a good dance.

Marnie's lips curled. *In my heart, I wanted to be with you,* she said.

It's good you stayed here. You'd laugh.

I'd not laugh at you. To me, your dance is all times beautiful.

Smiling, he leaned down and kissed her lightly on the cheek. His lips were like ice, and he was shivering.

You are very cold. Did you swim in the sea? she asked.

No. The fields are all over with white smoke. I saw deer, and fox.

When we are in a different house, you don't have to all times sleep inside. I know you like to be under the moon and stars. I don't want you to be different from the way you are now.

Why?

Because I want you to be happy.

I'll be happy if I can see your face. That is all I want.

One day my face will get old and ugly.

It's ugly now, he said, grinning, and she shot out a fist to punch him. But he caught her hand, laughing, and when she tried to pull free he lost his balance and fell across her. Giggling, she tried to push him off, but he lay half over her, his face buried in the pillow beside her head, as he discovered the scents of white linen and lavender. He inhaled vigorously, reveling in the fragrances, then he turned to Marnie's hair and neck. He passed the tip of his tongue over her skin, tasting her, then softly sniffed her, as he had the rabbit, enjoying her with all his senses. She lay very still, lost between laughter and deliciousness, feeling his face cool against her neck, his beard soft and still damp from the mist. Slowly he lifted his head. His face was just above hers, and his eyes were suddenly grave, full of longing. He wanted to talk to her, but could not without sitting up. So he stayed where he was, his fingers smoothing back her hair, while he tried to read her expression. She was smiling a little, unsure.

Tenderly, he pressed his lips to her forehead. Hardly breathing, she closed her eyes. His mouth was gentle as it moved across her eyes and slowly down her cheeks. It was not a kiss; this was something infinitely more tender, a brushing of her skin, a touching so light it held her spellbound, powerless. He was moving his mouth along her jaw, across her lips, his breath warm, sweet. He stopped, and she lifted her face, wanting more.

"Ah, Marn," he said, amazed, and slowly moved over her, covering her with kisses featherlight. Entranced, she did not realize he had pushed away the blankets and undone her clothes, until she felt his mouth on her shoulders and throat, moving down, exploring, his lips exquisite on her skin.

With utter trust she gave herself to him, to his mouth, his hands, all of him. Just once memories of Isake tore through her and she tensed, waiting for the sudden roughness, the hurt. But there was only gentleness; only Raven, groaning quietly with pleasure, saying her name over and over, his voice full of adoration and wonder, his touch so tender it made her weep; Raven, innocent and unhurried and in perfect harmony with her, telling his love at last, in ways beyond words, in ways that were moon-good beautiful.

Chapter 29

ATHER BRANNAN LOOKED up from digging the grave in the churchyard, and stared in astonishment at the couple standing just beyond the carved stone crosses. The young woman wore a white dress with green leaves embroidered on the bodice, and a garland of wild flowers on her hair. The youth was in a snowy shirt, black hose and shoes, and a quilted jerkin of indigo silk. Smiling, radiant, they both had blue-black hair still wet from washing in the sea, and their eyes shone. They looked stunning.

"Well, you two polish up all right," remarked Father Brannan, trying not to smile too widely, as he leaned his spade against a tombstone and wiped his hands on his dusty habit. "Going to a wedding, are you?"

"Aye," said Marnie. Raven signed something to her, and she giggled and blushed.

"And whose wedding is it?" asked the priest gruffly, though his eyes sparkled. "It wouldn't be the wedding of that young widow—the one who said she wouldn't buy a wagon without seeing if the wheels turned?"

Marnie's blush deepened, and she did not reply.

Unable to keep a straight face any longer, Father Brannan chuckled. "Oh, Marnie, child!" he said, striding over and hugging her. "The wheels spun fine, did they?"

"None of your teasing, father," she said, "or we'll go elsewhere to be wed."

Father Brannan hugged Raven as well, then stood back and admired him. "Well, you're a brave man to be taking her on, and that's for sure," he said.

Marnie signed to Raven: *Father Brannan said you are strong, like the bird that flies in the storm, to be my husband.*

Grinning, Raven said, *Tell him, maybe I am stupid.*

She punched his arm, and they laughed.

"Come, now! You can't be clouting him yet, you haven't even said your vows!" cried Father Brannan, leading them over toward the church.

Marnie looked back at the grave he had almost finished digging. "You're busy, father. Shall we come another time?"

"Nay—I wouldn't hear of it! If I made you wait, you'd be bound to change your mind! I have a burying in an hour or so. I've time for your wedding, before then. But I won't be able to celebrate with you after, I'm afraid. The funeral is a child's, and her parents are needing me to spend some time with them, after."

"That's all right, father. If you'll just marry us, we'll be grateful forever. Besides, I want to see Pierce Isherwood after, about the house. I won't make a deal with him. I'll just ask what he'll pay, and then talk it over with you. And, if you don't mind waiting for it, we'll pay you the penny for marrying us after he's bought our house. I don't have a penny now."

"All your life's great enterprises done in one fair morning, eh, lass?" Father Brannan smiled. He added, seriously, "I hope Raven knows the significance of what he's doing, and that it's for life."

"I told him, father."

"Aye. No doubt you did," muttered the priest. "There's one thing I'll say for you, Widow Isherwood—you know how to give a man a message straight, and no mistake."

The church was quiet, full of incense and holiness, with yellow morning light coming in through the small windows set deep into the walls. The roof was lost in shadow, but Marnie could just see the rafters, their harmonious patterns unfolding in the quiet dark.

Father Brannan went up to the altar, and bent his head in prayer for a while. Marnie and Raven waited behind him, their hands linked. When Father Brannan turned to face them, Marnie said, "We only want a short wedding, father. Not the whole thing, like I did with . . . like before. And can you talk slow, and make the words easy, so I can tell them to Raven?"

"I'll do my best," promised the priest. "We'll have the wedding in the little porch, as usual, and then come inside the church for the Communion. I'll keep everything short."

"I think we'll miss the Communion, father," she said. "It would remind me . . ."

"I understand, child, and I don't think the Good Lord will love you any less for it. But there are a few other things to be arranged. We need two witnesses. I'd like your own mother to be one, but you're not giving me time to fetch her."

"She wouldn't be a witness, not for me and Raven."

"What about Old Finian and his wife? They took no part in bringing you to your trial, and they helped me look after Raven sometimes, when he were little."

"They'll be fine, father."

"And we'll need a ring. I have several that I keep for occasions such as this. You can choose which one you want, while I wash and get on my vestments, and talk to Finian." They waited in the porch while he hurried to his house, and returned with a small box of rings. "Choose which one you want," he said, giving it to Marnie. "And maybe you and Raven should do some praying—if he knows about the Almighty, that is."

"Raven knows him very well, father; he always has. I only gave him the name."

"Aye, I thought he might," murmured Father Brannan. "I can't tell you how happy I am to be doing this for you, lass. But I wish I'd had some warning; I'd have made myself handsome, and put flowers in the church."

"You're always handsome, father, and the church is always beautiful."

"Ah, you're a sweet saint, Widow Isherwood, and that's my true and unbiased opinion." He kissed her forehead, and hurried back to his house.

Marnie and Raven stood in the picturesque little porch, and looked through the rings in the box. Morning sun filtered in through the leaded windows, making soft halos about their bent heads, and glinting in the rings. At first Marnie looked for one large enough to go easily over the scarred finger on her left hand, but then changed her mind.

I'll put your ring on my right hand, she signed. *It's the hand I make many words with, and the only good hand.*

They are both good, he said, lifting her left hand, and kissing the scars very softly. Kissing her right palm as well, he noticed that the gold band was missing. "Why?" he asked.

I gave it to Father Brannan, so he can get gold. I gave it for all the things he gave us.

We want that ring, now.

No. It was Isake's. I want a different ring for us.

I have one! Suddenly excited, he felt in Isake's velvet purse, which was hanging from his belt. Marnie had given it to him, and in it he kept colored stones and other assorted treasures. *I'll give you this,* he said, slipping a large ring on her finger.

It was the ring he had found in the ashes the day the chimney had broken, bringing down the nests and debris from the sooty recesses. In the morning light the colored glass glowed red and gold and white.

It's too big, Raven said, disappointed.

It's a man's ring, she told him, relieved because it was so crass and ugly, though she would have treasured it, for Raven's sake, if it had fit.

Raven tried the ring on his own fingers, but as always it fell off, and he dropped it back in the purse.

They chose a plain brass ring, and Marnie gave it to Raven to hold. *When we have made our big words together,* she explained, *you will give me this ring, and after that I will be your wife, and you will be my husband.*

I don't want a ring, to know that, he said.

It's for other people to know. Other people must hear our big words. Two people, and Father Brannan, and the Maker of all things. We must hold him in our hearts a little time now, and make us right and strong for the huge thing we do.

They went into the church, holding hands as they walked through the dimness to the stone altar. Kneeling, they closed their eyes. After a time Raven made soft sounds, and Marnie looked at him. Tears were streaming down his face, and he was talking with his hands, though his eyes were still closed. She looked away again, her head bent. For the hundredth time since she had known him, she wondered how much he understood, and suspected it was more than she would ever know.

Closing her eyes, she prayed, whispering, "Thank you for Raven, for our love, and the joy it is. One day let us have words enough to tell everything that is in our hearts. Thank you that, for the loving part of it, we need no words. And pardon me for saying that, Lord, but I wanted you to know that with Raven it's fine, and I won't be asking you to let me out of it again. And I'm glad you forgot that I asked to be ugly or plague-ridden, because that would have been calamitous, seeing as you had Raven waiting for me. And please bless the souls of Isake and Eilis, because without them I wouldn't be here this day, beside this friend."

After their prayers they went back and waited in the porch. Father Brannan returned, wearing clean vestments, and carrying a holy book. He had brought too a large pitcher of honey mead, which he set on the grass just outside the rustic wooden gate. "The honey mead's my gift to you both on your wedding day," he said. "I know it's the custom for your parents to give it to you, but seeing as they're not here, you can have it from me."

"Thank you, father," Marnie said. "We'll think of you while we drink it."

"I doubt you will," he said, smiling.

Old Finian appeared, hobbling through the long grasses between the tombstones, with his wife clutching one arm. Very gravely, they came up and shook Raven's hand, and nodded to Marnie.

They faced the church door, and Father Brannan opened his book. He was about to speak when there were voices in the churchyard, and a group of villagers approached. They were mainly elderly women, for the younger women were minding their children, and the men were out fishing in their boats. They clustered behind the gate, staring at the beautiful young widow with the white dress and flowers in her hair, and the youth they used to whip, looking handsome as a prince. They began to murmur among themselves, then caught Father Brannan's frown, and fell silent.

"Are you happy if they stay, Marnie?" asked Father Brannan. "I can ask them to leave, if you wish."

"I don't mind, father," she said.

The priest smiled, and his eyes shimmered as he began: "Beloved friends, we be gathered here, before God and before these witnesses, to join together this man and this woman in holy wedlock . . ."

At the end of every sentence he stopped, and Marnie repeated the words with her hands, for Raven. He watched and listened, his eyes grave and comprehending. When it came to the time for him to make his vows, he wept, and Marnie wept, making hers; and they both were so solemn and joyful that Father Brannan cried, watching them. By the time Raven slipped the ring on Marnie's finger, the priest could hardly speak.

Then it was done, and Father Brannan said, "Raven, you may kiss your wife."

Raven looked to Marnie, to have the words interpreted, but she only stared at him, nonplussed.

"What is it?" asked the priest softly. "You have kissed him before, haven't you?"

"Aye," she said, confused, "but I don't have a hand-word for kiss. I don't know what to tell him."

"Just do it, lass!" said Father Brannan.

So she did, in front of them all, and Raven put his arms around her and would not let her go, and it was a kiss such as never had been seen before, in Torcurra.

At last, red-faced and breathless, Marnie managed to disentangle herself from his embrace, and the women behind the gate twittered and sighed, and thought wistfully of their own sweethearts of long ago. Old Finian and his wife beamed at one another and, clutching each other's wrinkled hands, followed the newlyweds and the priest into the church. Father Brannan said a formal blessing and a prayer, then went over to a table beside the altar to record their names in the book of marriages.

Dipping the quill in the ink, the priest wrote for a while on the old yellowed page. Suddenly he looked up, disquieted. "I've a problem with the names, Marnie," he said. "I don't have a family name for Raven that you can take instead of Isherwood. And I need a name; this is a lawful document."

"Can't we make up a name?" she asked. "He's Raven of the fields. Call him Raven O'field."

Father Brannan looked at Finian. "I'm happy with O'field as the name, but what are your thoughts on the matter, man?" he asked.

"Well," quavered old Finian, "I quite like the name O'field. And that's how most of us got our names, come to think of it—Thatcher, for thatching roofs, and Smith, for the smithy, and Miller for the miller. It makes sense. Raven O'field. He lived in the fields all his life.

I think the name's a good one, and I'll not hem and haw about witnessing it."

And so Marnie and Raven received their new name, and they marked their crosses beside their names in the great book in the ancient church at Torcurra, and were married.

Chapter 30

PIERCE ISHERWOOD OPENED the dark bottle of costly wine, and poured the rich crimson liquor into three goblets. He gave one to Raven, and handed Marnie hers. He was congenial, generous, and his good will worried Marnie more than his acrimony had.

"Here's a toast, then," said Pierce, raising his goblet. "To the newlyweds. May your lives be long and happy." They drank, and he went on: "I never thought to be toasting you twice as a bride, Marnie. I admit, you look even more ravishing now than you did the first time. I'm honored that you've come to visit, straight after your wedding. I thought you'd be with your friends, celebrating."

"Father Brannan has a funeral to do," she said. "We wanted to see you while we were in the village. It's about the house."

"Well, sit down," said Pierce, indicating two chairs.

Marnie and Raven sat, though Pierce remained standing, sipping his wine and regarding them with that sly, infuriating smile of his.

The room was sparsely furnished, though everything in it was of excellent quality, handpicked from the manor house. A delicate polished table stood between their chairs, and Marnie put her wine on it so she could talk to Raven. Without speaking, she signed: *The man says good words, but his eyes say different things. His words will most like be lies.*

"I see you still use your strange magic," remarked Pierce pleasantly. "I thought you'd have loosened his tongue by now, so he could talk."

"I have no sorcery. The ordeal proved me innocent, and I'll not answer to you about any of it," said Marnie. "I've come to talk about the property, and that's all I'll talk about. And I know it's not the house you want, but the cove, because of the business you want to start there."

"Business?" repeated Pierce, a black eyebrow raised. "And what business is that, Marnie?"

"The shipping business, for the wool. I heard talk when I was working on your land, before Sir William died. I heard talk about all the sheep you wanted to own, and how you planned to ship out the wool to other places. I know that's why you want the cove, and that it's worth a good amount."

His face inscrutable, Pierce finished his drink, then poured himself another. He lifted his goblet again. "You're right about the good amount. Here's to it, and my new property," he said.

"It isn't yours yet, sir," said Marnie.

"Ah—but it is!" said Pierce. "And I thank you, most sincerely. I wasn't expecting such a generous move on your part, not after all your fighting talk. I would have paid you that good amount, if you'd sold the place to me. I thought you needed money. But as it is, you've just handed the property into my hands, free, and I'll not show ingratitude."

"But I haven't," she said, the color rising in her face. "I'm not giving it. I want to sell."

"But it's too late for that!" he laughed, running his hand through his dark hair, as if he were perplexed. "I don't know what you're up to, Marnie! You do realize, don't you, what you've done?"

"I've come to sell my house!" she cried, standing, angry because he was laughing at her, and she did not know why.

"You don't realize, do you?" he said. "Oh, Marnie Isherwood! What a beautiful, blessed fool you are!"

"I'm not a fool! And I'm Marnie O'field, now. That's my new name."

"Marnie O'field. Well, now, that rolls off the tongue smooth and lovely, like red wine. Marnie O'field. Lawful wedded wife of the village madman, and no longer widow of Sir Isake Isherwood. You know what you've done, my sweet? In marrying your madman, you've forfeited your house. It's in the will my father wrote: If any of our wives are made a widow, they inherit whatever we leave to them; but if they marry again within ten years, the inheritance returns to the Isherwood estate. All you ever got from Isake reverted back to his family the moment you made a vow to someone else."

Marnie sat down again, speechless. "You're lying," she said after a while.

Raven went and crouched by her, asking something, but she held his hands still, and shook her head. He waited, confused and upset.

"I'm not lying," said Pierce. "If you've any doubts, I'll send a lad to Fernleigh with a letter for my brother Gerard, asking for a copy of our father's will. It's there in black and white. What a pity you didn't come and see me on your way to your wedding, instead of after it. It would have made all the difference. But you couldn't wait, could you, to get rid of that ring Isake put on you? Well, you're rid of it now, and him, and everything else he gave you. I wish you happiness with your fine new husband and his wide estate. Now, if you're not going to finish your wine, maybe you'd like to leave. I have some things to box up for moving. I'll shift into the cottage at noon tomorrow. You'll be out by then, or I'll throw you out—and even your obliging priest won't be able to stop me."

Marnie stood, and without looking at Pierce again, or saying a word, walked out. As Raven followed her he picked up the jar of honey mead Father Brannan had given them, which he had left on the step. *What did he say?* he asked, tucking the heavy jar securely under his arm, and hurrying after Marnie.

He said, because I have your ring now, and not Isake's, the house is not mine. It's his. He will not give me gold for it. He will take it tomorrow, and shut us out. We must go, and have nothing.

She was furious, devastated, and Raven did not know what to do to comfort her. They came to the church and saw the mourners going in, carrying the dead child on a bier. People stopped to look at the newlyweds, and began to whisper. Marnie clutched Raven's hand and looked straight ahead, at the long grass track to the cove that was no longer hers.

A little farther on were the graves outside the churchyard, where Eilis was buried. Three boys and a girl stood around the headstones, talking. They stopped as Raven and Marnie drew near.

"You're the witch, aren't you?" called one of the boys, his expression a mixture of fear and audacity. He was about twelve summers old, and the oldest of the group.

Marnie did not reply, but walked on, her fingers tight about Raven's, her face expressionless. As she passed the graves she looked at the grave of Eilis Isherwood. The pitted stone was stained with something dark. She looked at the children, saw the guilt in their faces. Then the boy said, his chin jutting out, "We didn't do no wrong. We're stopping it, the evil in our village."

"What evil?" asked Marnie.

"*Her* evil," said the boy, kicking the headstone. "The curse of the old witch. We killed a black cat and put its blood on her stone. It's a powerful thing, cat's blood; it'll stop the evil coming up out of her grave."

"That's foolishness!" cried Marnie. "There's no evil in her grave."

"Aye, there is too!" cried the girl. "It's her ghost! It went back to her cottage, and put itself in you! That's what my mother says."

Marnie's hands shook as she told Raven what the girl had said. The children watched her strange gestures, and retreated.

"Your mother's wrong," said Marnie. "There's no ghost, no witch."

"There is so!" shouted the first boy. "It's in her house! And we're going to do something about it!"

Afraid, the others tried to hush him, but he burst out, his face red with defiance and zeal: "Tomorrow, after church, we're going to burn it!"

They ran off into the village, and Marnie watched them leave, her face sad.

It's good that we are going, she signed to Raven. *All the people, children too, do not like me. They say they will put fire on our house tomorrow.*

Are you afraid they will?

No. It's only words from children wanting to be strong. But we will go at sunup, and have all day to journey.

She picked some daisies from around the graves, and spread them over the blood the children had poured on Eilis's headstone. But the blood still showed, so she removed the wedding garland from her head, and placed that too on the stone. Then she took Raven's hand again, and they started walking back.

As they descended into the cove and saw the cottage shining in the sun, Marnie covered her face with her hands, her grief sharp and unbearable. She stumbled on, sobbing, and Raven stopped her. He put the jar of honey mead down on the grass. Lifting her chin with his hand, he made her look at him.

I have you, and you have me, he said. *A house is only stones and grass. We have all the stones, all the grass, the sea and the sky. All the far fields, they are ours. We have a wagon and horse, and chickens and bread and clothes. We have everything we want for our journey, and we are together all times. Why are you sad?*

Looking at him, seeing the love in his eyes, Marnie slowly smiled. *I'm stupid sometimes, that is why,* she said.

Very stupid, Raven said, smiling. *We have this day here, and tonight. I want it to be a good time.*

This time, she said, *it's what people call our honeymoon.*

Honeymoon? he repeated, puzzled, thinking she was joking. *What has the moon to do with honey?*

Under the moon, we drink the honey mead. Everyone drinks honey mead on the first night they are husband and wife, and the time is called their honeymoon.

Raven laughed. *Sweet-moon time,* he said, picking up the jar again. *I like it.*

They kissed and walked on, their arms around each other, down to the sun-warmed sand and the secluded house and the honey-sweet afternoon.

Chapter 31

RAVEN PICKED UP the basket of bowls and cups from the floor, and took it outside. The sun was barely up, the skies vivid blue, cloudless again. It was a good day for a journey. He pushed the basket to the back of the wagon, wedging it between the chests of clothes, and called Marnie. She was under the trees feeding the hens.

You can bring the chickens now, he signed. *I have made their house.*

The "house" was the little table Isake had made, turned upside down so the top formed the base and the legs the four corners, with a blanket tied firmly about it for the sides. Marnie came over, a speckled hen in her arms. Gently, she placed it into the enclosure.

It's a good house, thank you, she said to Raven. *Isake's table is good in many ways.* Her face was flushed from the dawn, and the sun burned in her eyes and in the specks of sand still caught in her hair from yesterday's loving on the beach. She glanced at Isake's grave with its rough wooden cross. *Maybe Pierce will get a stone cross for him,* she said.

If you want to sit near Isake a little time, I'll get the other chickens, said Raven. *Everything is on the wagon now, but not the chest with Isake's making-things. We must put them all back in.*

I don't want to sit by Isake, but I want to be in the house alone, to put his making-things away.

Understanding, Raven went to catch the other hens.

For a few moments Marnie leaned in the open doorway, looking at the empty room. Only Isake's toolbox remained, the tools piled beside it; and the straw where the bed had been. Marnie knelt by the toolbox. Raven had set the rabbit free, and emptied its droppings from the box. Only a dark stain remained on the wood where the animal's injured leg had left a smudge of blood. Marnie looked at the hearth, and remembered the day she had washed away Isake's blood, scrubbing the hearth until her knuckles were raw. Bending her head in her good hand, she sighed deeply and was quiet a while, thinking. Then, slowly, she picked up the first tool. Holding it between her knees, she polished it carefully on her apron with her right hand, then fixed it into its special place in the box. When all were cleaned and put away, she closed the lid and stood up.

Everything was finished, now. The cottage was bare. But the floor was dry and clean, the roof was thatched, and the fireplace tidy. "Thank you for letting me live in your house, Eilis," she whispered. "I loved it well."

When she went outside, Raven came over and put something into her hand. *I made this. It's yours*, he said. It was a piece of wood, broken at the ends, but smoothly curved between, and on it he had etched a little boat like theirs. *The wood*, he said, *it's from our boat. It's a little thing from our time here, to take away.*

Speechless, she kissed him, and put the precious gift in the basket with the bowls and cups. Grunting with the effort, Raven brought out the box of tools, and Marnie did her best to help him put it on the wagon. Then Raven got the goat, leaving the tethering rope around its neck so they could lead it back to Father Brannan's place.

You take the wagon, said Marnie, *and I'll walk with the goat.*

That was the way they left, not looking behind them, with Raven driving the wagon and Marnie scolding the goat for being unruly and too slow. They were almost at the village when they saw Pierce Isherwood coming toward them. He was walking in a leisurely way, as if enjoying an early morning stroll. He stopped by their wagon, and Raven halted the horse.

"Good morning, sweet sister-in-law!" Pierce said cheerfully to Marnie, ignoring Raven. "I was on my way to make sure you were keeping your side of the bargain, but I see you are."

"We had no bargain," said Marnie, struggling with the goat, which decided that the edge of Pierce's tunic looked like interesting fodder. "But the house is yours. I hope you're satisfied with it."

"I'll be very satisfied, once I've found what is hidden there," he said. "You were wrong about the shipping business, and me wanting the cove for that. My father thought about the wool business, but changed his mind. You shouldn't listen to gossip, Marnie—it brings nothing good, and you should know that well."

"Then why do you want the house? What do you mean—what is hidden there?"

"You've no idea what you've been living with all this time!" he said, laughing. "Have you heard those old stories about Eilis, and how she had a king for a lover?"

"Aye. Father Brannan told me."

"Well, they were true. He gave her a gift once. A king's keepsake: jewels and gold. And that's what makes the cottage worth more than all our father's lands—that treasure Eilis hid there. Obviously Isake never told you."

"No." Marnie's voice was small, dry in her throat. Then she remembered. "He did ask me once if I found anything! I thought he had lost some money. He said if I did find anything, to give it to him, and not to deceive him. It was the last thing he ever said to me."

"You should have listened." Pierce smiled, enjoying her anguish.

"You had so much time to look for it, Marnie. You could have dug up your whole floor, taken the place to pieces stone by stone. But you didn't. You prattled on about your pathetic new thatch and how much you loved the hovel, and never thought of anything better. Well, I'll be finding it now."

"If you knew about it, why didn't you look before?" she asked, hating him, hating the way he sneered, mocking her.

"We only knew about it after our father died," said Pierce. "We knew our grandmother had a cottage here, but it was worthless. We wanted nothing to do with it, since she died by the fire, dishonorably. When Isake inherited her old cottage and nothing else, we were angry for his sake, and thought our father was a miserly old devil—and mad into the bargain. But he left Isake a letter, and when Isake read it he didn't mind so much. He never told us what was in the letter, and I didn't know till I found it here that day. I knew then I had to own this house, by fair means or foul. And now I have it. So you go on your merry way with your new husband and your little goat and your precious belongings; and in the years to come you can tell your children, as they crowd starving around your knees, how you spent a whole summer living with a king's treasure, and you didn't know it."

He bowed mockingly, and began to go on.

"What is the treasure, sir?" asked Marnie. "Is it gold?"

"Aye, a bit of gold," said Pierce, stopping again. "But it's what's set into the gold that matters, Marnie. There are rubies, each one worth a manor house, and jasper, and diamonds beyond price. 'Tis a small thing, I believe, a piece of jewelry most like, but worth a life spent in looking."

Suddenly Raven called out. "Marn! Marn!" he cried, pointing back up the hill toward the cove. From behind the hill, from the cove itself, rose a pall of black smoke.

"The house!" cried Marnie. "'Tis your house, Pierce! Oh, Lord! The children! The children! They said—"

Pierce did not wait to hear more. With a cry of fury and despair, he ran toward the cove, stumbling, falling in his haste, his hopeless yells like sobs.

Raven got down from the wagon, and touched Marnie's arm. Transfixed, she was staring at the smoke, her eyes moist.

It's not our thing to hurt about, Raven said. *It's not our house. What did Pierce say?*

He shook her arm, and she looked at him, shocked, not comprehending anything except that the house she loved was on fire. Then, slowly, that other thing dawned across her mind—the thing Pierce had said, about the king's keepsake.

Raven, she said, her fingers shaking so much she could hardly sign, *where is the ring you got from the fire, the day the storm came?*

Why?

Where is it?

Bewildered, he felt in his leather pouch. Then he searched a second time, and shrugged. *It's lost,* he said. *No matter. You said it was ugly, and—*

"Find it!" she shrieked, forgetting to sign. "Find it!"

Alarmed, catching her panic, he leaned over the wagon and opened his chest of clothes. He pulled out a shirt, and felt in the silken folds. Throwing it on the ground, he pulled out another, and another. Jerkins, leggings, and colored tunics flew through the air. He came to the belt he had worn yesterday at his wedding, and pulled it out. He felt in the velvet purse still tied to it, and held up the ring, beaming. *Why, Marn?* he asked.

It is . . . she stopped, frantic, trying to think of a word for worth. Fumbling, her signs jumbled, she said, *Pierce said there was gold in the house. Gold, much gold that will get houses and fields and—*

But this ring is not gold, he said, mystified. *It's ugly. You don't like it.*

We must take it to Father Brannan, ask him what it is. The red and yellow and white things, maybe—maybe they are not ugly. Maybe they are beautiful. Father Brannan will tell us.

Raven scratched his head, and dropped the ring back in the purse.

Marnie grabbed it out, and held it tightly in her right hand. "Quick! Pick up your clothes! We have to see Father Brannan!" she cried, and Raven, watching her mouth, fathomed most of her words.

But Father Brannan had seen the smoke and was already on his way to them, running fast, his holy books still under his arm, for he had just finished the morning service at church.

"Your house is on fire!" the priest yelled, panting hard, drawing alongside them and waving his arm toward the smoke. "Haven't you noticed?"

"Aye," said Marnie. "What color are rubies, father?"

In astonishment, Father Brannan surveyed the clothes strewn across the ground. "What on earth are you two doing?" he cried. "If you're thinking of holding your own market, you can't—it's the Sabbath. But your house! What are you going to do about your house? 'Twill be nothing but blackened stones, by now!"

"What color are rubies?" she asked again.

The goat was chewing one of Isake's embroidered shirts, and Father Brannan snatched the garment back, scowling at the animal. "Rubies are red. Are you blind? Don't you see what's happening?"

"And jasper, father?"

Father Brannan gazed at her in disbelief. Beside her, the goat started on a costly tunic, and in yonder skies the black smoke spread, ink-dark and appalling.

"All right, I'll play your silly guessing game," Father Brannan said. "Jasper is yellow, maybe brown. What's your next question, while your worldly goods are being destroyed?"

"Diamonds, father. What color are they?"

"Diamonds are clear and pure as Christ's own tears."

"Like these?" she asked, dropping the ring into his hand.

Father Brannan's holy books slipped to the ground, and he went so pale Marnie thought he was going to be ill. Seeing the shock in the priest's face, Raven grabbed the nearest thing, which happened to be his clothes chest, closed it, and set it on the ground for him to sit on.

Father Brannan sank onto it, still staring at the ring on his palm.

What are you saying? Raven signed to Marnie. *What is going on?*

I don't know, she said. *Maybe everything. Maybe nothing.*

Raven rolled his eyes heavenward, and began picking up his clothes. *Stupid!* he signed furiously, to the goat, to Father Brannan's back, to the stunned villagers outside the church, to anyone who might be interested. *Marnie is stupid today! Stupid! Stupid!*

Marnie knelt in front of the priest, looking into his face. "What is it, father?" she asked. "Is it worth anything?"

"Aye, a small kingdom," he murmured. "Where did you get it, child?"

Smiling, crying, she told him. And she told him what Pierce had said about the king's gift Eilis had hidden. Father Brannan listened, shaking his head, sometimes near tears himself. "I think we'd better go to my house," he said. "I'll give you a piece of leather to thread this on, and you must tie it around your neck and make sure you never lose sight of it."

"It's Raven's," she said, "not mine. I don't like it."

"Ah, you have poor taste, Marnie, excepting in my cooking, and in your choice of husband. And at the moment I have my doubts about him, the way he's reverting to his former ravings. I'll go home with this and find something to thread it on, and you and Raven come on when you've sorted out your little bit of domestic bedlam. And, just in case you've forgot, I feel it's my bounden duty to remind you that your house is on fire."

"It's not my house," said Marnie, and told him why, and what the children had said.

"I suppose that's divine justice," he remarked, gazing at the black smoke. "Still, there'll be enough rubble left to keep him busy for a year or so, searching."

"You won't tell him we have the ring, father?"

"What? And ruin his blissful ambitions? I might even do the neighborly thing, and go and help him look for it!" Chuckling, Father

Sherryl Jordan
258

Brannan picked up his books, took the goat's tether firmly in one hand, and began walking back.

Marnie opened the chest he had been sitting on, so Raven could put his clothes in. He was still snatching up the garments from the ground, tight-lipped and angry. Marnie tugged at his arm, but he pulled away, stuffing his belongings violently back into the chest. He expected Marnie to complain, because she was fussy about folding clothes; but she only watched, a wide smile on her face.

I don't like it when you don't make words to me! he signed, then slammed down the lid and heaved the chest onto the wagon again, dropping it with such force that the whole wagon shook, sending the hens into a flutter, and seriously tempting the horse to bolt. *I'm not stupid! I want to know what is going on! I ask you, and you say, Maybe everything, maybe nothing. And now you laugh, and I'm angry. Very, very, big, huge angry.*

I'm happy, she said. *Very, very, big, huge happy.*

Why?

Stop, and I'll tell you.

Haltingly, because she did not have all the words, she explained about the ring, and what Father Brannan had said. As Raven watched her hands his anger evaporated, though he did not fully understand. It was enough that Marnie was happy. *Now we have everything,* she finished, elated.

Shaking his head, unable to comprehend her excitement, Raven told her: *We all times had everything.*

Chapter 32

FATHER BRANNAN ROLLED up the letter he had written to his friend, and tied a red ribbon around it. He handed it to Marnie. "Give that to Father Seamus, in Killacureen," he said. "It'll introduce you, and gain you a loyal helper."

"What have you said to him?" asked Marnie.

"I told him Raven's an extraordinary young man with emerging brightness."

"And me? What did you tell him about me?"

"I told him you're a crotchety, mutinous saint, who's caused some near-calamitous upheavals to my spiritual peace. I also warned him not to argue with you, because you always win."

"I'm not crotchety!"

"I'm begging your pardon. Maybe I should have used a stronger word."

She laughed, and signed to Raven: *Father Brannan made parchment-words to his friend in the big village where we go. He said to his friend, Raven is good and Marnie is bad, and he will like us.*

Raven grinned, though his gray eyes were narrowed, astute and suspicious. *I watched his mouth,* he signed. *Father Brannan did not say those words.*

I'll tell you after, she said, speaking as well. *It was lies, what he said, and his words don't matter.*

"Lies, was it?" muttered Father Brannan, picking up the priceless ring, which he had knotted securely onto a thick leather thong. "I don't think I ought to be giving you this, Marnie. You simply don't appreciate diamonds when you see them." He put the leather over Raven's head, hiding the ring inside his shirt. "Look after this ring," he said, and Raven, watching his mouth, nodded.

"For Marn," Raven said. Looking into the priest's face, he signed, trying to speak as well: *You are my mother and father. You made me strong and all right, before Marnie came. If you did not look after me, she maybe find me hurt all the way to dead. All times, I will hold you in my heart.*

Marnie interpreted, and the priest embraced the young man. "I'm glad I kept you all right too," he said huskily. "I don't know which of you needs the other the most. You're kindred spirits, born for each other, and that's the truth."

When he was composed again, Father Brannan told Marnie, "I haven't mentioned the ring in the letter to Seamus, in case the letter's seen by someone other than yourselves. People murder for less than what Raven has around his neck. Keep it hidden. Tell Seamus about it yourselves, and ask him to help with the selling of it. You won't be able to sell it all at once; there's not a person in this land could afford it, excepting maybe a king himself."

"If this is so valuable, why did Eilis not sell it? You said she died poor, with nothing."

"She couldn't sell it for the same reason it'll be difficult for you. You'll be able to sell it only in a town, such as Killacureen, and then only a stone at a time. But don't break up the ring yourselves; get it done proper. Don't sell even a little stone without asking Seamus, first. He'll know where you can go, where you won't be cheated.

What are you going to do with it all, Marnie? With your great fortune?"

"I owe you some of it, father. And we still haven't paid you the penny, for making us wed."

"You owe me nothing. You've already given me your old wedding ring, and that's worth far more than anything I've given you. Will you buy yourselves a great piece of land, and a grand manor house?"

"I was thinking, maybe we'll buy another horse and a little house on wheels, such as the Gypsies have," said Marnie.

Father Brannan laughed. "Aye—I can see that suiting you better! Now, before you go, there's something I want you to have."

He picked up a gift from the table, and gave it to her. It was a little book with a cover of velvet-soft brown leather, and the name embossed in gold. With great care, Marnie opened it. The parchment pages were pale as cream, fine and smooth, with golden edges. The script, beautifully written by hand, was small and flawless, and the letters at chapter beginnings were wonderfully decorated. Marnie stroked the pages, then sniffed them, and put her cheek against the leather cover.

"'Tis lovely," she said. "I love it, father. Thank you. I'll keep it till I die."

"Then I hope it's yours for a long time," smiled Father Brannan. "'Tis the Holy Gospels, copied by an old monk I loved well. I was planning to teach you to read them, but for reasons of his own, the Almighty's decided that's not to be my joy. But I don't doubt you'll learn to read, and to write as well. And when you can read the Gospels, you can tell the stories to Raven, and that'll be my gift to him. It's for you both, Marnie."

She discovered something written, in a larger hand, on the first page. "Did you write this, father?"

"Aye. I want you to read it for yourself, one day."

"Won't you tell me what it is?"

"No. And now you'd best be going, and make the most of a fine day for traveling."

Sherryl Jordan

"I feel terrible saying this, father, but I need to ask you for something else. I seem to be always asking, and never giving."

"You give more than you know, just by smiling. What is it you need?"

"Can you lend me a few pennies, so I can buy bread from the alehouse before we leave?"

Amused, Father Brannan went to a pottery jar on a shelf, and took out a piece of silver and several copper coins. "This will keep you going," he said, "until you get your first sack of gold."

"Don't say that; you frighten me," she said. "Thank you, father."

"Now don't you start on your thankings," said Father Brannan, going outside with them. "I want you to go, and go fast, or else you'll see me overwrought and blubbering, and that's not a pretty sight."

He embraced Raven, and the youth climbed onto the wagon and took up the reins. Then Father Brannan turned to Marnie. "Don't say a word, lass," he said hoarsely, holding her close and kissing her hair. "Just go. God bless you both. I'll never forget you."

She got up beside Raven, and he flicked the reins, and the wagon rumbled off. Marnie looked back at the priest, and waved, but her sight was so blurred she saw only a brown form and a hand raised in blessing. Then she faced the front, and Raven took her hand in his, and they went along the rough road to the beachfront cottages, and down onto the stony track along the shore, where the road passed the sea wall and the alehouse.

Marnie wiped her eyes, and signed, *Stop here. We want bread from the house with the words over the door.* Giving him one of the copper coins, she added, *You go. Ask for bread.*

I can't. They will laugh.

No they will not. You can ask with your mouth. All you say is, Bread please. You have said it to me many times. She repeated the two words, very clearly. "You say them," she said, without signing.

He swallowed nervously. "Braird pileaze."

Marnie smiled, and kissed him. *Your mouth-words are good like mine.*

Now go and get the bread. Give the gold, and they will give you bread.

He jumped down, and stood for a few moments facing the ale-house, gathering his courage. At last, with shoulders back and head held high, he crossed the pebbly beach to the steps that led to the weather-beaten door. He turned and looked at Marnie, and she blew him a kiss and waved him on. Ducking his head, he passed into the darkness within.

Marnie sat holding the reins, looking at the door and the sign above it creaking as it swung in the breeze. THE SAGE AND FOOL.

A hundred summers, it seemed, since she had sat in this place, on this wagon, waiting for another man. She looked the other way, at the ocean, and thought of the time she had first sat here and watched it, marveling. And the mad boy had stood on these very stones, the blood running down him faint-colored in the rain, and his eyes full of hunger and pain . . .

"Marn!" she heard. "Marn!"

She looked back at the alehouse, and saw him running down the steps two at a time. Laughing, triumphant, he came leaping over the stones toward her, brandishing a loaf of bread. He put the bread and money away, and checked that everything was secure. Then he climbed to his seat, gave Marnie a joyful kiss, and took the reins.

The wagon rumbled along the track, and Marnie hummed to herself and did not look at the people as they came out of their houses, silent and unsmiling, to watch the departure of the madman and the witch. Raven drove the horse up on to the inland road, and they passed the last grim houses, and the stony field with its unused whipping post; and on they went, away from Torcurra, toward the shining hills.

Author's Note

THE *RAGING QUIET* began, as all my
stories begin, with the arrival of the main char-
acters, who appear suddenly in my mind, as
vivid as a dream or powerful memory. I cannot
describe the excitement of that moment, that
first seeing; it is like a meeting with long-lost
friends, in whose shining company I shall
spend the next months of my life. The entire
story is like a remembering—a series of images
flashing across my mind; a gift to be treasured,
experienced in the imagination until it is fully
known; then recorded as faithfully as possible.

Marnie and Raven came to me like that, so
charismatic and real that I felt I had known
them all my life. Their story too came to me in
a few moments, so vivid and complete that I
found I could not force it into a particular time
or place in history, for fear of distorting what I
had been given. So I left their tale in the freer
atmosphere of myth, and simply wrote a fantasy set in an ancient time.

But although their story is fantasy, there is much in it that is true. Marnie's trial, for example, is authentic, and the words and rituals recorded here were used in such ordeals. Marnie's life on the manor land is typical of the lives of many people long ago, and the festivities and customs are drawn from history. Also, I drew on my own experience in writing of Marnie's difficulties as she tried to communicate with Raven, who is deaf. For several years I worked with profoundly deaf children in schools, and spoke with them through signs. Marnie's dealings with Raven—her difficulties, frustration, despair, joy, and triumph—are all things I have experienced. The sign language Marnie invents is obviously different from the official sign languages used today, though some signs are based on natural gestures, and are therefore similar.

This tale belongs to any time, even our own; it is about prejudice and ignorance, and a young woman wrongly accused, who is guilty of only one thing—the unforgivable crime of being different.